JOURNEY TO THE CENTRE OF THE MIND

– a Particularly Mental Gap Year

FSC
www.fsc.org
MIX
Papir fra
bærekraftige kilder
Paper from
responsible sources
FSC® C105338

By Eilidh C. Richards

Journey to the Centre of the Mind – a Particularly Mental
Gap Year

Genre: Fiction

Cover design: H. Chruicshank
Proofreading/editorial guidance: J.M. Ferreira Bardal & Kris C.

© 2025 Eilidh C. Richards
Publisher: BoD · Books on Demand, Postboks 354 Sentrum, 0101 Oslo, bod@bod.no
Print: Libri Plureos GmbH, Friedensallee 273, 22763 Hamburg, Tyskland

ISBN: 978-82-938-7320-4

Prologue – How it all ends

'Oh my God, will you fucking MOVE?!' As the slow-walker turned to watch her in confused horror, Hannah realised – far too late – that the words had in fact escaped her. 'Move, you fat fuck! I'm going to miss my train!' she screamed. 'What the hell is wrong with me?! Shut up, shut up, shut up!' More people had stopped to stare at her now. Sweat started pouring down Hannah's face as well, her voice trembling as she yelled, 'This isn't real! La-la-la-la-la-la-la-laaaaah!', realizing that in fact it was very real. She incredulously pinched her arm. 'Ouch! I'm legging it!' As she made a run for it, her right toe caught on a seemingly invisible obstacle on the station floor, causing Hannah to stumble onto and over the railing between herself and the parking garage three floors below. As the filthy, oil-stained concrete hurled towards her face, bag contents flying through the air – pens, gum and tampons hitting onlookers in the face – Hannah screamed one last time: 'So this is how it ends?!' As her jaw hit the ground and shattered, rattling her brain, pain shooting through her like explosive sensory diarrhoea, Hannah awoke, mid-air. 'Shit!' she exclaimed – not quite able to shake the feeling of falling – 'it's gonna be one of those days.'

Meet Hannah Higgins, 41 years young – not young because of her gorgeously youthful appearance, mind you, merely due to her complete inability to do anything grown-up or even mildly productive in her life – eternally single and now seemingly lacking the ability to keep an inner dialogue to boot. Her brain still foggy from last night's wine-binge, she checked her phone. 6.15. Phew, at least her high-level anxiety had kept her from oversleeping. She stumbled out of bed, sheets soaked from nightmare sweats and drunken slobbering, and started getting ready for work. As she caught a glimpse of her haggard face in the bathroom mirror, she wondered aloud; 'What am I even doing with my life?'

Part 1: Winter

Chapter 1 – December: Into the abyss

Shutting her front door firmly behind her, Hannah was reminded of the grim fact that it was already mid-December. Decorations in red, green and gold dominating every shop window, sparkling crimbo lights in dubious arrangements aloft on every street. Every coffee shop tempting passers-by with peppermint flavoured coffees on special offer, tinsel wrapping every door and window frame she passed. Nice way of suggesting a perfectly festive way of hanging oneself, Hannah thought to herself, slip-sliding her way toward the train station. 'All hail Jebus Moneybags Christ', she muttered under her breath.

Hannah had always taken pride in her punctuality. As a matter of fact, she was one of those people who considered herself to be late if she wasn't at least 12 minutes early, so when she spilled into the office through the back door – having taken the stairs in order to not stink up the lift in her vino-marinated state – promptly at 9.17, she was more than an hour late *and* two minutes late for the torturous weekly team gathering. Hannah looked around the open-plan office for a free desk, careful to avoid meeting anyone's gaze, and opted instead for one of the booths in the silent zone so she could sign in to the team meeting "remotely". Having done this exact thing far too many times in the past six months, she made sure to change her IP address before logging on, typing in her usual, 'sorry guys, bit late, had an issue with the Wi-Fi again. I'll head in after this and go through my emails on the train.'

Now, before you start judging her, Hannah hadn't always been like this. In fact, she had always enjoyed working just a little bit too hard and put in a few more hours than what her superiors demanded or even expected. The only problem was that, since she wouldn't dream of telling anybody of her extra curriculars, they never noticed and, hence, she never got the praise she so desperately ached for. (It's alright, you can feel free to judge her now.) But with an ever-increasing workload, there was never any time for Hannah to stop and wallow, so she pressed on, diligently; always on time and forever overachieving like a good little worker bee.

It seemed as if, under the right amount of pressure, Hannah could do almost anything. Which was why, with a severely diminished workload, she now found herself unproductive, underachieving, stressed out and at a complete loss for direction. Unfulfilled and hungry for something she couldn't quite put her finger on. So, she filled the void with booze and casual, too often booze-fuelled and completely unnecessary and/or unremarkable, sex – you really couldn't have the latter without the former in Hannah's world – and when she'd managed to reach a respectable level of self-loathing, she had taken to self-harm. As if the constant blackouts and STI scares weren't harming her enough. Yet, true to her slightly neurotic personality, she kept it up, subconsciously trying to hurdle herself over the edge instead of just constantly inching towards an edge that only seemed to get further away from her as the nights went by. Anyway – back to reality and today's team session.

The meeting went by in its usual blur, her colleagues all blabbing on about numbers, ROIs, SCM, market value, how to exploit resources and a whole horde of other terms that made Hannah's anti-capitalist stomach turn. You see, always the idealist, Hannah had wanted to change the world for the better for as long as she could remember; she believed in a just world, where everyone was treated with compassion and respect. In this environment, she was rapidly losing herself in a soul-sucking sea of self-assured millennials with too loud voices and no integrity. Never one to cry, let alone in public, Hannah had lost count of the times she had to run to the bathroom in recent months on account of the lump in her throat and tears pressing against her eyelids throughout the day. Yet, despite her aversion to her colleagues and their seemingly exploitative worldview and disregard for bettering the environment, she still yearned to fit in. Additionally, she quite fancied Drew in Legal, and would take any chance she'd get at being in his presence. (Funny how these urges surface when you're not drowning in deadlines, eh?) Which was why, when she received an invitation to the after-work event two days from now from the HR rep, she accepted with a smile.

Hannah went about her day, making sure she left sharply at 3pm, so she could fit in a solid workout before heading home. She'd better start making room for the extra calories that would no doubt be consumed in liquid form on the day. Upon inspecting her developing muffin top in the mirror after her workout, she decided a 48-hour fast and another gruelling gym session was sorely needed for her to look her absolute best for the event as well.

The fast kept Hannah from having her usual two bottles of wine that evening – and the next, so she managed to get to the office with time to spare the next two days. Feeling quite pleased with herself for having gotten her life back on track in just a couple of days, she decided she had reason to celebrate and so she left the office an hour early on Thursday, saying she had a dentist's appointment but would be able to get to the event for when it started. She then promptly took herself to the nearest pub and ordered herself a large red wine, forgetting all about her empty stomach. Downing the wine over the course of 15 minutes, she ordered herself another for good measure, taking her time to savour it before heading off to meet the others. Stopping by the bathroom on her way out to top up her makeup and undoing a few buttons on her work cardigan to reveal the lacy top of the Ann Summers corset underneath, she could already feel the wine starting to work its magic. She winked at herself in the mirror, taking a quick selfie to commemorate her grey mouse-cum-office vixen makeover, before stepping out into the icy December afternoon.

The place they were meeting was just around the corner from the building her work shared with a few other businesses and was largely frequented by suit and dress clad people in their late 20s and early 30s. Hannah always thought they looked like toddlers playing dress-up, the younger lads with their patchy facial hair and boyish shoulders and the girls' obvious attempts of looking more grown up with elaborate updos and expensive designer frames with no prescription lenses in them. Yet she always observed them with a little bit of envy and a dull pain in her gut, as her eyes fell on their wedding bands and when she'd overhear them talking about their families, newly bought houses and significant others. Hannah, having fled the country when her friends had started breeding and buying property, had none of these material things in her life and, although she never really yearned for such things to begin with, felt increasingly and utterly out of place in the company of these people that were at least a decade younger than her.

The warmth of the bustling place hit her as she opened the door to the busy tavern, which was starting to fill up with shiny, smiling patrons, enjoying an after-work tipple with their office pals. Spotting her coworkers at a long table out of the corner of her eye – Drew already deep in conversation with one of the girls from accounting – before they had a chance to see her, she bee-lined to the downstairs bar for a quick shot of whisky for courage and a handful of mints from her bag before joining them.

Everyone around the table were patiently nursing their respective half-pints of artisanal lager and small white wines with soda, all of them already chatting as you would with old friends. Feeling a bitter bout of jealousy, Hannah ordered herself another large red wine, explaining with a laugh that the pain suffered from the dental work needed dulling. After all, she didn't dare getting anaesthetised before going out drinking! They all nodded in approval, and, for a minute, Hannah felt pleased with her own ability to manipulate her surroundings. Confidence boosted by the wine, she figured she would start climbing Mount Drew. Spotting a space on the bench across from him and his lady friend from accounting, Hannah decided she'd have another go at this newfound ability of hers. She pulled her top down slightly to reveal some more of the padded lace cradling her breasts, fingers lingering for a few seconds on her small but inviting cleavage, making sure Drew would catch a glimpse and planting the seed of her naked body in his mind. As Drew's eyes wandered in the direction she not so subtly pointed out for him, she cleared her throat just enough for him to look up at her. "Eyes up here, pal," she giggled, smugly, thinking he was checking out the merchandise she so blatantly had laid upon the table, and sat her perky-for-forty bum down on the bench.

Hannah enjoyed the sense of freedom and confidence – however false they may be – the wine had given her. Therefore, she downed a few more glasses in quick succession. Before long, she was fully intent on monopolising the conversation Drew was already having when she first entered the tavern. His judgement had been somewhat clouded by his own penchant for strong microbrews, which left him slightly intrigued by Hannah, who was a good seven years his senior. A couple of hours went by, and their colleagues started to excuse themselves from the table, all needing to head home to their awaiting families. The girl Drew was talking to initially had already left, and Hannah had nabbed her place on the bench next to Drew. One of the women from Hannah's team was getting a taxi and urged her to join her as they were going in the same direction, but Hannah declined. She had Drew within her grasp now, she thought to herself, and there wasn't a chance in hell she'd let him slip away from her this time. 'I'm alright', she barked. 'I need to swing by a friend's on the way home and wouldn't want to be a burden. Just you go ahead, and I'll see you in the morning'.

Drew then jumped up and said he'd take Hannah's place in the cab. *What the hell?!* Hannah was aghast. How dare he leave her when they were having such a good time? He clearly didn't know what he was missing, so she decided to let that fact be known. She got up to give him a brief hug goodbye, whispered 'I'll be seeing you later' seductively into his ear, gently brushing the top of her thigh against his crotch as she went. As he eyed her incredulously, she sat back down and hinted at the waitress that she was ready for another drink and that she would be having it at the bar. 'Just one last one for the road', she winked at her workmates and left the table.

'Lightweights', she sneered as she glanced down at her phone to check the time. It was only 7.30 and she was just warming up. Might as well hit one of the old watering holes in town. Already numb enough to not care about the fact that she really couldn't afford getting a taxi, getting one was exactly what she did. 'Scruffy's, please, on the corner of Dale Street', she demanded as she got in. The cabbie gave her a look that indicated he reckoned she would be better off putting herself to bed – or maybe off to pasture – but did as he was told.

As she approached the steep stairs going up to the dimly lit rock bar, she hesitated a bit. The cold had sobered her up a bit and she was having doubts. Maybe this wasn't such a good idea? After all, she did have work tomorrow. Wait – she'd told everyone she was going home, so they'd be none the wiser. Fuck it. I'll just see who's in and have *one* beer.

She shrugged off the cold and started on the stairs.

As she entered the pub, she could already feel everyone's eyes on her. As the only one there not part of any group, apart from the odd alkie that was sat at the bar, she was no doubt object to scrutiny. Something bordering on guitar heavy power metal was blasting from the speakers as she hastened towards the bar. 'Chappy in yet?' she asked the barmaid, attempting to sound as sober as possible. Claiming you knew the owner always worked wonders anyway, and as the staff confirmed he had just left but would be back she replied that she'd have a pint while she waited. She could feel eyes burrowing into her back now. 'Oh, and a shot of whiskey too, please', she added, just to shake off the sudden desperate feeling of someone or somewhere to belong to.

The whiskey started working its magic quite quickly, and before long she could feel her shoulders relax. She started scanning the room for a replacement for Drew, but the few eligible ones that did not resemble someone off the cast of a Tolkien novel were already in the company of corset clad female versions of Robert Smith. She pounded another two shots in quick succession and ordered herself a second pint. When Chappy arrived half an hour or so later, she was already on fire. She dashed over to greet him with a hug and then made her way to the DJ booth to work her magic on the playlist, knowing he wouldn't kick her out as long as she made sure to add a few of his favourites. She might have been paranoid about people looking at her when she arrived, but all eyes were on her now. The only difference was that the booze filter convinced her that they looked at her with admiration and jealousy now, and not in disgust and annoyance, as was the reality. There is nothing cool about a 40 plus uninvited girl DJ, off her tits on wine and spirits, out by herself and looking to paint the town brown on a Thursday evening.

She quickly tired of her DJ set – after all, being in faux aux demand *is* rather tiring. Returning to the bar, ready for another drink, she was pleased to find a fan there. It was the sort of bloke you kind of smelled before you saw him, and certainly someone Hannah would avoid talking to when she was out with *actual* people. 'Let me get you a drink, luv', he uttered, through his near toothless grin. 'I thought that sounded great. Smashing that was. I never get to hear my old favourites out on the town anymore'. And, in Hannah's defence, her DJ skills were unparallelled in today's scene. She had once been an excellent DJ and had drawn quite the crowd back in the day. But that was 15 years ago now. Either way, the compliment had put her in a good mood and so she accepted his beverage with a smile and joined him at the bar. Celebrating her triumph, she decided shots were in order, so she got them each a shot, as well as for everyone at the Tolkien table. 'They look like they need a stiff one' she harrumphed. 'Wink, wink! Nudge, nudge! Am I right?' she laughed, only to have her Monty Python reference fall on deaf ears.

The rest of the evening went by in a flash. Or a blur, more like. In fact, when she woke up on her couch the next morning (her go-to when drunk, as she'd found it prevented her from over-sleeping), fully clothed, she had no idea how she'd gotten there. But she took comfort in the fact that she hadn't woken up next to the toothless old man. She vaguely remembered running for the bus, as she couldn't afford another taxi. The kebab sauce stains on her coat told her she's stopped for food on the way (although you didn't really have to be Sherlock Holmes to solve that mystery). Now, if she could only find her phone, she'd know more about how she got there – and be able to let her boss know she'd be working from home today. What time was it anyway? It was still dark out, but for December that didn't really give any indication of anything. It could be anywhere between 5pm and 10am.

A sudden flashback hit her like a lightning bolt through the skull. No, it couldn't be! She jumped up and headed for the hallway and started going through her jacket pockets. No phone. Handbag? No phone. Surely, it must have fallen out and was laid behind the shoe rack or something. She upended the whole thing, ransacking every single shoe like a woman gone mad. No. Fucking. Phone.

Flashback time again. Having been startled awake by the bus driver at the last stop, she'd ran out the door as quickly as she could. She had no idea where she was but had started to drag her feet through the snow, towards something that resembled civilisation. This was when she discovered she wasn't wearing her headphones and, hence, had no idea where her phone was. She backtracked her steps to the bus stop and must have spent about an hour looking for it in the snow. It was really coming down now as well, and the part of the road her phone would have been had it fallen out of her pocket was now covered in a thick and fluffy layer of cottonwool-like carpeting. 'Fuck!' she cried out. 'FUCK!!' She could feel her shoulders starting to shake. Tears welling up in her eyes. 'No, you're not going to cry, you pathetic, dumb little bitch', she said to herself. 'I'm just going to keep looking and it'll turn up. It has to'. And, as an answer to her prayer, she saw light out of the corner of her eye. There was a small service building at the bottom of the hill, that she hadn't noticed before, and outside the service building was a man, on his way into his car. 'Wait!' Hannah shouted. 'I need help!'

Back in her hallway again, she fell to her knees, remembering now. The very kind man outside the service building had somewhat reluctantly helped her look for her phone some more but had insisted on giving her a lift home when it became clear it was nowhere to be found. He worked for the bus company and his shift had just ended but said he would let the people at the lost and found know about her missing phone. It could still be on the bus or there could be something on the CCTV. He tried calling her number and as it was still ringing, there was still hope. That had calmed her down quite a bit, so when he dropped her off, she took herself to the couch and slept like a baby – for a full three and a half hours – completely in denial of the fact that her phone was her only way of logging onto her work laptop when she wasn't at the office. Now she'd be forced to go in, and everything would be on the line. She'd been able to hide this side of herself for so long, as she was highly capable of doing her job quite well – even despite the hangovers from hell. She loved her work, and she had gotten more than decent at it. She just wasn't very good at having this much freedom *outside* of work. And now she was completely and utterly screwed. And not in a good way. Not that she would know; she hadn't had sex sober once in the past decade.

Remembering that without her phone she had no concept of time, she went to look for one of her many discarded watches in the bathroom. 8.05. Shit. No time for a shower. She quickly changed her clothes and topped up her eyeliner. Luckily, most of the clown makeup from yesterday was still glued to her face, so she didn't bother too much with that. She grabbed an old phone and charger from her office drawer – thank fuck she always kept the old ones for emergencies – and decided to get a new SIM on her way in. As she locked the door behind her, she worked on her excuse for being late and tried out a cough. A lot of people in the office had been ill with covid over the past few weeks, so that would be her excuse for getting people to stay at an arm's length. Maybe she could even score some points with her boss for showing up even in this near-death state of affairs.

As she was approaching the train station, it quickly became apparent that last night's snowfall had caused quite a delay on all lines. Hannah, already in panic mode, realised there wouldn't be enough time for her to stop by the phone shop on the way. She'd have to stick it out until lunchtime at least. This meant having to talk to IT about the lost phone and having them override the two-factor authorisation from their end. 'Just my bloody luck' thought Hannah. At least it was Friday. This meant that most of her coworkers would be working from home and that her boss would be stuck in meetings for most of the day. She could actually get by only having to interact with the IT department, which consisted of individuals who – by some sort of miracle – never seemed to indulge in the office gossip. Also, because it was the end of the week, there were no meetings to attend today, so she could grab one of the private offices to work on some content for the team's website. When it comes to losing one's phone whilst on a blacked-out bender, this was not the worst way to go about the aftermath. In fact, she felt as if she'd been touched by an angel or something. I guess this is why other people win the lottery and not me, Hannah thought to herself. I spend all of my good fortune on getting myself out of these drunken, bloody messes.

This, too, was of course a low blow for Hannah, and she could feel herself starting to dig herself further down by the minute. No, not when I'm working. She gave herself a sobering slap across the face and made a note of getting a box of wine on the way home, so she could have some emotional release when she got back. She made a list of items to get her through the day:

1. 9-11.30: Update website content
2. 11.30-12: Pop to the shop for new SIM and get lunch to have at desk
3. 12-3.30: Edit website and prep for Monday's meetings

After the initial debacle of having to get IT assistance, the first few hours at the office flew by. Hannah made such progress on the website that she decided to do all of her other shopping when she popped out at lunchtime as well – including the wine and a bottle of bourbon for good measure – so as to save time on the commute after work. There might still be delays and she didn't want that cutting into her drinking time. When she got back from the shops, new SIM in hand, she made sure everyone could hear her coughing

on her way to her office. 'Sorry for being so antisocial
today, I just don't want anybody else getting whatever
this is', she said, when passing a few of her coworkers
that were stood having a chat at the coffee machine.
Should she feel the need to take Monday off, she was
laying down the groundwork now. She looked around
for Drew, but he was nowhere to be seen. *Weird*, she
thought. He never used to take Fridays off. She got back
to work, and as she had practically worked through
lunch, she wondered if she should bunk off half an hour
early but opted not to, although she'd finished
everything on her list already. She waited until the last
of her coworkers left, collected her bags and went to set
the alarm. "TGI friggin' F", she muttered to herself as
she stepped into the lift. "I can't believe I got away with
this".

As luck would have it – again, wasting her luck
and good karma points on pointless things – traffic was
back to normal. But on the train, she couldn't help but
feeling overwhelmed. All around her were people in
pairs or groups, smiling and chatting about their week
or their plans for the weekend. Without her normal
aural armour of her headphones, there was no way to
block them out and she could feel every last bit of joy
from having smashed her deadlines leave her body. Her
negative thought pattern once again reared its ugly
head; why can't *I* have what *they* have? Why can't I be
pretty like other people? Why don't people like me?
Why don't *I* deserve love, too? Deep in destructive
thought, she was snapped back to reality by her phone
vibrating in her pocket. A text from Chappy: 'Good to
see you, trouble. Although having to drag people out of

the utility closet doesn't happen every day. Maybe not drink us dry next time, eh? LMFAO!!'

LMFAO?! Hannah felt her hands grow clammy and her lunch getting ready for a swift exit the way it had first entered. *This is my life he's talking about, and he thinks it's laughable!* And she hated it when people called her *'trouble'*. She could feel a familiar twitch in her left eye, as the tics she'd struggled to hide since she was a teenager made themselves known. The more anxious she let herself become, the more they'd take over, and soon her head was twitching uncontrollably. *God, I hope no one notices*, she prayed quietly.

As her stop approached, finally, she was more than eager to get off the train, but this too was now a struggle, as she couldn't take the three steps down to the platform without backtracking herself to make the number of steps even. 'Fuck this magical thinking bullshit!' her inner voice shouted. Angrily, she pushed through, growing increasingly anxious, and accidentally elbowed a fellow passenger in her path. 'I'm so sorry!' she mouthed as she headed, once again, for another spree in her local wine shop. What she had in her bag already really wasn't going to cut it.

Now finding herself back at her front door, Hannah was glad to be able to set down the heavy bags that she'd dragged up the hill of horror. When she'd found the place online, she'd fallen in love instantly. A tiny, wee red cottage, with white sconces and its very own terrace overlooking the sea in the distance. Hidden in the garden behind the main house on the property, it was perfect for an introvert such as herself. It was small enough that she'd have an excuse for not opening her doors to overnight visitors and large enough for her to have the space she needed, as it stretched across two floors. The living area had a lovely exposed brick wall and original wooden floors, as well as large windows, one of which overlooked the water. The kitchenette and bathroom were both rather rustic as well, but she'd found that rather charming in the beginning. Her bedroom and home office space were up a narrow, steep set of stairs – an area which was fully furnished with a bed, set of drawers and a freezer when she moved in, so that she didn't have to worry about making any extra purchases in that department at the time. Never mind lugging a king-sized bed up those narrow stairs. There was also the free parking and Internet at no cost, but the car was now long gone, and the Wi-Fi was unreliable at best. And, since the house was hardly insulated, the electric bill had become an increasingly large money pit, which had her scraping the barrel in her once growing (albeit slowly) savings account. Add to that the fact that she was living in her landlord's garden – that they were of course putting to good use every single day, even in the winter – and she had come to resent the place. What was meant to be a fresh start for her had become just another reason to feel worthless. Like a prisoner in her rented palace. Rapunzel without the luscious locks. We'll no doubt come back to the hair situation later, of course. But yeah. Like so many times before, she had fallen out of love when the novelty wore off.

So, as she was gearing up for another freezing Friday night in her money pit, she was feeling rather glum. She was trying to look at the one bright side of having bought too much booze to carry any additional shopping; the fact that she hadn't succumbed to her yearning for sweeties and crisps. And there was no way in hell she was walking down and back up the hill of doom again today. The fridge and freezer were both pretty empty, bar half a bag of frozen mango chunks, so there was also no chance she was in any danger of blowing her calorie budget on food. So, she bundled up on the couch in a teepee of blankets and wearing her woolly hat and a knit jumper and enjoyed a delicious dinner for one; a very boozy mango smoothie at about 70 percent prosecco and bourbon and 30 percent fruit, which – judging by the taste – could likely double as a highly effective paint stripper.

One of the great things about December, Hannah thought, was that she finally had a legitimate reason for watching romcoms. And much thanks to the Hallmark empire, her streaming services added new crimbo themed chick flicks every single day of the week. Perfect for an evening of emoting without having to connect with your own actual feelings. Sometimes all you need is a good cry.

About halfway through *Christmas Magic on Mistletoe Farm* (or something of the sort), Hannah couldn't help but starting to feel sort of joyful, though. This movie was ridiculously feelgood and had almost completely ruined Hannah's bad mood. She half-blamed the smoothie as well. Prosecco was definitely an upper, and the evening she had planned for was in dire need of red wine and her aptly named *Sad Shit* playlist.

She switched off the festive film and put the music on. Then, she poured herself a hefty glass of red and took a selfie for "the gram", on her nouveau-old device, with the caption *You know it's December when*

you need a hat and a gallon of wine just to keep warm
and one of those tacky emojis the Zoomers had
cancelled. Adding a sarcastic music track to the story,
she chuckled at herself. She did enjoy her own sense of
humour.

Now, Hannah's little pity party might seem sad to
some, but she oftentimes preferred the solitude of her
own company to that of others. Tonight was no
exception. She didn't have to put up a façade with
herself, didn't have to choose her words carefully so as
not to offend anyone. And she found that music would
always provide great company in the odd event that she
actually started to feel lonely. So, she was enjoying
herself. A little too much perhaps, but she needed to
feel something that wasn't her own pain, and this was
just the ticket.

Once again, Hannah started to feel the warmth of
the alcohol spreading through her veins, like a hug
coming from inside. As she was singing along to the
music, the day that was slowly coming to an end behind
her began to feel like a distant memory. There was of
course the odd jab of flashbacks here and there, but
none so bad that they couldn't be subdued by alcohol.

And so, she went about her business. Vocally
wanking along loudly to her playlist, then getting her
guitar out as well. As she was strumming along, she
found that it wasn't sounding too bad, so she recorded a
little play-along. Upon deciding that it sounded
fantastic, she opted to film the next attempt and post it
to her story on Instagram. Very clever. After the brief
success of having broken the mould as a cover artist
and influencer, she went back to watching the
Christmas movie again, wine in hand. It no longer felt as

cheery as it did to begin with, so she allowed herself to wallow in the pain of the lead character, who had now been dumped by her fiancé and thrown out on the street by her landlord, her large suitcase bursting at the seams with designer dresses, proving far too challenging for a heartbroken city girl to drag along the cobbled streets of the big city.

Hannah saw this as a good point to start a drinking game for herself. She'd have a shot of bourbon for each time the main character mentioned her ex, her landlord or, indeed, the big city. After about 45 minutes of this and very little else, Hannah was invested. But the combination of the wine and the bourbon seemed to have had a gnarly effect on her and as the main character's luck shifted and everything sorted itself out on Mistletoe Farm, she found herself pissed off. Shouting at the TV now, for shoving such unrealistic crap down people's throats, Hannah wanted to take her anger out on everything that was wrong with commercial filmmaking. No one made artsy, well thought out – and largely more realistic – cinematic pieces like *Harold & Maude* or *Love Story* or even *Leaving Las Vegas* anymore. She grabbed her guitar again, attempting to write a three-chord punk anthem and failed miserably at even hitting the strings in a proper manner. Furious, she banged her guitar against the floorboards (might have been more successful going for the bricks) to smash it up in protest. The result was a few splinters – might have come off the floor – and a couple of scratches in the varnish on the guitar. 'GAH!!' Hannah growled.

This was the last thing Hannah remembered before blacking out at approximately 10.22pm that

Friday evening. Yet, the 2.45 missed call from a food delivery service, one she noticed upon waking up around noon, made it abundantly clear that she'd managed to stay somewhat lucid long beyond that. The chips scattered around her, along with a half-eaten brownie, was testament to the fact that she'd been able to get her hands on the food in the end.

Hannah dreaded checking her banking app, as she had just been paid and the next pay date wasn't due until January. With the accumulation of drunken antics in the previous days alone, she knew she'd be in trouble already. She opted instead to check her Instagram, starting to diligently delete her stories, one by one. God knows what else she'd been up to on that thing. Worst case scenario she'd sent some distasteful nudes to a couple of the few people she knew would respond favourably to such an uninvited gesture, best case, she'd started an *Only Fans* and gotten some actual money out of her alcohol-fuelled narcissism. Either way, now was not the time to find out. She dragged her body upstairs to put on her winter running gear and made her way outside to make room for today's calories – or even get rid of some of those consumed last night.

Whoever said you shouldn't work out with a hangover is wrong, Hannah thought to herself, as she brushed snow off her shoes after her half marathon. For one, she'd burned off quite a few of last night's calories and, additionally, she now felt invincible. She was even bothered to start cleaning the house after a quick shower, which made her feel quite accomplished. Celebratory drink and a matinée? Yes, please. Although, she would have to get some food to avoid falling down a wormhole similar to last night, so off to the shops she went. Here's the kicker, though – you should not go shopping on an empty stomach, especially after a half marathon following a boozy night.

When faced with all of the sweet and savoury goodness of the special offer section in her local supermarket, Hannah succumbed to her hanger and got EVERYTHING she'd so valiantly resisted for the past few weeks (calories consumed during a blackout don't count, obviously); glazed donuts with sprinkles, choc chip cookie ice cream, pick & mix, cheesy crisps, popcorn, pizza, guac and crackers – the lot. And some spinach and tomatoes for a salad. Grabbing a couple hard seltzers and a coke for the hangover as well, she was trying to convince herself that she'd be able to just have the one donut and not all six, and if push came to shove, the two-hour run would cancel all of the rest out. Oh, Hannah. Quite naïve for a self-proclaimed realist and former hobby bulimic, eh? And, to make matters worse, she got a notification from her banking app that she was overdrawn as she was leaving the shop. SHIT.

Braving the aforementioned hill of doom at an admirable speed, considering her increasingly hangry and hungover state, she was trying to not let the overdraft bother her. She had her credit card, right? Rent was paid. It would be FINE. Also, anything you eat when you're on the move doesn't stick, so she popped one of the donuts in her mouth as she powered through the now sleet battering her cheeks. Actually, better have another one – eating items in odd numbers is just plain crazy.

Going down the hill normally took about seven minutes on a bad day. Going up it, on the other hand – and in a snowstorm to boot – was a different story altogether. Hannah struggled to find her footing and her vision was beyond compromised. Her body's response to these conditions, however, was to move along in a half jog half power walk fashion, and as her ankle suddenly wrapped itself around a hidden curb stone, she yelped in pain. But she was halfway home by now, and there was no way she was going to lay down and die in the middle of the road. What would the neighbours say? Hannah sped up, grateful she'd opted to bring her own recyclable bags to the shop instead of having to use their paper ones, which would surely have burst in this apocalyptic weather. She could just about make out her driveway now and let out a low 'thank fuck' in sheer relief. Time to pop a couple of ibuprofen and hard seltzer.

'Pain is an illusion!' Hannah more or less shouted to herself, as she was trying to remove her now skintight boots, revealing an already purpling ankle that had more than doubled in size in the past few minutes. It was really throbbing now. The ibuprofen wasn't going to cut it, so she decided to have them team up with two paracetamols for effect. Boots finally off, she limped towards her kitchen counter with her shopping and pulled her painkillers out of the fridge. Lubricating herself with an entire can of the alcoholic soft drink, she downed the cocktail of pills. Sweet, sweet relief. If she was going to be able to get back out there tomorrow – weather permitting – she really needed to be able to at least stand on the bad leg by the end of tonight.

The mini-injury had taken her mind off her financial troubles and so she resumed her behaviour from the previous night, but as it was still light out, it didn't really count as drinking-drinking. It's the same with staying in instead of going out-out. Good lord, how she loved day drinking. Pain and worries gone by 6pm and likely in bed by 9. Ideal. Having ticked off all the items on her mental to-do-list as well (run, house cleaning, shopping), there was nothing that she had to do, so she could actually relax for the rest of her Saturday. Another thing for the pros column in regard to hungover training – as long as you get out there whilst still slightly under the influence, you won't even notice you're doing the work and it will give you enough endorphins to get through the following couple of hours thinking you are some sort of wonder woman. If Hannah were a superhero, she'd be the Mega Livertron – super resistant to any kind of cirrhosis and words of affirmation. Her title was a bit of a mouthful, but at least that would keep her out of the multiverse that shall not be named. And for now, this superhero was about to put her organs to work, yet again.

As predicted, Hannah's Saturday went according to plan. She spent her first few drinking hours downloading her apps and syncing photos to her new old phone, making sure to log out of everything on the missing one. She tried her luck with *Find My Device,* but as she'd already transferred the number, it was a dead end. After this, she put her phone away and started on her mountain of snacks and booze and was fast asleep in a food-induced comatose state by 9.

The following morning, Hannah woke up from a dream of three evil looking elves pinning her down and drilling a sharpened sugarcane into her leg. The pain was unreal, and it was in fact her own screaming that had woken her from her slumber. Right, that bloody ankle. Looking down to check the damage, the swelling had already gone down, and the discoloration wasn't half as bad as it had been yesterday. She lifted up the curtains to check the weather; snow still coming down hard. Phew! Forced rest day – exactly what she needed.

No longer numbed by alcohol, Hannah was attacked by her own brain. There was no shortage of name-calling and self-blame this morning, but she managed to use it for some good. There would be no more drinking for the remainder of the month. It wasn't like she could afford it anyway, right? Remembering her overdrawn account, she began to write a list of essentials for the month. She could cover that with some of her savings and then do her Christmas shopping on her credit card. Sorted. She'd be at her sister's for Christmas anyway, which meant she'd only had to spend money on the train there and back. Just two weeks remaining until her office shut for the holidays and she'd be golden. She could do this. All she needed to do was stay off the booze and avoid online shopping for a while and payday would be there before she knew it.

Monday looming on the horizon, Hannah made sure she stayed busy for the rest of the day, starting with a workout session (low impact for the ankle) she found on YouTube. She then went on to organise her closet. Surely, donating some of her lesser used gems would score her some good karma points? Making a list – but unlike our pal Santa, she didn't bother to check it even once – she blasted through things she'd avoided for months. Procrastination was one of Hannah's worst habits, but the good thing about it was the sense of accomplishment she experienced when she accumulated the tasks and completed them all in one

day. This was, in fact, how she managed to impress
people in her work life as well; her unique ability to do
every and anything in no amount of time. She quite
enjoyed the instant rewards it gave her. So, although she
would have to go back and correct mistakes she'd
occasionally make, these were minimal and seldom
discovered by others. As long as everything looks good
on the outside, there's no limit to what can be under-
rug-swept in the process. This applied to all aspects of
her life. Just keep it to yourself and put an airtight lid on
it, and you'd be golden.

Come Monday morning, her ankle was almost
good as new. Public transport was back on track after
having had to deal with the weather all weekend (who
knew it would *snow* in December, AGAIN, this year?!).
As she entered the dark office, she put in her alarm
code and took in a quick hit of joy – or was what she felt
in fact relief – for starting this week off right. She found
a spot in the corner of the open plan office, switched
her laptop on and logged on. 7.59am. Hell yes.

Hannah didn't see Drew all day. This wasn't
unusual, as he tended to work from home on Mondays,
so she tried to ignore the dull feeling in the pit of her
stomach. Surely, she hadn't come on too strong? She
was convinced he liked her too, as he'd always take time
out of his day to talk to her or sit with her at lunchtime.
She tried not to think about it. Her day mostly consisted
of meetings and if she was going to get anything done,
she would have to pay attention to find out what might
be a good strategy for the week. No one ever told her
exactly what to do and Hannah found this excruciating.
With no instructions or guidelines, how would she
know what was expected of her? So, she had learned to

read her boss and colleagues during these meetings, just well enough for her to get a good view on what they were all working on. That way, she could feed them articles relevant to what they were doing or lend them a helping hand before they had to ask. Nowhere in the job description had they mentioned people-reading as a desired skill, but here she was, spending 75 per cent of her time deciphering people's gestures in order to get anything done. Great.

Tuesday rolled around and still no Drew. Maybe he was ill? It didn't really matter. She had work to do and got to it. She didn't stop for lunch but made a point of telling her coworkers this was due to the heavy workload. If she wanted to have everything done by Christmas, it didn't look like she would be coming up for air anytime soon.

The week went by in a similar fashion; work, home, dinner, workout, sleep, repeat. Autopilot was the best option and keeping busy kept her intrusive thoughts at bay, making sure her workouts were just tough enough to drain her completely. The weather stayed much the same, making running outdoors impossible, and so her ankle slowly stopped bothering her. Due to the enormous amount of booze she would normally indulge in during a normal week, she could also see results from abstaining after just a few days, which was brilliant motivation. As she left the office on Friday, she felt confident that next week – the last push before Christmas – would go by just as swimmingly.

No booze meant the weekend went by rather uneventfully, but it also meant her brain had started to wake up and repressed memories and intrusive thoughts were now coming out swinging. When it was revealed in Monday's staff meeting that Drew had decided to work from home until Christmas, she had a proper anxiety attack and had to isolate herself in the quiet zone for the rest of the day. Her 90-minute post work treadmill run didn't help much, as she felt fat and disgusting. The next four days seemed like an unsurmountable wall that stood between her and the time off with her family. Any spare minute she had was spent picking at her face with the pair of tweezers on the Swiss army knife she kept in her bag, often picking until she pulled off small pieces of skin and started bleeding. On the second of the remaining days, she'd gotten explosive diarrhoea, forcing her to use the office facilities every half hour. Sitting on the toilet and having brown liquid squirting out of her like her bum was some sort of flesh mitral valve, she got to thinking about that old song, *Your Body is a Wonderland*. More like, *Your Body is a Horror Movie* in my case, she thought to herself, feeling – for once – quite fortunate that Drew wasn't there to overhear anything.

Packed and ready, Hannah went straight to the train from work once she clocked out Friday afternoon. Just a couple of hours stood between her and some quality time with her nephews.

As she made her way through the crowded central station, packed with holidaymakers – some going home and some arriving – she was finally starting to get into the Christmas spirit. Although walking through the station made her anxious on a good day – remember the dream – she was able to find some joy in the smiling faces surrounding her for just a second, before her dismay of global capitalism, slow-walkers and people's inability to walk properly got the best of her. Once on the train, sweat was pouring down her back and this morning's attempt to look somewhat presentable had proven completely futile.

Hannah managed to squeeze in some shuteye on the train, so when it pulled in at the station, she felt well rested and ready to deploy full auntie mode. Hannah hadn't wanted to live for as long as she could remember. In fact, she'd been actively suicidal for the better part of the past decade – until these two arrived. As soon as she stepped off the train, she spotted her two favourite little weirdos running towards her, shouting 'Auntie Hannah!' from the top of their lungs. These little guys, sharing her blood, had stirred up something deep within her. For the first time in her life, Hannah actually cared whether she lived or died. She actually *wanted* to live. As she was kneeling down and spreading her arms out wide to greet them with a hug, nothing else mattered. Not even the shiny new Tesla that was waiting for them, with her sister's partner at the wheel, was bothering her now. With the boys still in her arms, she got up to have her sister joining them in the cuddle. 'Happy Christmas, kiddo', Hannah whispered in her sister's ear.

Hannah's younger sister Helena was doing adult life in the proper way. She'd met her partner, Shirley, at work a decade ago and once they'd tied the knot, Hels had gotten pregnant with their eldest son on their first try with a carefully selected donor that they've opted to go for the second time as well.

Despite the donor's genetics, the boys had so much of their sister in them. In fact, they'd inherited all of their family's genetics and mannerisms as well, so Hannah saw her own darkness in their eyes whenever she had some time with them. This, quite frankly, scared her absolutely shitless, so she had decided she would do her absolute best in preventing them from turning out the way she had.

Five years her sisters' senior, much of Hels' rearing had fallen on Hannah when their parents were overworked and under-stimulated when they were growing up, so the fact that Hels, very much her sister's opposite, had become such an accomplished adult – and a fantastic mother to boot – delighted Hannah to no end. Unfortunately, Hels had chosen a partner that seemingly took a lot of joy in putting her down – possibly due to the fact that she hadn't been the one to birth their children – and suffered the consequences of staying with her regardless. Naturally, Hannah felt much resentment towards Shirley for this reason, but despite that they got on quite well. Shirley's distaste for her children's love of Hannah over her own siblings, however, was not lost on Hannah. For that reason, Hannah remained on her toes whenever Shirley was within earshot of her.

The boys were five and three, and the younger sibling loved getting on his brother's nerves, so to avoid any crying on the way back to the family's home, Hannah had them sing carols and tell her about the goings on in the nursey. Apparently, the five-year-old had become quite the ladies' man and was already on his second girlfriend. Although Hannah suspected he'd be more inclined to – like his parents – end up with a same-sex partner eventually, Hannah was thrilled her nephew trusted her enough to divulge such personal information and sat back and relaxed without the aid of alcohol for the first time since the last time she'd seen them. She made a mental note of somehow teaching the kid that it was alright to not follow the norm of set gender roles, despite what they were imprinting on them in nursery, before it was too late. As the honorary bedtime storyteller during her visits, Hannah decided to incorporate this in one of their stories to remove any stigma attached to so-called teachable moments. Christmas was off to a great start.

Waking up from a dreamless slumber in her sister's guest room, she was saddened to hear the sound of Hels and Shirley arguing loudly upstairs. She kicked off her duvet, put her clothes and face on and went upstairs to intervene.

This had become more and more of a habit over the years. Shirley was constantly nitpicking at Hels for seemingly no reason. Hannah obviously knew enough to realise this is quite common in any kind of adult relationship – and one of the many reasons she refused to be in a relationship herself – but she could tell her eldest nephew had started to act out because of it. He had a lot of frustrations and no real outlet, as he was so often placed on the couch with his iPad whilst his parents were snapping at each other over seemingly banal things, such as how they cleaned the coffee machine or why they had used one of two identical blocks of cheese in the making of last night's pizza instead of the other. Hannah could tell they needed a proper adult talk, but with their schedule, it was difficult to find the time. Also, Hannah reckoned they both feared the outcome of such a conversation, as they continued to add activities on top of the other to eliminate any breathing space. This had resulted in exhausted children and irritable adults and a complex mess of short, entangled fuses. It was impossible to tell which bomb would go off first and the damage it would cause once it had gone off. Hannah was very grateful to be there to help when all of this was going on, but she couldn't help feeling guilty as well, as she was one of the elements that clearly added to the list of things they kept piling onto the chaos. This was one of those things that really got to Hannah when she was left to her own devices, so she did what she could to diffuse the situation whilst she was there.

'Good morning!' she said cheerfully in a sing-song voice. 'Alright if I take the kids out to build a snowman after breakfast?' The relief she saw on her sister's face said it all. This would give the both of them some time to do whatever it was young parents need just a few minutes to themselves for in a day, and there was a temporary ceasefire. Breakfast went by without any negative comments or jabs – at least from the adults' side of the table. The youngest heir, however, decided it fitting to tell his brother and everyone else that they were all giant, brown poos with hair in them. 'I'm gonna poo, poo, poo, poo on you!' he exclaimed, getting out of his chair and running towards his auntie, who at this point was struggling to not die of laughter and encourage this behaviour. She took a mental snapshot of the scene that was playing out before her and held it in her heart. At what point had she become such a sentimental old lady?

Days of playing in a dreamlike snowscape unfolded before them. Lots of snowmen, swordfights and bedtime stories brightened their days, and the promise of Christmas morning gifts was used heavily to subdue any starting fights between the kids. There was the occasional fit of tears and rage, of course, as we are dealing with young children here, but no trips to A&E or any permanent scars.

Christmas Day was spent with Shirley's family, where her parents and siblings had pulled out all the stops for a truly magical time. The table décor was delectable and the food plentiful and scrumptious. A lovely time was had by all, until the time for gift-giving came. The absence of Hels and Hannah's side of the family was palpable. The two sets of grandparents had sent gifts beforehand, but they lived all the way across the country and couldn't find the time or resources to join in on as many important occasions as Shirley's family could; her siblings and their respective families lived just a couple of houses down from theirs, and their parents – still together – lived on a farm on the outskirts of town. As lovely as Shirley's kin were, Hannah felt the weight of having to represent a family she did not much care for all on her own, and with her finances in tatters, she was unable to spoil her nephews with the latest Lego sets, robots or Apple products that Shirley's more affluent siblings could. I addition to this, Shirley and her siblings would also give each other lavish gifts, such as gorgeous winter coats, designer shoes or packaged holidays they all went on together. So, when Hannah handed her sister the box of chocolates that she knew she loved and the pair of mittens she'd asked for, in all its at-home-wrapped glory, Hannah couldn't help but feeling like dogshit. She was the oldest out of the lot yet had the least in financial terms. She was already very fucking good at putting herself down for this, and now she had to feel their pity on top of it. Soon, her nephews would be old enough to pick up on this, too, and she didn't know if she'd be able to bear it when the time would inevitably come. So, when the kids had been safely tucked away in their beds, she accepted the nip of whiskey offered to her by Shirley's dad.

Just a few more days with this lot, and she would be back home, where the absence of invitations to any New Year's parties was hanging heavily over her head and the fridge was ready stocked with a magnum bottle of prosecco and two boxes of wine, that she'd put on her credit card that was now dangerously nearing its limit. She needed the next few days to top up some happiness, to shake this feeling of not belonging in their seemingly far better world.

Chapter 2: January – There is no bottom

'OH. GOD. NO. NO! NOOOOOO!!!'

As Hannah awoke to the sound of her own screams on New Year's Day, all she wanted to do was to crawl up her own rectum and disappear. How on earth was it possible, or even allowed, to be so fucking stupid? Taking in her surroundings (she was not on the couch this time but had actually made it to bed for once); shoes, coat, bag scattered across the room, as well as a bloody traffic cone (what was she, 12?!), she shook her head in disbelief. The shaking of the head summoning an orchestra of bongo drums and crash cymbals in her head, adding to her agony. This 'no drinking ever again' schtick sure as hell hadn't stuck this time either. 'FAAAARK', she groaned and pulled the duvet over her head in an attempt to go back to sleep.

Of course, last night's festivities had been planned. She'd been invited to someone's party for once, and due to the fact that the other attendees were all a decade younger than her, she'd opted to down an entire bottle of prosecco *before* she left the house. Which was the best option, she'd decided, as she was starting to feel a bit fluey. Might as well kill off any bacteria before they started breeding. To add insult to injury, she'd used the bottle to break a 36-hour fast, *after* a 10-mile run – also taken in a fasted state – which she'd embarked on to decide whether or not she was too ill to go to the party. She'd survived the run, so now she had to woman up and go socialise like a functional human being. She should've consulted her magic eightball instead. She'd contemplated staying in and not drinking, keeping up the sober streak, but had decided she didn't want to start the new year off with any booze in the house, so she might as well go. She'd already made enough enquiries to the host that she was absolutely certain she wouldn't be the only single person there, so this could actually turn out to be a nice evening. She'd just take it easy on the drink. Tomorrow was a Monday, after all.

She arrived at the party just after five, and she found she was glad she did. Greeted at the door by her new pal Jen's partner, Justin, she was relieved to see that, a) he – much like herself – didn't seem too fussed about dressing up as some sort of Met Gala reject either and, b) he seemed to have been out of his nappies for just about as long as she had. And none of the people there were of the breeding kind, so all of that sort of inane small talk would be unnecessary, and they were all there because they had something in common, rather than their kids attending the same nursery, or some equivalent of the latter. It was really nice to not be the odd one out for a change! So, Hannah handed over a bottle of red for the hosts and began to relax. When she was offered a welcome drink, she accepted with a smile, forgetting she had yet to eat, and that dinner was at least an hour – i.e. at least three units – away. Needless to say, the party had been great. Until it wasn't.

So, what actually happened last night? How did she get home? Had she been asked to leave? She vaguely recalled trying to pull one of Jen's female friends – drunk Hannah wasn't one to discriminate –

after not getting anywhere with the boyfriend. Whether that had been before or after they had gone outside to see the fireworks was anyone's guess. She started to remember brief bits from their little outing, during one which Hannah had approached a child, asked its "owner" to pet *it* and then winded up having a full-on philosophical conversation with the poor child. Surely, no amount of therapy could ever be enough to help them get past the trauma. She felt absolutely disgusting. How was she meant to bounce back from this? How was she going to fix this? She'd have to start by putting out some fires, she decided, and pulled out her phone from underneath her. Apparently, she was an either/or person; she'd either leave her phone on a bus or couldn't get it close enough to her person, so she'd try to insert it into her own damned self. Just lovely.

Four missed calls, six unread messages and not one, but two UNANSWERED VIDEO CALLS to Helena from herself. Thank the good Lord Satan that they were missed calls, but how was she going to justify calling her in the middle of the night, knowing Hels had been on the night shift? She made herself go through her call history. Jen and her partner. Messages from the both of them: 'Where are you?' 'Are you still alive?' 'PLEASE ANSWER YOUR PHONE SO WE'LL KNOW YOU'RE ALRIGHT!!!!' 'Justin's just got back from looking for you outside for an hour… please just call us when you see this'.

Hannah groaned. She wasn't going to call, but the least she could do was message them. She felt her anxiety levels rise as she typed: 'I'm so, SO sorry, Jen!! I've no idea how I got here, but I'm at home now. Are you guys OK? I really hope I didn't offend anyone yesterday. Proper blackout from about 10pm here. I feel terrible. Really sorry. Won't happen again. XX'

She didn't expect a reply anytime soon, but she was too anxious to go back to sleep now, so she got up and went downstairs to get her life in order by making the following list:

1) Exercise
2) Shower
3) Repent, repent, repent
4) Make list for fixing life (starting tomorrow)

She had to start taking some responsibility for herself now. One more of these slip-ups and it would be too late. She could feel it in her gut. And you could probably say a thing or two about Hannah's gut, but it was never wrong.

Always one to rise to a challenge, Hannah loved ticking things of her list, so after completing the initial one, she made a start on one for her self-improvement as well. Jen had replied just moments after Hannah had messaged her, saying not to worry and that they were all glad she was all right. 'Everyone gets hammered once in a while and this was just one of those occasions'. Delighted and relieved by this response, Hannah decided to forgo going into detail about this being the norm in her case. The less Jen and her pals new about her more tragic personality traits, the better. Also, she was about to change all of this defeatist behaviour anyway, right? She still felt bad, but she figured she had a choice; she could let this get to her and continue the tradition of digging herself the world's biggest hole, or she could try and adopt a healthier attitude. She was just so goddamned tired. Knackered, in fact. Feeling like all of the energy had been completely sucked out of her all of a sudden, Hannah collapsed onto her couch and just laid there, staring at the ceiling, until it got dark, and she had to get up to turn the light on.

Her feet felt like blocks of cement as she dragged herself across the floor. She should probably make a bathroom pitstop as well, as who knew when she'd be able to get back to the upright position if she were to sit down again. Once in the bathroom, what looked back at her in the mirror shook her. A shade of dark purple sat around her once bright eyes, which were now sunken so far back in her head, it was hard to spot any life in them at all. Her hair was filthy; greasy at the roots and dry and split at the ends. Her forehead was creased, and her lips were red raw, as if she'd been rubbing them on a hedgehog. (She hadn't, had she?). The inside of her mouth felt like she'd tried to blow a nuclear device. She gagged and switched the light off, did her business, brushed her teeth and took her broken self straight to bed, leaving her phone downstairs and not caring that it was just gone 6.30. And then Hannah slept for a full 24 hours.

Waking up on the eve of the second day of the year, Hannah was shocked at the fact that she'd been able to sleep for more than her current standard of four consecutive hours. As a result of her micro-hibernation, everything hurt and she was in agony, but her mind seemed clearer than ever. As a bonus, the prolonged fast had left her belly flat and tight. Alas, that was not quite enough to dub herself a renaissance woman just yet. There was no way she was going to work in the morning. She went to get her phone so she could email her boss about not coming in tomorrow and to book a consultation with her GP, to ask for an extended period of sick leave.

The next morning, Hannah awoke promptly at 6am, ready to make some changes. A few hours later, she found herself sitting across from her GP; a lovely woman about her own age, and slightly intimidating due to the fact that she was both physically gorgeous and accomplished in so many areas that Hannah could only dream of ever reaching. The fact that she was genuinely nice as well was downright unfair.

As they were going through the usual how's and why's of her appointment, Hannah felt compelled to put everything on the table. Caffeinated out of this world, Hannah started talking. About EVERYTHING.

After a ten-minute bout of verbal diarrhoea, Hannah's GP concluded that she was indeed in need of some time off due to burnout, put her on an initial two-week leave and then referred her to a specialist for treatment of severe PTSD, self-harm and concurrent obsessive compulsive behaviour, exacerbated by the trauma. Due to the 'severity of her case' and 'nature of her injuries', it shouldn't take long before she'd hear back from the specialist. Then they'd take it from there. And under no circumstances was she to do anything work related – including checking her emails.

Hannah felt both empty and terrified but was somehow relieved at the same time. She had never taken more than a couple of days off in a row and hadn't taken a proper holiday in yonks – how did people do this? When someone is physically ill, there is very little you can do about it – you'd stay at home or in hospital until the symptoms wore off (or Death found you). But when it's all in your head, quite literally, and there's nothing stopping you from roaming around and having to face the thoughts you so stoically avoid when you're constantly working… it's just a different matter altogether. But she could feel this was the right decision. She hadn't really thought she'd be put on leave. She wasn't used to talking about her personal problems, as people either didn't take her seriously, or they were too set on talking about themselves instead of asking how *she* was, so this whole situation felt very odd. But she would try to make the most of it. Stay away from people, work out and keep her bankrupt self out of the wine shop.

On the bus journey home, she emailed her boss and team to say she was going on sick leave. Despite still reeling from the shock of her own openness and honesty during her doctor's appointment, she was already starting to feel a bit better about the whole thing. At least now she could finally log off the bloody work apps for a full fortnight. All her deadlines were met and since no one really knew – or cared about – what she was doing on a daily basis anyway, there'd be no slack to pick up when she got back. She waited until her boss confirmed having gotten notice of her leave before logging off, and as she went to click on the 'log off' icon, she saw a familiar face popping up in the team chat. Drew was online. 'Fuck this shit', Hannah mumbled through gritted teeth, logged off and shoved her phone back in her pocket, slightly blushing at the surprised stare from the elderly lady sitting across the aisle.

Now what, thought Hannah as she shut the front door behind her after her journey home. She supposed she could have a sit-down with herself and try to come up with some sort of plan, but she didn't feel like making any big decisions at the moment. Her mind was full of chaotic thoughts, and she was just too riled up. She'd been in and out of psychotherapy before – ever since high school – and look how well that had turned out for her. Who's to say it was going to do her anything but harm this time as well? She was starting to feel rather dismayed about her decision now, and just when she was about to succumb to the familiar embrace of darkness, she was blinded by an absolutely brutal ray of sunshine, and it stopped her destructive train of thought. It was as if she saw the sunlight for the very first time – and, to be fair, it *was* the first time she'd seen it this year – and it beckoned her to go back outside. Some movement to clear her mind was exactly what she needed.

Hannah peeked through her curtains, looking for excuses to stay indoors but found none. It had since long stopped snowing, and it looked like the roads had been completely cleared of snow and ice. She felt around her own self for any remnants of the New Year cold – no joy there either. Her mini hibernation had seemingly restored her body. Even though her desire to go for a run was pulling at her, she decided to have some breakfast. Perhaps the weather would turn in the meantime? She checked the forecast on her phone as she made her way through a bowl of stale granola and yogurt. All sunshine for the next five hours. As usual, she could feel the calories multiplying in her body, adding to the layers of fat around her gut as she ate. The only way to get it to go away was exercise. If she was going to deal with her mind, all she could do was lace up and get going.

The bright light burned Hannah's retinas as she stepped outside for the second time that morning. The cold air felt like knives in her lungs, so she pulled her snood up and hat down, leaving her eyes as the only visible part of her face. Shoving her in-ear headphones deep into her skull and sticking on her favourite playlist, she was off.

She wasn't planning on going very far or for very long, but as she left her street and got onto the path going down towards the water, everything started to feel very light and easy, somehow. It was as if the previously chaotic thoughts in her head started compartmentalising themselves, making it easier to pull them out one by one and giving them a proper look. Each song on the playlist gave her an extra boost, and before she knew it, she was already over halfway into her regular route.

As the smell of salty seawater found its way into her nostrils, she could start to see the water glistening between the trees. There was something about being near the open ocean that had always seemed to make her feel calm and centred. On a day like this, with not another soul in sight, the atmosphere pulled at her heartstrings and made her emotional, and as Ludovico Einaudi's *Experience* started playing, Hannah took the lid off all of her bottled up emotions and let the tears flow down her cheeks. As some of the salty secretions slowly made its way in between her lips and into her mouth, Hannah felt free and in touch with her innermost self. This was a kind of meditation for her, as the only way she would allow herself to look inside was when she was utterly exhausted, physically. She kept on running and didn't stop until she was back at her house almost three hours later.

After a long stretch and a shower, Hannah began to feel close to human again. It was as if she'd shed excess skin and found herself in a sort of embryonic state. She had no intentions of – or desire to – being born again, but perhaps a fresh start with herself was just what she needed. And as she opened herself up to opportunities, she looked down at her phone as it lit up and an unknown number flashed across the screen.

'Hello?' Hannah very rarely answered calls from unknown numbers – or at all – but she had a feeling this might be important. The voice on the other end belonged to Andrea Kowalski, a psychiatric specialist a couple of years older than Hannah. She'd just received the referral from Hannah's GP and thought it would be best they'd set up an appointment as soon as possible. Would Tuesday be alright?

Hannah let out a breath of air she hadn't realised she'd been holding in. She almost wanted to cry. This person on the other end had seen the symptoms of her struggles and decided she was worthy of a helping hand.

Dr Andrea found a time that would suit them both and that would give them an opportunity to carry on should they need to after the first hour. She explained there'd be a screening process and quite a few forms to fill out, but the most important thing about this first session was that they could have a proper chat and figure out whether they were a good match.

In all her years in and out of the public health system, Hannah had *never* encountered such a level of care and compassion. Hell, not in her life, full stop. She almost had to pinch herself. But this day was already beyond surreal, so she opted not to. If this was all a dream, she might just stay asleep for a while.

The weather remained chilly but sunny over the next few days, so Hannah managed to get a few runs in. She knew she wouldn't worry too much about next week's appointment if she exhausted herself enough, so she stayed active. Having decided to do Dry January, there was nothing around to help her self-sabotage either, so Hannah slept, worked out, ate, watched films and got started on the stack of books she'd been meaning to read that had been gathering dust by the coffee table for months. She discovered how much she'd missed getting sucked into a good – or terrible – book. Just like when she'd read *The Lion, the Witch and the Wardrobe* as a child, she took great pleasure in getting lost in the pages and letting the story swallow her whole. By Monday morning she was halfway through her third bestseller and not really sure where the stories ended and her own life began, or indeed which of her thoughts were her own and which were the characters'. But, right now, that didn't matter. All that mattered to Hannah in this moment was that she'd managed to get through a full week without doing anything that would cause her to feel shitty in the long-term. No small feat for an expert self-saboteur.

Yet, when it was time for bed, Hannah simply couldn't get to sleep. She tried everything, from breathing exercises to long division and even guided meditation. She was terrified she'd fuck up and oversleep and miss her appointment – having overslept precisely once in her entire life, over a decade ago, this was obviously a fear that was rooted in reality – and thus kept fidgeting and analysing every noise she heard. She must have gone to the toilet at least 22 times, but still felt like her bladder wasn't empty. What if I fall asleep and pee myself in the middle of the night? Isn't that what happens to people my age? That we automatically start *Benjamin Button*ing in terms of losing control over our bodily functions? This of course started an avalanche of similar thoughts; what if I stop breathing? What if I can't hear the alarm if I do manage to go to sleep? What if I go blind in the middle of the night and fall down the stairs and break my coccyx? How will anyone ever find my body? The only people that know my address are former one-night stands and my landlord – who's going to check up on me when I lay here, slowly dying in a pool of my own faeces?

Needless to say, this line of thinking didn't help, and by 3.20 Hannah gave up and got up. She got herself ready and sat down to do Sudoku puzzles until it was time to get going, at which point she was so knackered she could hardly remember her own name.

The psychiatric hospital was a 50-minute bus journey away, so in fear of falling asleep, Hannah opted to stand the whole way there. She had forgotten all about her initial impression of Andrea and was now dreading the appointment. Surely, this would be another one of those job interview-like scenarios in which she was judged on her greatest shortcomings, put on medication and filed away as just another ungrateful loon. Ten minutes into the journey, she was already fighting the lump in her throat and could feel her head starting to twitch. When she finally got to the reception at the hospital, she was a wreck and in no mood to make light of the situation. The receptionist being rude certainly didn't help. *Twat*, thought Hannah, as she scowled at the insignificant little shit that butchered the pronunciation of her middle name; Kuikman (thanks, mum, I really loved growing up with this Dutch delight).

Feeling smaller than ever, and also feeling bad for having thought such bad things about slowly decapitating the receptionist with a set of rusty nail clippers, she sat down on one of the chairs in the waiting room, rubbing her hands violently with hand sanitiser, as if she was going to catch more crazy from the other waiting patients. *Nutjobs*.

'Higgins?' came a voice to her right. Hannah looked up to meet the gaze of a rather statuesque but slender woman, just a few years older than her, with sparkling dark eyes and long dark hair in a plaid, wearing an absolutely massive moss green cardigan and a warm, caring smile. 'Hey, I'm Andrea', she offered, sticking her hand out to greet her. Hannah took it and felt herself smile, despite herself. 'Nice to meet you', she managed, and followed the good doctor up a set of stairs to her office.

As it turned out, Andrea (or Dr Kowalski) was very easy to talk to. She was as welcoming as she looked and, to Hannah's great relief, wasn't too focused on pushing her own agenda – or that of big pharma. She genuinely wanted to know how Hannah was doing and how she could help. So, for the first time with a therapist, Hannah removed the lid she'd welded so firmly shut to hold her thoughts, memories and emotions in and let it all spill out, not caring what Andrea might think of her. The thing was, she could not feel any judgement being passed on her at all from this unicorn of a human being. What's more, she felt that she could trust her. Trust being one of Hannah's main issues, especially with women as they are prone to constantly negging each other behind each other's backs, this was a huge step for her. But in this moment, she didn't even consider this to be a milestone. She just talked. Forty years of trauma, abuse, "leftoutedness", intrusive thoughts, self-diagnosis, official diagnoses, ineffective treatments, her experience with being medicated; everything. She had nothing to lose and everything to gain from this. She didn't know if it was the lack of sleep that had unlocked this little miracle, but she was grateful that there was something within her still capable of standing up for her.

As per public health services standard, there were quite a few standardised diagnostics forms to fill out, but Hannah knew these tests like the back of her hand. She'd filled them all out before, so there shouldn't be any surprises there. What did surprise her was Andrea's way of going through the documents with her. She was open to input from Hannah, who was no stranger to psychology, and spoke to her as if she was her equal instead of a helpless leper, unlike so many other healthcare professionals before her. This made Hannah feel profoundly safe and valued as a human being, which was an entirely new sensation for her. The fact that she'd been at such a low point that she'd actually asked for help probably had a thing or two to do with the fact that she was so open to trying to explain things properly as well, but shutting down and up when you can feel that the health service provider isn't really listening is far too easy. And when Andrea brought up

the subject of medication, she really listened when
Hannah tried to explain why she would never in her life
go back on meds. She'd rather be dead than have all of
her emotional input being put to rest.

She'd been 17 when her then psychiatrist had
put her on a high dosage of sertraline antidepressants,
and her complete lack of regard for consequences or
even feelings had seen her plan, and halfway execute,
her very first suicide attempt – which was only halted by
the fact that her live-in boyfriend came home from work
half an hour early that day. She'd carefully towelled the
bathroom floor so that she could easily bleed out
without staining it – he wasn't the best at cleaning, so
she'd spare him the trouble – and laid out her
razorblades on the toilet seat, ready to put herself out of
her own and everyone else's misery. She'd just managed
to force the blade half an inch into her left arm as she'd
heard the key turn in the lock of the front door, so she
was forced to abort her mission. Not because she'd
changed her mind about wanting to end her life but
because she realised that her then boyfriend would not
be capable of dealing with disposing of her body.

She had then decided she no longer wanted to
see this particular psychiatrist, mainly because he kept
making sexual insinuations that made her incredibly
uncomfortable, but nevertheless, she declared herself
'cured'. For some reason, he never cancelled her
prescription – nor did he mention that you would need
to slowly decrease the dosage over a rather long and
controlled period of time, so when she just stopped
taking them, she woke up one morning to find herself
and her surroundings utterly unrecognisable. She took
one look at her boyfriend, whom she'd started dating

whilst on the meds, and was immediately sick to her stomach. No offense to him as a person, but he was so removed from her personal tastes that she had no idea how she had let him sleep next to her, let alone *inside* of her.

While Hannah was regurgitating random information from her four decades of attempting to be a functional human being, Andrea simply regarded her and listened. She never interrupted her or interjected, she just jutted down a few notes and waited until Hannah was done before she said anything. And, instead of interrogating her or questioning Hannah's integrity in any way, she asked a few follow-up questions and told her that she would put a note in her journal not to put her on any medication in the future. Most mental health professionals Hannah had been in contact with previously had been big pill pushers, which was good enough reason for Hannah to stay clear of them altogether.

Realising they'd surpassed their allotted time by a full 40 minutes, Hannah started apologising profusely. She was 'never like this' and didn't know what had gotten into her. But Andrea hadn't checked the time once and she didn't seem to mind now that she'd been made aware of the fact either. She expressed an interest in starting a thorough diagnostics process and asked if Hannah thought she'd be up for that. If so, they'd make an appointment for next week.

On her way back home, Hannah was staring at nothing in particular out the bus window. By some miracle, someone seemed to be genuinely interested in what she had to say, what she'd been through and how she could start dealing with how she'd been coping (or not) over the years. Tired but ready to change her life for the better, she could feel herself opening up to the possibility of a life worth living. Not only for herself, but also for her sister and her young nephews that gave her role in life real meaning. She wanted to be stronger without constantly fearing that she'd crack and fall apart. And as she deeply exhaled, she was brought back to the present by accidentally letting out an, albeit completely silent, extremely vile-smelling fart that she realised she must have been holding in for the past two hours. Humiliated to her core, she desperately pounded the stop button to get away from the, quite frankly, shocked looking people around her. *Let me out, now!* she screamed inside her head. There was still a good fifteen minutes left until her stop, but she needed to get away from the shame before it got the better of her.

After what felt like an eternity, the bus finally pulled over and opened its doors. As she was rushing to get out, she slipped in a puddle on the floor and slid out the door in the most unladylike fashion before hitting the pavement, bum first, with a squishy thud. Feeling liquid seeping through her jeans, she was truly embarrassed now, as she looked in horror at the rolling metal gas chamber as it pulled away from her. 'We just can't have a full good day, can we?' she muttered, got up and started walking.

I can't believe I shat myself.

Hannah was still shaking her head in disbelief as she frog-walked her way through the slippery streets of the until now never before visited part of her neighbourhood. Her plan had been to simply jump on the next bus after her escape, but that was obviously not an option now. So, she walked.

As she walked, Hannah had begun to contemplate – as she often did – the proverbial rock bottom. Because it had become clear to her, in her previous attempts at sobriety, that there really is no such thing as a *bottom.* Very much like in a game of *Super Mario,* every time you think you cannot possibly get any lower, the floor falls out from underneath your feet and there is another surprise level of bottomness. What was even more frustrating, she found herself equally surprised every time this happened. Was it like this for everyone, or was she the only part of the species that had encountered this?

She could vividly remember the first time she thought she'd hit her low point; in her own take on *How to lose friends & alienate people,* she had woken up next to her flatmate's crush – in his bed – stark, bollocks naked (obviously), with her phone in her hand. As if having had sex with this guy wasn't bad enough for her to want to move away and become a Mormon, she'd somehow managed to film the pair of them as he was violently taking her from behind and send it to her flatmate as a *'fuck you'* for leaving the weekly cleaning duties to her every single week for the past year. Not exactly your standard eye for an eye approach, but what else could you expect from a brain that was thoroughly marinated in dark rum and cheap beer.

Oh, yeah, did I mention that drunk Hannah is *extremely* tech savvy? A skill that always comes in handy when you're trying to get to the next level of extreme shittiness. But more on that later.

Either way, as bad as that might have been, she had somehow managed to go on another bender a few days later, during which she had gotten obliterated and went home with another lovely young man, with whom she'd wound up smoking heroin – come on, he looked like an even more tortured Kurt Cobain, how could she *not*. Although, that might not be worse than stabbing your flatmate in the back. But it certainly made Hannah feel as if she had taken the knife to her own hide that time, and she was going to have to live with the fact that she had done both of these things very willingly – and some might say fully intentionally, as she had been the aggressor in both scenarios.

Hannah had no idea where she got the energy from, but she somehow managed the 3-mile walk home in just over half an hour. She might have been propelled by the faeces running down her legs, making her jeans stick to her like tar – as well as not wanting to have anyone see her – and she was grateful for her body's ability to shift into an extra gear in desperate times. She was also grateful that New Year's party Hannah had polished off all the alcohol in the house – along with her funds, so that she was unable to get more – because this would certainly have been one of those moments where Hannah felt that she could in very good conscience have a drink.

After the initial horror of her faecal incident had subsided, Hannah's anxiety escalated. This was to be expected, of course, because she was quite adept at digging herself a deeper hole once she was in one – especially if she'd had something good happen to her. It was like her subconscious refused to believe she would be capable of handling good things and thus protected her from receiving any positivity at all. And so, the self-deprecation ritual began; *what sort of self-respecting grown woman shits herself, and in public at that? No wonder I don't have any friends, who would want to be seen with me. I'm so ugly, people are offended when they see me. People treat me like I'm a burden.*

Hannah knew deep down that this wasn't helping and that it was in fact making matters worse, but she couldn't help herself. It was so much easier to sit and wallow in her own (now literal) shit, than to dust herself off and try to change her mindset. No amount of cognitive behavioural therapy could fix that. And this is what brought her face to face with herself in the bathroom mirror, with the cold metal blade of her scalpel pressed into her wrist. But, as she felt the sharp, exquisite sting of the razor making its way through the top layers of skin and small droplets of blood started to appear around the small incision, it was as if she could see something worth saving in herself and she was pulled out of her trance with a jolt. *What the fuck am I doing?!* Surely, just another thing she would have a hard time forgiving herself for, but she was still here, at least.

Chapter 3: February – I am not an addict

How is it that the shortest month of the year always seems the longest? Hannah had dreaded this month every year for as long as she could remember – not that she really had any reason to justify this, that she could recall – and now it was here. At least she'd pulled through Dry January, so she was allowed to have a drink again. So, when her pal Kim had texted her saying she needed a night out, Hannah was happy to oblige.

Kim was one of Hannah's friends from Uni, who had become one of those *proper* adults, with a real and important job, her own flat and, although she had no children or partner, she had a dog and a sense of entitlement and self-justification that made Hannah more than a little bit reluctant to hang out with her without any booze in her system. Moreover, as Kim was a proper grownup, she always relied on Hannah when she wanted to go out drinking, as her other adult friends wouldn't stoop to that level. And, since Kim had this alternative sort of sad friend that still went out binge drinking, she was highly regarded as a Samaritan among her peers when she was feeling generous enough to donate her time to the less fortunate.

How on earth a social worker with little more than a BA had come to think so highly of herself was a mystery to Hannah, who had an MA and none of that same entitlement, but they found themselves on two completely different rungs on the social ladder, nonetheless.

Naturally, Hannah had come to resent Kim for the above reasons, yet as much as she tried, she could never seem to shake her. She had tried cutting Kim out of her life for years – pretty much since they met – but no matter what she did, she was harder to shift than toenail fungus. Hannah reckoned that Kim was just about desperate enough to have someone in her life that would always be beneath her on the caste system, that she felt more than happy being the only one in the relationship that would initiate any sort of social interaction.

Hannah did realise that she had her own selfish reasons for going along with these sporadic meetings as well – she wasn't completely oblivious to her own shortcomings. Kim was overweight and utterly allergic to exercise, and refused – as a self-proclaimed feminist – to put in any effort whatsoever on her appearance, meaning all Hannah had to do in order to pull next to Kim was to put on a bit of eyeliner and clothes that didn't resemble something you'd use to carry potatoes in. In addition to this, Kim was incredibly loud and opinionated, and had a tendency to blame any of her own – or indeed society's – shortcomings on men, and she would always find a reason to call people out purely based on them owning a pair of testicles. She also firmly believed that women should get better pay and jobs based on their womanhood alone, even when a male candidate was better suited to a job or promotion. These were just a few of the many reasons why Hannah couldn't handle being around Kim in a sober state.

Don't get Hannah wrong here, she is fully for equal pay and human rights, but she doesn't believe that men today should be punished for something that was carried out by other men – often not even their ancestors – during something that belonged to our culture 60 years ago. And also, men have always been expected to get an education and go to work, while women were allowed to stay at home and run the house. You don't hear all of them resenting women for staying at home and not contributing to the household now, do you? There will always be exceptions to any rule, of course, but as a whole, men are not responsible for everything bad that happens to women. In fact, women largely try to sabotage other women on a daily basis, despite walking around claiming sisterhood and wanting to "take down the patriarchy" *together*.

Alas, despite Hannah's disregard of Kim, she needed a night out and didn't feel like going out alone. She also desperately needed to get her leg over, as a month of sobriety had stirred up a longing she'd normally numb with alcohol. She hadn't had intimate relations sober in at least a decade, so this was a more than terrifying thought. The introduction of alcohol into her system would do one of two things; remove the urge entirely or allow her the brief confidence she needed to get someone to come home with her. A win-win situation if Hannah ever heard of one.

As they had agreed to meet in town Thursday evening, naturally at Kim's favourite kitschy place, Hannah was having a few pre-drinks as she was getting ready. Upon receiving Kim's text – and this month's pay – Hannah had taken herself to the wine shop to get some prosecco. Having completed *Dry January* was a cause of celebration, surely?

It was ridiculous how much effort it took trying to look like you were effortlessly semi-hot. Well aware of her own physical shortcomings – reiterated on a daily basis by both parents and the rest of the world throughout her life – she did the best she could with what she had, meaning something to augment her not hideous eyes and enough alcohol to stop from caring about her lack of boobs and extra back fat. (Why couldn't the fat distribution have been a bit more fair and bloody *natural* in her case? The fat should go in the front, for God's sake!)

Despite her lack of ability to grow breasts, Hannah found that most men could be drawn to the flattest of chests when properly lubricated, so she put on one of her low-cut band tees that showed off some of her lacy (and subtly padded) bra, along with a pair of black skinny jeans that accentuated her bum. Years of heavy squats in the gym had given her a perky pair of glutes, which were the envy of most women her own age – and as long as the jeans staid on, no one could see the cellulite developing underneath. Yet another thing an inebriated male would seldom notice should the jeans come off.

Done with her hair and makeup and her confidence fuelled by the prosecco and strange sense of purpose, Hannah took a selfie, winking at herself in the mirror. *Not too bad for a middle-aged chick,* she thought to herself.

She got a text from Kim, saying she'd be stuck at work for a little while longer, but she could meet her at the place at 7. Seeing as that was two hours away,

Hannah decided it would be safe to have something to eat; any bloating from the food should be eliminated by the time she got there. Also suspecting her tolerance may be lowered due to not drinking for a month, this was indeed a fortuitous change of events. She got some crispbread and Brussels style pâté out of the cupboard and started the countdown to the night's festivities.

Having timed it so she wouldn't be too early or too late, Hannah arrived at the hipster-infested bar at 6.58pm. Not wanting to go in alone, she swept her gaze across the venue through the windows and spotted Kim at one of the tables in the back. She seemed to be thoroughly enjoying the massive sandwich in front of her, clearly not giving a single shit about judging eyes in the already busy place. Hannah had to admit she felt sort of jealous of other people's ability to eat in public, without caring if anyone should see them and being able to manage to put the food into the face hole and not poke themselves in the face with the eating utensils. Going out to eat was Hannah's definition of a nightmare. In fact, she'd rather be penetrated anally for a full 45 minutes instead of going out to dinner (and by some miracle she was STILL single!). Hannah took a settling breath and stepped inside.

'Hey!' Kim boomed at the sight of her. 'So nice to see you, it's been ages! I was so hungry I just had to get some food. Do you want anything?' Hannah looked at Kim's plate and half-empty pint glass. 'Nah, I'm good', she replied. 'I'm getting a drink though. Can I get you one?'

Taking care of the first round meant she wouldn't have to feel the pressure of finishing her first drink too quickly in order to pay for the next round. *Well done,* she told herself, as she got in the queue for the bar. She scanned the bar for any potential conquests for later, but most of the blokes in here seemed either younger, into each other, or very married. Or all three. Fuck it, no one in this place was her type anyway; all man bun, copy/paste hipster metrosexuals. Made her lady bits dry right up.

When her turn was up, she ordered pints for Kim and herself, as well as a couple of shots. 'Oh, and my friend got promoted today, so if you could bring two more shots over to our table in 30 minutes time as well, that'd be lovely. We're celebrating', she winked at the barman. It was good to have an excuse on hand in case things would get a little out of hand later. Or if the hot barman should fancy joining them once his shift was over.

As she sat the drinks down on their table, Kim shouted: 'Shots?! Really? You know we're both in our 40s now... Jesus, Hannah!' But she didn't seem to need any convincing downing the shot that had been placed in front of her. Hannah also knew that it would only take a couple of these to make Kim lose a bit of her well-rehearsed adultness and assume her old role of party lover – Hannah was pretty much doing them both a favour. By the time the second round of shots was brought out, Kim didn't even question why the barman was congratulating her, and as soon as they'd both finished their round of drinks, she jumped up and beamed; 'My turn!'

Taken aback by this unexpected turn of events, Hannah excused herself to go to the toilet when Kim returned with a fresh round of shots. Kim was doing shots voluntarily now? On a school night, no less?

Still shaking her head as she was walking back to their table, Hannah spotted something equally shocking unfolding in front of her; sat next to Kim was Susannah, one of the girls from their study group, whom she had not talked to – and quite frankly had tried to avoid – for at least a decade. Lovely. Also, come to think of it, didn't she have an even more grown-up job than Kim?

'Look who's here!' shouted Kim, excitedly. Hannah approached the table with extreme caution. She was in no mood to be judged by the pair of them, or to sit there and listen to them complain about their wonderful lives. 'I thought I'd message her, it being the school holiday and all and we're all off tomorrow.' *Off? Holiday? WTF?!* As if Hannah was meant to have any control or indeed interest in people's kids' school holidays. And now she was stuck with Kimannah – the two-headed man-hating fembot from the land of Werebetterthanyoutopia. Great. There are just not enough shots in the world, Hannah thought, unless they're coming out of the barrel of a gun. Despite her better judgement, she took her seat at the table. 'So, what are we having, then?'

It turned out Susannah was in no mood for shots, as she had a screaming toddler waiting for her at home. 'And Richard is actually looking after the baby; can you believe it?!' Referring to her husband and father of said toddler, as if he were completely bereft of aptitude when it came to the care and rearing of their offspring, men were apparently only good for one thing, and that was the donation of viable sperm. If Susannah could have her way, they'd all be hooked up to some sort of milking device via their scrotums, like in *The Matrix*, but with more jizz and less coding.

Instantly saddened by the thought of a world sans Keanu, Hannah made an excuse to get back up and made a beeline for the bar for an emergency shot. Why on God's green earth she'd given up smoking, she had no clue. She was dying for a cigarette now, if only for the short five-minute break from the conversation. Maybe she'd try to bum one off the barman later, should she get really desperate.

It was now gone 8.30 and the bar was heaving, full to the brim; it would appear most people had the day off tomorrow, as she could see more than a few shirt-clad hipsters double-fisting the IPAs. Why had she agreed to going to this place again?

Back at the table, Kim and Susannah were still discussing the uselessness of men. Frustrated by the aspect of having to keep on listening to this, Hannah decided to interrupt them with a little rant on how feminists like them were just as – if not more so – obsolete than the men they were referring to, pointing to the fact that parental leave fell mostly to mum and that men have to give up pay if they wanted to bond at all with their child. This didn't sit well with the fembot, of course, but Hannah couldn't help herself. Fuelled by Patrón and a sense of injustice, she hammered on about how they should look up the word equality in the dictionary when they got a minute. Pleased with herself, she went off to pester the barman for that cigarette she so desperately needed.

Normally, when Hannah went off on one like she just did, the normal reaction was for the "adults" to laugh at her for being pathetic and juvenile behind her back until she returned, yet this time she sensed a disturbance in the force as she joined them after her cheeky cig – which totally didn't count, by the way, because she didn't inhale properly. As she sat down, she could see that Susannah had been crying – Hannah had no clue as to why – and just as she was about to ask what was wrong, Kim rushed to her feet and said they'd better go. 'But you're welcome to stay here, of course', she added.

What the fuck? 'Um, alright then…? It was really nice to see you both. Let's catch up soon, yeah?' Hannah said. They both looked at her rather blankly and said something along the lines of they didn't know when they would next have the time to go out drinking like this. They had other priorities. Hannah shrugged. Oh, well. She said her goodbyes and joined the barman – who had informed her that he'd finish his shift in a few minutes – at the bar.

She was looking at her Instagram when her phone buzzed with a message from Kim: 'I know you couldn't possibly know this, but Susannah and Richard are in the middle of a custody battle right now. He's been emotionally abusive towards her, and she's been trying to leave him for months now, so leaving her daughter in his care is a MASSIVE deal for her. Maybe you should try to think before you speak next time.'

SHIT.

Needless to say, Hannah felt terrible. Although the two of them had never been close, it didn't mean that Hannah was devoid of empathy regarding Susannah's situation. No one deserved that. She didn't have Susannah's number, so she couldn't call to apologise – not that she would've if she *had* had it, but she would have at least texted. Instead, Hannah went for the next best option. Shots with the barman and big trek to a steady stream of pints in *Scruffy's*.

Hannah had always had the ability to hang out with just about anyone, which was one of the reasons why so many said they knew her; she was a cheap psychologist and an even cheaper date, so why not, right? And most people found her to be a happy-go-lucky extrovert that was always up for a laugh, seeing as they only saw her when she'd had a few.

Hannah's new pal, the hipster bar barman, seemed to be more than happy in her company, and having never been to *Scruffy's* before, he was impressed to see she knew everyone in there. Now intent on getting rid of the bad feeling in the pit of her stomach, Hannah was really hitting the bar in a big way. Gone was the urge for pulling, now replaced by the desire to kill off as many brain cells as possible so the voice in her head would give her some peace. But for some reason, the alcohol just didn't seem to be doing its job tonight, and just around midnight she decided to tap out and head home, not even stopping by the 24-hour shop for her guilt trip binge on the way home.

Hannah woke up reasonably early the next day and decided to text Kim and apologise for her behaviour, reiterating of course that there was no way she could have known and that she was in the midst of getting into psychotherapy at the moment and that she wasn't as sensitive to her environment as she'd be normally. Kim immediately rang her back to say she may have overreacted slightly due to the amount of drink they had all had – and, *really*, Hannah should know better than to order shots – and did she want to come for a drive on Saturday? Kim was going to the big outlet store a couple of hours away and she could use the company. And maybe Hannah could tell her what was going on with the psychologist? She said she'd apologise to Susannah on Hannah's behalf, as she was probably the last person she wanted to hear from right now. *Thanks for that, by the way*, thought Hannah. But feeling the urge to have a real friend stir up inside of her, Hannah agreed to have Kim pick her up tomorrow morning and hung up before she had the time to regret saying yes. She then put on her running kit and braved the icy roads of the neighbourhood for an aerobic cleanse.

Hannah still had that empty, sort of out of body-like feeling when she got back from her run, so she kept herself busy with cleaning and listening to Gustav Holst's *The Planets*. She was a bit worried about tomorrow's drive, as she very much felt like she had taken off the lid on her jar of extra nutty when she was at the psychologist's and now she had somehow misplaced it so she couldn't screw it back on. Like, if someone would go against the norm and ask her how she was, she would tell them exactly how messed up she was on the inside. What had initially made her feel free and open to changing her outlook on life now just made her feel like she was missing the top layer of skin and had nothing to cover herself up with. Alcohol had lost its appeal, and she didn't much feel like eating until she couldn't help but making herself sick either. It was stressing her out. Her normal coping mechanisms seemed what they were; completely and utterly meaningless. And, ironically, she didn't quite know how to deal with that.

Knowing Kim, they'd probably stop by the massive sweet shop tomorrow, so there was one way of coping still available, Hannah figured. Having found a loophole leading back to her true nature and depressed self – like in a real life game of chutes and ladders – she decided to have an early dinner and then do a 24-hour fast so she could burn through the sweet shop calories like a forest fire the next day, neglecting the fact that stopping eating at 2pm would surely make it near impossible to get any sleep when the time came for her to go to bed. Little or next to no sleep also had a tendency to make her very thin-skinned the following day, so there really was no telling how the upcoming road trip would unravel. Or, if indeed it would lead to her unravelling entirely. Only time would tell.

Of course, Hannah struggled to get any sleep that night, despite her having gone to bed just after 10, so when her alarm went off at 8am, she had just managed to fall asleep and had to drag herself out of bed. Off to a great start.

Three cups of very strong coffee, a shower, a bout of caffeine induced explosive diarrhoea and two hours later, Hannah found herself legging it through the garden to avoid having to say 'hi' to the landlord on the way to Kim's car, which was already waiting for her in the driveway. To her chagrin, she discovered that Kim had put on her favourite road trip playlist, consisting almost entirely of pop punk – the kind of "musical" torture that made Hannah's stomach turn. And seeing as her recent behaviour hadn't exactly been stellar, she wasn't about to start complaining either, so she grinned and bared it. 'So sorry again for Thursday', Hannah exclaimed as the car pulled out of the driveway and onto the street. Already an expert on self-deprecation, she added 'There's obviously no excuse for that type of insensitive behaviour, and I really should have known better'.

'Don't worry about it', said Kim. 'Sorry, I just have to focus on the GPS for a bit, this isn't my normal route, you know'.

Two minutes in and Hannah was already enjoying her first guilt-trip. Lovely!

After what seemed like an eternity in silence, they finally got onto the main road, and they could both relax. Hannah asked Kim about her work, a subject she in fairness always seemed keen to talk about, which got the conversation off to a start. Maybe she'd lucked out and Kim had forgotten she'd taken a brief interest in Hannah for once? But just as she was starting to lower her shoulders and assume her normal role as the great listener, Kim surprised her by saying: 'But what's been going on with you lately? You're on sick leave and seeing a therapist now?'

And, despite herself, Hannah blurted out a lot – if not all – of what she had kept bottled up for the past 20 years that they'd known each other. Seeing as Kim's eyes were on the road and not on her seemed to make it even easier for Hannah to let her guard down and give Kim some credit. She did use to have a job where she had a vow of silence, so surely Hannah wouldn't have to tell her that this needed to remain between the two of them? Hannah wasn't even sure she cared at this point, so she just talked. More surprisingly, Kim seemed to understand her as well, so she didn't have to repeat herself or explain a lot – she just talked. She even talked about how she couldn't remember the last time she hadn't blacked out while drinking, which was why she so rarely went out these days. She did make sure to keep reminding Kim that depression and this air of darkness had been her life for as long as she could remember, and that the biggest change in her life was the fact that she now had every intention of *not* ending it. And as the urge to purge was more or less starting to subside, Hannah didn't feel so miserable anymore. Perhaps this friendship was in fact a real one, instead of the one-way street she had gotten used to over the years? After all, it had been *her* assumption that Kim wasn't likely to be interested in her life and had thus failed to provide much information about herself. Nevertheless, she did have the common sense to realise that this was more than enough sharing for one day, so she more than happily turned the conversation back to Kim's life, asking about her dog and such. She just needed something lighter to focus on, which Kim seemed pretty happy about as well. After that, the conversation went between Kim's home and work life and their respective shopping lists, and they both agreed that a trip to the sweet shop was much overdue, where they both got enormous bags of all of the things that Kim loved and lots of the stuff Hannah enjoyed throwing up. Top tip – marshmallows are NOT good for throwing up; they'll clog up your toilet something fierce.

All in all, they had a nice wee trip and parted ways with a hug and a promise to hang out again soon.

Which made the call from her psychologist two hours later come as a total surprise and stab in the back – it seemed Kim had made a phone call to her former colleagues on the psychiatric crisis unit, saying she was worried Hannah could be a danger to herself. For them to ruin her psychologist's weekend – not to mention her own – was unforgivable to Hannah. She was filled with an enormous rage, which in turn refuelled her need for numbness and alcohol, so after having spent the better part of her last hour trying – and ultimately succeeding – to avoid having herself be committed to an overnight stay at the nearest psychiatric hospital, she was seething with anger. Clearly, Kim was not worthy of the trust Hannah had given her. She had to agree to spend the rest of her weekend reporting her whereabouts and mood to her psychologist every couple of hours as well, knowing that the van with the men in white coats would show up at her door if not. *So, this is what you get for taking a chance on someone*, Hannah thought to herself, bitterly. *Figures.* At least she could stop feeling guilty for thinking she'd been too quick to pass judgement on Kim within the first five minutes of their first meeting all those years ago. Although she was quite cross with herself that she hadn't severed any ties before there had been any, based on that initial gut feeling.

Hannah's plan for the evening had been to turn her phone off, shut the world out completely and do some drawing, but since she was now on constant reporting duties, there was no way she would be able to relax enough to do anything remotely creative. The only positive thing was perhaps that she opted out of having any of her emergency wine that was now tucked securely behind her upstairs freezer. She refused to let this become one of those occasions where Kim would be proven right in her efforts to sell her out.

Hannah resisted the urge to change Kim's contact name in her phone to *AntiSocial Worker Cunt* and instead began her least detrimental form of self-harm/coping ritual; eating every single sweetie in the massive 700-gram bag as quickly as she could, only to projectile vomit them back up again within the 20 minutes it normally takes for the calories to be absorbed into the system. But instead of making her feel clean and empty, the binge and purge left her laying on the bathroom floor, with her throat red raw and a sense of having been covered by a layer of filth that had seeped through her skin and into her bones, making it impossible for her to scrub herself clean. But I suppose that is what you both get and deserve from letting matters you cannot control getting to you. In any event, her psychologist would be calling soon, so she scraped herself off the floor, brushed her teeth until her gums bled and headed back into the living room, where she sat in complete darkness with her water bottle, waiting for the next call.

Hannah called it quits and trampled up the stairs to bed after another call and two texts from her psychologist. *Bless her*, thought Hanna. *She really doesn't deserve to have her whole weekend ruined because of me. She's the first person that seems to actually understand me, and now I'll probably lose her because of this shit.* She really was terrified this might happen, as medical professionals had expressed their incapability to handle someone like herself in the past. She was simply 'too much' for them. *If you think I'm too much, what do you think it feels like living inside my head? At least you're just a bystander and you can clock out when the end of the day comes. My day doesn't have an end unless I end it myself.*

Hannah could feel herself spiralling now. If she wasn't able to get to sleep soon, she was unlikely to get much sleep at all, so she pulled out her phone, opened the *BuzzFeed* app and went through so many *Can you believe I can guess the colour of your soulmate's aura* quizzes that her brain finally put itself out of its misery and capitulated to the Sandman.

Waking on Sunday morning to a splitting headache, thanks to the sugar overload, it was still fairly early, so Hannah decided to text her psychologist before she got the chance to get up and text *her*:

Hi Andrea, so sorry again about yesterday. I really am alright. Just heading out for a run now, in case you call and I don't pick up straight away. I'll message you when I get back. Thank you for caring and checking up on me. H'

And she really was alright. It's not as if she was going to do anything stupid yesterday. She just wished she hadn't opened her big mouth. It seemed to her that hanging out with Kim made her feel extra shitty about herself – it almost always had. And she was well aware of the fact that this was down to her own insecurities and not necessarily something that Kim had done. In fact, the real betrayal Hannah was experiencing was her own, where she'd willingly put herself in a situation where she knew that she would end up dreading the event before it happened, feel miserable throughout the meeting and then feel guilty about her own behaviour towards both Kim *and* herself in the aftermath. This simply wasn't sustainable. So, she made a fairly sober and grownup decision – the first one of the year – to message Kim to tell her that she needed some space and that she wouldn't be in contact with her whilst she was getting her life back on track. Or onto any sort of tracks, for that matter.

She waited until Kim had read and replied to her text that she completely understood before lacing up and hitting the road. And for the first time in a long time, she knew in her gut that she had made the right decision.

Monday morning began with a follow-up session with her psychologist, so by 8am, Hannah found herself in the waiting room, really quite anxious to get on with things. By the end of this week, she would have missed a great chunk out of work's team meetings, and she knew she should try to get back sooner rather than later. At the end of the day, her contract with the company was temporary and if she wanted to make it permanent, she would need to show them that she was needed. It was either that or looking for a new job, but her boss had already told her, on several occasions, that she had started lobbying for a fixed position for Hannah. Unhappy as she was at her work, down to simply not fitting in as well within her own department as she did all the others and always being taken for granted and generally being quite desperate for any other job that wasn't *there*, she felt like she couldn't afford to start over yet again. She didn't have the energy.

In any normal circumstances, Hannah would have gone with her gut – that was convinced her boss would go back on her word – and started looking for a new job ages ago, but this time around, just the simple task of writing up cover letters seemed utterly exhausting. Fuck, she was tired. *Anyway, must get back to it,* she thought, as she heard her name being called from the top of the stairs.

'What?!' Hannah stared at her psychologist in disbelief. 'You're not serious!' Andrea adjusted her glasses and smiled at her, somewhat apologetically. 'Hannah, I really don't think you should be working at all, and I am going to recommend to your GP that we put you on sick leave for at least a year, starting now. The episode this weekend is just another indication that adds to my list of why you need to take a real break. You're burnt out on top of everything else, and the type of ongoing treatment you'll need is quite frankly something that you shouldn't have to be dealing with in addition to a full-time job.'

Hannah, who hadn't taken more than a long weekend off work in over a decade, was flabbergasted. She felt sick. What was she going to do for money? It wasn't as if she had any savings worth mentioning, having spent what little inheritance she got after her granddad passed already due to the mere fact that she wasn't planning on living a day past 27. And getting paid sick leave was sort of contingent on you having a job in the first place. With her contract being up in the next few months, she wasn't sure HR would get on board with a renewal if she took out any more leave during this quarter.

As if she'd been reading her mind, Andrea continued:

'I know you're worried about your contract renewal, but there are processes already in place to support you through periods of illness. We won't have to deal with any changes in your income until the initial 12 months are up, and then we will assign you someone to help with applying for continued financial support when the time comes. I'm afraid you won't get any better unless you start addressing some of what's been bothering you for so long. And for us to help you do that properly, we need to follow protocol and all the steps to make sure we don't leave anything out or unaccounted for. I just want you to be happy and healthy.'

A younger, less knackered, Hannah would have smiled politely and said 'thanks, but no thanks' and walked out. Instead, she slumped back in her chair – the air going out of her as if she were a balloon – and started making a plan with Andrea. She only had one demand, and that was the chance to go back to work and complete her assignments before she clocked out for good. She couldn't take another failure now and really didn't have it in her to see the company wasting a whole year's salary on a project that would end up not bearing any fruits. She didn't want to be remembered as someone who came in and didn't do the work. So, Andrea agreed to compromise. Hannah would work for another month, then take a few weeks off and then go back to her final weeks part-time before the contract was up.

On the bus on her way home from the appointment, Hannah emailed her boss to say she'd be back next week and that she was eager to start showing her some results. Her boss instantly replied that there was no rush but that it would be nice to see her back in the office and to take care. Hannah felt her face contorting into a fake smile. Did she always do that? Put on a front with work stuff? Maybe taking a year off wasn't such a bad idea after all.

Hannah stuck some music on, put her phone away and looked out the grimy bus window. Bright rays of sunshine were starting to penetrate the thick layer of heavy clouds that had previously threatened to shower them with another slab of sleet, and cracks revealing blue skies were starting to form. *Wow,* thought Hannah. *Blue skies and sunshine, and I haven't shat myself even once today. I've either died from the embarrassment of last week, or there's some good about to come from this whole therapy thing after all. Maybe I'll celebrate with one of my pink prosecco mango smoothies. It's not like I'm going to work any time soon.*

Part 2: Spring

Chapter 4: March – I can do this

By Monday morning, Hannah had started to get some of the old fire in her belly back. She now had a deadline, and there was nothing quite like pressure to make Hannah go above and beyond. Which was probably why she burned out completely when two decades of pressure was finally lifted off of her, with her current workload. But that whole problematic situation, we'll save for another day.

The day hadn't got off to the best start. When she was on sick leave and didn't have to set her alarm, she'd wake up, fresh as a daisy, at 5.45 sharp. Every morning, like clockwork. But today, knowing she *had* to be up at a certain time, she'd hit the snooze button at least four times before managing to drag herself out of bed half an hour before she had to be out the door. She had struggled to get to sleep as well, as usual, and due to her snoozeathon she only managed to put on her clothes and makeup before having to head out the door, so she was now on the train trying to function on about four hours of sleep and absolutely no coffee. They did have a machine at work, but Hannah's ritual of two double espressos to kickstart her BMs was now making her contemplate going without. She rummaged through her bag to see if she had any glucose tablets left, but no luck there. Luckily, her brain thrived on four to six hours of sleep and no food for fuel, so when she finally got to the office just before 8, she just went into autopilot and got through her entire to do list before most of her colleagues started turning up about an hour later. *The perks of living with crippling anxiety*, Hannah smirked to herself.

Despite the shitty start to her morning, she had really gotten into a groove workwise now, but as soon as her colleagues started to infest the open plan office like a colony of incredibly loud-chewing termites, her mood started to drop. The room was all too soon bursting with inane laughter and banal chatter about what everyone had been up to over the weekend. Could they not see that she was working? Also, couldn't they catch up over lunch instead? She knew how they would all waddle into the lift in just two hours anyway, so why not squeeze in some actual work on a Monday morning? Every trace of her earlier glee over crossing things off her list had completely vanished, as if the noise was a flame and her joy an odourless gas. All gone.

She could hear her stomach growling now as well. Of course, she'd fasted since yesterday to counteract a weekend of bingeing, so that didn't help the mood much. She wanted to look good in case Drew dropped by her desk as well, but she could feel the double chocolate cookies in the lounge area calling her name now. Screaming her name, actually. Hannah would normally sneak a handful (or three, rather) of stale cookies that had been sitting out over the weekend *before* her coworkers showed up, to avoid being dubbed a gluttonous, fat sugar junkie looking turd, but she had really thought she'd be able to control herself until lunchtime today.

Hannah had a team meeting in ten minutes. She could do a lounge sweep and dispose of the evidence on the way if she got a move on. It would not be particularly wise to head into the first meeting of the day on an empty stomach, so she had to do something to lengthen her already short, quickly deteriorating and almost non-existent fuse.

Promptly unplugging her laptop from the docking station and grabbing her pen and paper, Hannah had already planned her route to the lounge area in her mind. She needed to avoid the overly chatty and always gossiping accountancy staff on the way, or else she'd be stuck in a conversation with them until the meeting started. She would need to time it perfectly to slip past all of them without them noticing, but this is where all her years working in hospitality came in handy – she was used to constantly analysing situations and people's behaviour, so she had everyone's pattern down to a T. In about 12 seconds, Rebecca from marketing would come booming through the door, having dropped off her kids at nursery after being stuck in traffic for 45 minutes, and Hannah would be able to hide herself in the wake of the flood wave that was Rebecca's personality.

The ding of the lift was Hannah's cue – and proof of her own impeccable timing. She could already see the reflection of Rebecca's bright yellow dress positively glowing like radioactive matter in the picture frame that hung opposite the lift and got into her starting position for darting through the room at a speed that would put Usain Bolt to shame. Her gait would make it clear to anyone who noticed her that she was in a rush to get somewhere, and she managed to avoid accounting by taking a left before the toilets and going the long way round. She stopped at the kitchen island in the lounge area, dove into the large cookie jar on top of the counter, grabbing no less than eight cookies and a handful of honey-glazed trail mix before swinging herself into the disabled toilets to dispose of her bounty. With any luck, she'd have time left over to grab a coffee from the machine on her way into the meeting. No such luck today though, because the one thing she hadn't counted on, was smashing into Drew that was coming out of said toilet as she was about to fling the door open. She was going down in a blaze of nuts and cookies as the hottest man within a 50-mile radius stared at her with a look she couldn't quite decipher. Fuck. FUCK!

In any scenario involving herself, Drew and nuts, this was certainly not what she'd ever imagined, as the back of her head smacked into the doors of the lift behind her. If only they'd been open, so that she could have at least fallen down the elevator shaft – or even better, been pulled into some sort of teleportation device that would carry her off to Titz, Germany. Or just any place where nobody would know her, and she could start afresh.

Drew was standing over her for what seemed like a lifetime before finally offering her – and the laptop she'd managed to hold onto in her fall – his hand to pull her up. Red-faced and chaotic feeling, she was suddenly face-to-face with him again. Just a little too close, and she breathed in the smell of him like some sort of psycho – his scent clean and crisp, like an early autumn morning. Realising now that she was panting with her mouth open, she quickly jumped back with all the poise and grace of a startled wildebeest, mumbled a 'thanks' and something about the meeting and stormed off, leaving the mess of foodstuffs behind her with just enough time to grab another handful of nuts to bring with her into the meeting. *Ick.*

Her caffeine deficiency was now palpable, as was the tension in the meeting room as she entered. It turned out the numbers for the end of the year had been made public and they were nearly disastrous. It had been made very clear by management that they all needed to up their game if they were going to meet the budget requirements for the first quarter of the year. It quickly dawned on Hannah that, in short, this meant the portion of the budget designated to cover her salary was now completely decimated. As the only one on her team with zero impact on sales or B2B interactions, there was nothing she could do to cover her own arse either. Even though her psychologist had reassured her that being on sick leave would cover her even though she would technically be unemployed, this seemed like Utopia to Hannah, who had been self-employed for most of her adult life, so the news sent her into a slight panic. She also knew that her boss would have sat on this information for months already yet had the nerve not to tell her to start looking for a new job. In fact, she had said the opposite when Hannah had asked her directly! The next couple of months ahead of her suddenly felt like the longest time yet still far too short and again, Hannah felt utterly drained of energy. Hannah must have zoned out, because all of a sudden, her team was wrapping up and had started talking about lunch. It was 11 already? She could hear the growl of her own stomach, having burned through the nuts like wildfire but there was no way she could sit at the same table as these people any longer. She declined their invitation to join them, saying she still had emails to get through

before she could in good conscience take a break.
Everyone else also seemed cafeteria bound and were all
queueing up for the lift, she'd so intimately caressed
with her skull only hours earlier. She watched them all
pile in, close-talkers one and all. She spotted Drew nose
to nose with the chatty disease of a human being from
accounting – the very same he'd been talking to at a
certain work do – just before the doors closed. She had
no reason to be jealous or even envious, yet she felt the
familiar feeling of inferiority starting to eat away at her
from within. A small victory, though, was that the office
was now nearly empty, and she could find one of the
small offices in the quiet zone and work from there.
Also, since no one was around, she was able to grab
nearly a dozen stale cookies from the kitchen island in
the lounge, as well as a mug full of nuts, to fend off the
hunger pangs. She also got herself a quadruple shot of
espresso, despite knowing it would more than likely rot
her insides and make her feel very nauseous and
bundled herself and her mini buffet into the quiet zone,
where she spent the next 20 minutes trying to come up
with a good excuse for working from home for the rest
of the day. Alas, as the first lift-full of coworkers started
pouring back in, her laptop screen flashed with a
notification; the first post lunch meeting was due to
start in 15 minutes. Somehow her brain had blocked out
her least favourite thing about Mondays in this office – it
was literally all meetings, from lunchtime until the end
of the workday. Which meant that there would be no
lunch break for Hannah today. Another quadruple
espresso and as much sugar she could stuff in her gob
in 15 minutes it was, then.

In a desperate attempt to show herself as the workhorse of the office, Hannah really did try to participate in the remaining meetings of the day. As she doubled as a sort of one-woman communications team within her department, she would attend the team meetings for the marketing and communications department as well. Today, she was dead set on relaying any information and wishes that wouldn't normally get to the marketing team in any sort of effective manner. If they could see what she was capable of, maybe there would be a job for her there instead? Although being around so many "look at me" people at all times was thoroughly exhausting, Hannah figured this would be the case in any other job where you'd share an office, so she might as well stay where they had sort of gotten used to her already. She couldn't stand the thought of having to introduce herself to yet *another* new place, where she would probably be unlikely to fit in anyway – like everywhere else in this world. And then there was Drew. He weighed on her shoulders like 83 kilograms of unfinished business, their latest interactions constantly at the forefront of her mind.

In no mood to stick around a minute longer than she needed today, she was out the door as soon as the last meeting finished. By some miracle, she managed to catch the 4.11 train home just as the doors were about to close, meaning she would be able to squeeze in a workout *and* eat something more nutritious than cookies before it got too late for her to start her fast. She hated the long commute that ate away at her precious free time. Everything seemed like a struggle when three of the day's hours were spent on a train full of hostile co-commuters. All the negativity was getting to her.

She'd wasted too much of her two weeks off work on worrying about what would happen when she got back, and her shoulders were already up around her ears with the stress of the first day. She put it down to her lack of energy in trying to tackle a day full of meetings with hardly any food or caffeine and tried to shrug it off – whilst at the same time kicking herself for setting herself up for failure by being stupid enough to snooze and skip breakfast, of course. She'd already forgotten her luck in catching the early train and was already knee-deep in the wallowing grave she was digging for herself. At the end of the day, she was the only one that she could rely on, yet here she was, sabotaging herself every chance she got.

An enormous wave of sadness hit her with such force that she felt weak in the knees and had to grab hold of one of the bars on the train just to keep herself from toppling over. One fall in a day was more than enough. The memory made her palms clammy, back sweaty and her breath uneven and she let go of the bar she was holding onto and instead jammed her fingernails into the thin skin on her left wrist, just to snap herself out of it. A public meltdown was certainly out of the question. Surely, she had been able to control herself a bit better in the past? She'd always been just fine with very little sleep as well, so there was no logical explanation for this sudden tiredness – especially as work was so undemanding. In the past six months she'd started to feel nauseous and feverish all the time as well, especially on the days she wasn't able to work from home and had to go into the office. In fact, just thinking about it now made her feel queasy. Yet, when she'd gone to her GP for a checkup, all her bloodwork had come back normal; there was nothing to indicate any infection or illness that would cause her symptoms. Not even one tiny ulcer. She was starting to think that the symptoms were linked to her mental state, but from where she was standing, she couldn't see any immediate way of fixing it. *Must push through*, she thought to herself, as she squeezed her eyes shut for a brief moment, pressed her nails even deeper into her arm and turned the volume up on her headphones in an attempt to centre herself and hold it together until the time came for her to step off the train and tackle the hill of doom towards her cold, filthy little home.

Halfway up the hill, Hannah was becoming increasingly nauseous. Well aware of it not being the case, she started using this as an excuse for not exercising when she got in, as well as ordering a massive kebab takeaway instead of cooking. (The nausea was obviously her body telling her that she was dying of hunger and would be far too malnourished to cook something healthy, right?)

Hannah stopped by her mailbox on the way in, only to find not one but two bills in there, one of which was from the electric company, and it was absolutely ridiculous. It was at least three times the normal amount and there was no way she'd be able to cover it without using her savings. Having splurged on a takeaway without factoring in the bills for the month, Hannah's stress reached an entirely new level. Breaking into a cold sweat now, her hands were shaking as she struggled to put her key into the lock of her door. The increase in the cost of electricity meant she wouldn't be able to work from home as much as she'd like. She definitely had to stop ordering takeaways, so she'd delete the app as soon as her current order had arrived. Not that she had a habit of ordering takeaways when she was sober, but she felt like she was doing something to cut back on expenses, at least.

Speaking of, she decided to check the app to see when her kebab was due to arrive. It appeared to be ready for pick-up, so that would give her about 15 minutes to try and calm herself down before having to interact with the delivery driver. Another reason why she hardly ever ordered in was that her house was incredibly difficult to find using the Maps app, which had resulted in her getting shouted at by stressed out drivers more than once. As if it was her fault that they didn't read the instructions properly. Either way, it made her feel bad in more ways than one and so she tried to avoid it when possible. Hannah's drunken alter ego obviously did not care about the lack of money or angry phone calls and was more than happy to find new and creative ways to order junk food online without having to use the app (extremely tech savvy, remember) – and sober Hannah was very aware of this – but that was an issue for another day. She had enough on her plate already, without having to think about what mischief her drunken self might get up to in the future. Nor was she planning on drinking any time soon, so at least there was that.

20 minutes later, the food had yet to arrive, and the app showed the delivery driver was driving up and down the street parallel to hers, clearly lost. She decided to put matters into her own hand, if only to avoid having to talk to someone on the phone and went out to see if she could find the car before they gave up. As she was dragging her boots on, her phone screen lit

up with an unknown number. Sure enough, it was the delivery driver. Clearly frustrated, he started shouting abuse at her for giving him 'the wrong address' before she'd even managed to say hello. Judging by the tone of his voice, all Hannah heard was 'how dare you making my life difficult by living in a house that's impossible to find, you useless, entitled, fat girl', and would likely be what she could see in his eyes once she managed to locate him. After apologising profusely for her own existence on the phone, she'd asked him to stay put as she could see his car on the map in the app, but he'd ignored this request and had made her track him down two blocks over from where he'd parked in the first place as some form of punishment. To add insult to injury, the only way she could make anyone ever deliver food to this area was by tipping in advance, so no matter how this driver acted now, he would still get his 30 percent. Seeing as this whole procedure of ordering was a bit of a hassle, not to mention a somewhat extravagant allowance for Hannah, this was not a battle that she had any interest in fighting, so she took the occasional abuse and paid up with no complaints.

As she approached the assumed car – it was unmarked, of course – she waved apologetically to signal she was the one coming to collect her order, upon which the driver simply leaned over his passenger seat, rolled his window down and dropped the paper bag with her food out of the opening and sped away. If she hadn't felt pretty useless and insignificant already, this might have put her, and any sane person, over the edge. Instead, she felt guilty about ordering food in the first place. No wonder he would try to prove a point. The fact that the wetness of the soggy snow was now seeping through the paper bag that was holding her Styrofoam-encased food was just another thing she deserved for being too lazy to cook on a Monday. And her wild goose chase to the car was simply another thing to teach her to skip exercise.

Finally back in the house and out of the cold, Hannah was surprised to find that the food was still warm. Well, tepid, but still far better than cold kebab. Starving now, she inhaled the entire thing within about seven minutes, not even stopping to come up for air. Had the offended driver tampered with it in another attempt at revenge, she would never know. A greasy kebab never failed to give her explosive diarrhoea anyway, so it wouldn't stay in her system for long enough to do any proper damage. Another testament to what an enormous waste of money this was, not only to get a kebab but to pay extra for delivery. She really shouldn't be surprised at having to pay a little extra for the indulgence, both in the monetary sense and in terms of sacrificing her own self-respect, the latter of which there was increasingly little left.

Her sense of self-worth didn't exactly skyrocket as she, only minutes after bingeing her dinner, was sat on her porcelain throne, giving birth to a seemingly never-ending projectile-like waterfall of extra hot kebab sauce, interspersed with pieces of bread and sweetcorn and trying to keep herself entertained with a language learning app on her phone.

When Hannah stepped out of her bathroom an unknown period of time later, bowels thoroughly emptied and having learned how to explain how a mouse and bear went about shopping for the perfect coffee table in German, it was already dark outside. Not daring to provoke the wrath of the Gods any further by turning any heating – or indeed lights – on, she lit every candle she could find in a hope that it would generate some heat in addition to light. One of the more positive prospects of living in this odd, little house that was far from up to code, meant that the smoke detector was less than functional; she might as well set all her shit on fire without having to worry about the alarm going off.

As she'd taken the laptop home with her, she reckoned she would work from home tomorrow, but in order to save on electricity, she would have to go in for the rest of the week. She wasn't looking forward to it, but at least she'd have one day where she could be productive and undisturbed in her little home office. If she could get to the shops after work tomorrow, she'd even be able to make her lunches for the rest of the week as well, meaning she'd save on what she'd normally spend in the cafeteria. Not to mention the fact that she'd be able to work through lunch so that she could leave half an hour early and squeeze in a few decent workouts in the small gym adjacent to her office building, before it reached capacity during the post work rush. Surely, this was a surefire way to set herself up for something other than failure for what little time she had left over there.

She made a list over what she wanted to get done workwise tomorrow and then proceeded to put together a shopping list with everything she could possibly need for the next fortnight. Pleased with having done something productive, she allowed herself to switch the telly on to see if *Prime* had something for her worth watching and spent the rest of the evening staring blankly at the screen, which was displaying one of those trivial, mind-numbingly stupid romcoms. Exactly what she needed.

Knowing that she would have to come up with an excuse for working from home the next day, Hannah had twisted and turned all night, only to fall properly asleep about 45 minutes before her alarm went off. But as she didn't have a single meeting today, she could pretty much just work from bed, so she allowed herself a ten-minute snooze before deciding on whether to throw something on and move across the room to her tiny office space. When she checked her phone, though, she found an email from her boss encouraging everyone to stay at home if possible, due to the 'adverse weather conditions.' *What*? In March?? Hannah lifted up her curtain and stared into a blizzard. Yeah, there was no doubt every single train would be cancelled. Outlook wasn't great for going for a run later, obviously, but that was a sacrifice she was more than willing to make, so Hannah went downstairs to make herself a strong cup of coffee and got to work.

Two hours in and Hannah was almost through her list of things that needed doing without any involvement from others. She realised she would have to slow down if she wanted an excuse to spend most of her time in one of the private offices when they were allowed back in. But she quickly found that she wasn't very good at pacing herself and before long was sat daydreaming and picking at imperfections on her face with a pair of tweezers that she kept in one of her desk drawers. She had a bad tendency to pick at her skin until it broke and bled, so when she discovered what she was doing, she decided to move away from the desk for a few minutes, if only to snap herself out of it. 15

burpees and an "abs in 15 minutes" video on *YouTube* later and she was back at her desk, looking for something productive to do. After asking everyone in her team if they needed any help, she gathered that she was either unwanted or not needed and had a look at the big catalogue of self-improvement courses that were offered on their company platform. She found a few that she reckoned might come in handy for positions in her own and other departments and got cracking.

Even though what she was doing was very much work related, Hannah felt as if she was slacking off, so she was constantly checking their team chat for any messages or notifications, only to find that a lot of her colleagues were showing as offline. She'd suspected for a long time that more than a few of them weren't really doing much in ways of office work on their days in the old home office, but to have it confirmed like this really bothered her, for some reason. She almost took it personally that she was sat here actually looking for more work to do rather than just take a break when there was nothing to do, but doing that just didn't sit right with her. She was also aware that their behaviour likely had nothing to do with her, but she couldn't help but feel like she was the only one pulling their weight. And when they were all in the office together, the others had a tendency to use her as their personal secretary, taking advantage of the fact that she didn't have it in her to say 'no' when someone needed her help. To be fair, she didn't see any point in being at work with nothing to do, so she welcomed the extra workload with open arms, but it was the most ungrateful task, as no one ever offered her a 'thank you' or showed in any way that they appreciated her sometimes hard work. As a matter

of fact, precisely because she was such a quiet, little
worker bee, they more often than not took credit for her
work. She was sick of it and had come to resent the
coworkers she had looked up to and admired when
she'd first started. Her background in hospitality didn't
help, nor did her fifteen years of being self-employed;
she always *had* to *please* and was incapable of
protesting or doing something that would invoke any
sort of reprimand or overt criticism. She had also been a
wailing wall for most of them when they'd had
something negative to say about their colleagues –
which was no rare occurrence – and knew for a fact that
they wouldn't hesitate to talk about her behind her back
if given the chance. Hannah couldn't stand gossip and
avoided it like the plague, yet somehow these smack
talkers always seemed to find her and pour themselves
out to her. All so very tiring and yet another reason to
self-isolate. Keeping to herself was very much her
preferred way of dealing with the general public, but in
a workplace where you would miss out on the small
details and the team bonding if you weren't there, it sort
of made you a pariah with no way to advance or work
around the social interactions. And the other teams
Hannah worked with within the company relied almost
solely on collaborative working methods, something
that her own department seemed oblivious – and
allergic – to. She sometimes wondered how all the
people that lacked basic people skills had somehow
wound up in the same sales team, normally these types
would be found in accounting, and very much lacking
the affinity for trashy small talk. She also wondered
how she had wound up in her current position. Was she
secretly a terrible person as well? Well, she knew the

answer to that last question. Bad karma harvested during times of drunken mischief had accumulated and started seeing to that she was being brought to justice. Or so it seemed. Hannah yearned for the times of yore when punishment was dealt out in the shape of a thorough lashing or a short spell at the stocks – or even the gallows, should you be so lucky.

A high-pitched ding broke her out of her daytime reverie. A message from Rebecca in marketing:

Hiya! Having as much fun as I am working from home? Assuming we're all allowed back in on Thursday, fancy going to the quiz together? Seeing as we've got the late production meeting, I figured Quizmaster Drew will wait for us if there's two of us. Can't wait! XX

Quiz? This was the first Hannah had heard about any quiz. Though unsurprised, Hannah was devastated to have been left out. And seemingly by Drew, no less. Nothing quite stings like an un-invitation from someone you so desperately want to like you – in fact, Hannah felt like this was up there with being asked to give a rim job to a rectally prolapsed sea cucumber.

On one hand, Hannah no longer had to worry about analysing Drew's look from yesterday. Yet on the other…maybe he'd forgotten to invite her? Due to her temporary employment status, her name didn't always come up in all of the team chat groups, or when you typed @all, so maybe he had wanted to and not been able? Or maybe he hadn't selected her team, because most of them worked remotely and wouldn't be able to attend. If so, she should really make an effort to go. Shouldn't she? She messaged back:

Hey! Having all of the fun over here. LOL. Haven't decided about Thursday as I'm meant to be somewhere after work that day. But will definitely see if I can get out of it! You'd better come up with a great team name. xx

Hannah felt a small part of what was left of her soul die as she typed the abbreviation. No one that has ever really laughed out loud has had the urge or need to make expressions of joy into shorthand. Case in point; people that will frequently use LOOOOL. If you think the emphasis should be on the preposition, you're already so far into your land of neurodivergent diagnoses that you can't even decipher your own emotions. If you have any at all, that is. Abbreviations for no reason other than economising the number of words in a sentence was something that infuriated Hannah to the core. She could feel her initial sadness slowly turning into anger now – which was quite pleasing, really – as her brain went on an inner rant. The term *S.O.* was truly the dumbest one of all. How significant is someone to you if you can't even say the words out loud? Or frigging *BAE*?! Firstly, it literally means *poo* in Danish. Secondly, she'd discovered only the other day that it was actually an abbreviation of 'before anyone else'. Hannah would rather bathe in a sea of fresh *bae* than use the term in referral to a romantic partner. An instant flashback from when she let the guy she was seeing a few years ago give her a golden shower suddenly ensued. She shook her head violently to rid herself of the memory. Good thing she wasn't in any position to use terms like that anymore, eh?

Hannah decided to set her chat status to Do Not Disturb, although it more often than not seemed to have the opposite of the desired effect, so she wouldn't have to deal with more shit that wasn't related to actual work. Or, if someone did message her, she would have an excuse not to write them back immediately. Unless it was Drew. She always had time for Drew.

The day went on and with an endless aching void inside her, Hannah managed to get through an entire loaf's worth of bread. With no prying eyes in her kitchen and not enough work to do, she quite felt like an endless void had opened up inside of her and the hunger wouldn't recede until there was nothing left to eat. She tried to calculate just how many kilometres she would have to plough her way through to negate the calories consumed but gave up pretty quickly. There was no way she'd be able to run particularly far in the still ongoing blizzard. If this weather didn't subside any time soon, she wouldn't be able to get to the treadmill either, so she would have to pull the plug on this gluttonous behaviour sharpish. As she was thinking this, though, she already had her hand down the freezer, about to pull up another two slices of toast. 'Stop it!' squeaked a familiar voice from within. 'Another one and you will never amount to anything. Everyone you love will hate you and you will never be able to pay rent'. Fucking OCD shit. Yet, as one that's lived with these compulsive thoughts of magical thinking for so long, they sometimes served a purpose as well. Like now, when it was the only thing that helped her stop eating when she was far beyond full. When the disease finally presented itself as salvation in form of a coping mechanism, why was she so eager to get professional help to rid herself of it? Sometimes that voice in her head was all she had.

Hannah sighed. Now she had stopped stuffing her gob, she could feel just how full she was. A quick look down confirmed what she already knew – she looked about seven months pregnant, full of buttered toast and no doubt enough gas to keep the oil companies going for another year. Why did she keep doing this to herself? No wonder Drew didn't want her if she couldn't even stay the same size for more than a few days at a time. Thoughts back on Drew, she checked the chat she'd muted hours ago. Nothing. And it was already quarter past four. *Time to log off and do something productive in the home improvement area of my life*, thought Hannah. *Just a quick nap first.*

Hannah awoke with a jolt to complete darkness. She had no idea where she was at first and she'd had one of those weird dreams that made it difficult to separate dream from reality that she only had when she slept during the daytime. It felt so real she could almost taste it, yet she still couldn't remember exactly what it was that she had dreamt – only the ambiance remained now she was awake and, boy, was it heavy with shame and unpleasantness. Hannah had no idea why these dreams kept occurring – or indeed why they only ever occurred when she was napping – nor did she dare googling it; she was terrified of what she might find out and suspected no good would come of it. Perhaps it was the universe trying to tell her she shouldn't keep taking naps when she had shit to do and needed to get a proper night's sleep. Who knew.

Hannah checked her phone for the time. Quarter past eight! How had she slept for nearly four hours? The only good thing about it was that it was far too late to eat, so that would have to wait until tomorrow now. She supposed she could do an hour's worth of HIIT circuits off of YouTube to tire herself out enough to get to sleep later, as her brain was far too scattered to do any home improvement. Disappointed in herself acting like a teenager, she pulled on her workout clothes and crept down the stairs to kick herself into shape.

Wednesday morning saw Hannah waking up all but freezing in the foetal position, with her pillow wrapped halfway around her head and her duvet mostly on the floor when her alarm went off. Another night of next to no sleep, yet she managed to drag herself out of bed after just two snoozes. There was still an orange warning level of blizzardly chaos outside, and she started mentally preparing for another day in the home office. Right enough, an email from her boss ticked in at around 7.30, ordering everyone to work from home 'if possible'. Hannah had no intention of skiing to work, so she supposed she would have to try and contain herself from braving the wintery weather conditions. Inspired by the shitty weather and her own incredible wit, she put on *Hell Freezes Over* by the Eagles while she put the kettle on and started getting her face ready for screen time.

Still feeling hurt by not getting an invite to tomorrow's quiz (that was surely hanging in the balance by now anyway), Hannah swiftly turned her status to Do Not Disturb as soon as she logged on and added a passive aggressive 'EDITING MODE' to the personalised message that would go out to anyone that did disturb her. She did have a few videos to edit, but the deadline for those was non-existent as she was doing them as a favour to a colleague in another department, but she might as well wrap them up, seeing as she was now leaving in a few months' time anyway.

Her bitterness from discovering her boss had kept crucial information about her future employability still bothered Hannah. Had it been her style to retaliate, she could have easily done so, but that sort of behaviour just didn't sit well with her. And she'd need her boss as a reference in the future. After a couple of decades in the hospitality industry she had gotten used to bending over and take it whenever it pleased her superiors, something that certainly didn't help when she tried to stand up for herself. Add to that her parents teaching her how worthless she was before she could walk, and you've got the perfectly preprogrammed employee that would do whatever anyone asked without hesitation or question.

What made it really sting, though, was that she was fully aware that she let everyone around her take advantage of her because she was unable to say 'no' and she was the only one that could change this pattern. Ipso facto, she was doing it to herself. And now she just didn't have the energy to rock the boat. The rebel in her only rebelled when others were treated unjustly, not when she was being treated unfairly herself. Also, changing a lifetime's worth of behaviour would take a LOT of cognitive behavioural therapy and a hefty dose of commitment from herself. Had she had any sense of self-worth, she would have gladly indulged in some CBT, but Hannah felt bad for the therapist that would have to monitor her treatment.

She knew firsthand how annoying it could be to have someone tell you all about their troubles and innermost feelings and wouldn't wish that on her worst enemy. She'd even had a therapist tell her that what she'd experienced as a child was simply 'too much' for them to listen to and refused to help her any further. That was the proverbial nail in the coffin for her attempt to get help the last time everything had gone to shit. The last thing Hannah needed was someone telling her she was 'too much' when she was finally ready to talk, and this had resulted in the self-harming behaviour that she was attempting to hide at the moment. She'd been able to cover up most of her scars with beautifully intricate tattoos – and the body art was meant to be a deterrent for Hannah when she was reaching for her knives and scalpels, but the closer she came to wanting to do more than just feel something that would take her away from the emotional pain, the easier it had become for her to find the gaps of naked skin between the lines that would do nicely for a swift end to it all. The only thing that had stood between her and death up until now was the fact that she'd been so inebriated the times she'd really tried that she'd missed the arteries completely or not been able to press shards of broken glass deep enough into her wrist for them to do any proper damage. Yet. Well, she wasn't perfect. And as she always delivered in her role as people pleaser, the only one that wound up suffering was herself. And we've already established that she doesn't count.

When the time came for her to take a quick lunch break, Hannah was absolutely knackered. She didn't have any meetings until later so she decided to take a powernap – the way things were going she was afraid she wouldn't be able to make any sense or remember much from said meetings. As of late, she had found herself so tired that her speech had started to become slurred after about 2pm on a regular basis – she'd dubbed this phenomenon her afternoon aphasia – so she tried to book most of her meetings earlier in the day, but that was very rarely convenient for her colleagues, who hardly ever did much of anything useful before lunch. Another thorn in Hannah's side. As with most midday naps, Hannah fell asleep as soon as she had become horizontal. Having set her alarm for 20 minutes, she was nowhere near awake once her allotted time was up and snoozed it for another ten minutes. And again. And again. After her fourth snooze, she very much realised she would have to get back to work, unless she wanted to work into the late evening, so she rushed downstairs to splash some water on her face, only to trip over her own tired legs on the way down the narrow staircase, managing to put her hands in front of her only seconds before her face was to hit the tiled kitchen floor. Her left wrist made the most pathetic little twig-like sound, but Hannah – who was now full of adrenaline – simply shrugged it off. She had work to do and a meeting in five minutes.

Hannah quickly realised she shouldn't have gone downstairs to freshen up, as she looked so haggard from her nap that it was difficult to improve the situation at all – especially in what little time she had. She instead made herself a tepid cup of instant coffee with the water from the kettle she'd put on this morning and jogged up the stairs, making it to her desk with only seconds to spare. Luckily, several of her colleagues were technically challenged, so Hannah pretended to have problems with the camera on her laptop until she could find a suitable filter to blur herself out a bit. Not that they would be looking at her anyway – she was willing to place good money (had she had any) on the fact that research likely shows that most people focus more on their own little square in a conference call than those of others – but in case there were any non-narcissists attending, she wanted to spare them from having to look at this 40 year old mess, somewhat resembling a human female, that had just woken up.

The team meeting dragged on, and Hannah watched on as her colleagues argued between themselves about the most trivial things. She was sick of this bickering. As an adult child of divorce, she was scarred from a childhood full of fighting, yelling and the occasional violent outburst, and their team meetings often triggered flashbacks in Hannah. She didn't tell anyone about this, of course, but she was terrified that her Id would one day take over and flip the table to make them stop the quarrelling. Or that one day, when they were all gathered in the office, her superego would act on her urge to stab them all through their eye sockets with her pen and pour dishwasher liquid down their collective throats whilst they bled out internally from the acid burns. She could hear someone saying her name in the distance and snapped out of her fantasy. Shit, had someone asked her a question? Ah, it was just her boss announcing that she was available if anyone on the team needed assistance on anything. (Erm, *what*?) No one seemed to care about this and started wrapping things up, chatting now about how they were going to win tomorrow's quiz now the trains were back up and running.

They had all been invited. Of course they had been – and of course *she* hadn't. It took everything she had not to slam her laptop shut there and then. Stone-faced as ever, she was pretty sure no one could see what was going on inside her, but she was very quick to say that she had another meeting to get ready for and therefore would have to log off. She did have another meeting, but not for another ten minutes, so she did whatever she could to keep herself busy and not think about what had just happened.

Her throat felt raw and thick, and her eyes were stinging. Hannah grabbed the closest thing to her – a ruler – and jabbed the sharp corner of it into her left thigh. Again and again until the initial pain gave her the emotional numbness she was looking for. For some reason, Hannah didn't bruise unless she had copious amounts of alcohol in her systems, so should she die within the next few days, there would be no trace of her mini battering to whomever would have the great misfortune of discovering her dead body. Because, by the looks of things, that would be the only way someone would see her naked thighs to begin with. No one fancied her or her disgusting body. They didn't even like her enough to be in the same room as her for a few hours. None of her team had invited her along to the quiz either, another testament to the fact that she was utterly superfluous in this world. She wondered what the meaning of her existence was and could find none other than to serve as something for others to make them feel better about themselves. No matter how lacking in qualities they may be, they were still better off than her, who had no money, no property, no friends to speak of and no 'other', significant or otherwise. Not even silverfish would hang out in her bathroom for long enough to see her fanny. She had become an undesirable on every level.

Any trace of her earlier desire to go into the office tomorrow, if only to use the gym afterwards, had gone. When Hannah slammed her laptop shut at 4.01pm, she quickly transferred a relatively large sum of money to her current account from her savings and embarked on a trip to the wine shop, where she would purchase a box of wine, along with two bottles of sparkling rosé and some spiced rum. Knowing she wouldn't want to brave the hills more than once this week, she also went to the next-door supermarket to get stuff for dinner for the rest of the week (to avoid another takeaway catastrophe) and about two pounds of pick & mix, ginger ale for mixer, low calorie ice cream, crisps and four chocolate bars. (2for1 – bargain). No one was ever going to see her naked again – not in this lifetime anyway – so she dove into her bag of sweets the minute she was out the shop door.

Realising she didn't have any beer, she nipped into the specialty brew shop as well, where she picked up an assortment of two hard seltzers and no less than three different very high alcohol content IPAs, two of each; two Chili-flavoured ones with a hint of tobacco, two with 'subtle undertones of elderberries and regret' and the final two so sour that they would surely make her insides tingle and tighten up. A feast for the palate.

Keen to make the most of her daytime drinking time count, having lost almost an hour to shopping, Hannah legged it up the hill, hoping her bottles would stay intact. She caught a glimpse of her utterly wild looking own reflection in a car window as she went, and a catchy German phrase popped into her head; *Mein*

Pferd ist kaputt. 'Very funny, brain. Yes, I know I look like a broken old mare, now shut up', muttered Hannah to herself and shifted her speed into top gear. She was wasting precious drinking minutes, and her intrusive thoughts could put a stop to them occurring at all if she wasn't able to start numbing herself soon.

Hannah burst through her front door only minutes later and reached for one of the seltzers, downing it in less than a minute. Belching loudly, she grabbed the next one out of the bag, poured it into a glass and mixed in a home measure of rum and started putting her shopping away, shovelling sweeties into her mouth as she went. She decided she would have a little movie night to herself – a little Hannah-centric extravaganza, where she would stick on the main tearjerkers, interspersed with listening to some choice tunes for when she needed a break from someone else's heartache. She'd managed to dodge the landlord for quite a few days in a row now. If they were away, there would be no chance of anyone seeing (or indeed hearing) any of her mid-week debauchery. She decided she'd eliminate the chance of herself taking to social media during her drunken stupor this time and turned her phone off and logged into the music player on her TV. As Lenny Kravitz' *Are You Gonna Go My Way* boomed out of the speakers, Hannah danced around the flat, drink firmly in hand and tried so very hard to shake off her tiredness, her melancholy and her disenchantment with life.

A couple hours into her little fiesta, Hannah started feeling a lot better. Or perhaps *less* was a little more accurate. Either way, she had made her way through four of the IPAs, feeling accomplished as she had done so whilst she was still sober. She was saving the cheap wine until taste was no longer an issue. She had made sure she always had a sip of rum and ginger ale every so often, so she wouldn't get nauseous before she was completely numb. Ginger settled her stomach and was her go-to for days like these, with limited drinking hours due to work the next morning. Speaking of; time *was* starting to become an issue, so she cracked open her first bottle of rosé, which she mixed with sparkling water and lemon, to get rid of some of the sweet fruitiness.

Despite the contradicting evidence, Hannah wasn't one for sweets and very much steered clear of things that would automatically give her the boak if not properly diluted. She only drank the stuff because of the uplifting effect it had on her. It was better than cocaine. And arguably less expensive – and illegal.

The first bottle disappeared far too quickly, so when Hannah had sat down with the first glass from the second bottle, she realised how drunk she was getting. She giggled to herself. She hadn't even started the first movie yet, as she'd fallen into a bit of a *YouTube* rabbit hole. Twenty minutes off the booze should do the trick. She got her guitar out and started playing and singing along to the songs she could play without looking up the chords. God, she sounded amazing today, didn't she? Maybe she should record herself and put it up on Instagram in case someone from a label were to come across her profile... She would need her phone for that, though. She decided that her mood was such that it was safe to switch it on for a little bit. As she was entering her pin, she could feel a familiar pang in her gut, something trying to tell her to stop whatever she was doing, but she ignored it. She wasn't going to let her shot get away from her. And she needed to do something productive while she was trying to get her bearings. She would be absolutely fine. As a matter of fact, so fine that she decided to mix a bit of red into her sparkling rosé. Maybe ten minutes would be a long enough break.

Hannah felt confident as she was posting her video to her social media stories and decided to finish the rosé/red combo in favour of the red. A well-known mood enhancer for Hannah, the red seemed a good choice in the moment, but as soon as she heard her phone buzzing with a notification, something in her switched and her vision turned to black.

Hannah awoke on her couch feeling sore. What had happened? She shifted to turn onto her right side and flinched. She opened her eyes and looked down towards where the pain came from and discovered she was covered in blood. Her wrist – where the initial pain stemmed from – had suffered some minor stab wounds, but when she saw her thighs, Hannah gasped as memories flashed back at her. It looked as if she'd been attacked by a wild animal. Another flashback. She hadn't taken photos of herself in this state and posted it online, had she? She reached for her phone, only to discover 12 missed calls, two of which were from a number she didn't recognise. Had she ordered a takeaway anyway? She googled the number and found it to be the emergency services. She could see that she had spoken to them and since she hadn't woken up in a room with padded walls, must have been able to somehow ward them off. *Fuck*. Had they really showed up at her door? She dug a little deeper in her missed calls log and messages. Fuck. The one person she didn't want wasting her time on her. Her phone buzzed again, with another call. Hannah hung up, not wanting to deal with real life. A message followed;

'You better pick up if you know what's good for you!!!!'

The screen flashed again, with the same number. Hannah decided she owed it to the person calling to pick up.

'Hello?'

Chapter 5 – April: You and me against the world

'No. You don't get to just *hello* me after the stunt you just pulled. What on earth is going on down there? You're scaring the fucking shit out of me and I'm 200 miles away! I'm really sorry I phoned the EMTs on you, but I had to do *something.'*

On the other end of the phone was Hannah's best mate – and only real friend through the last three decades – MJ. And she was *not* having any of Hannah's shit. Because, for some incomprehensible reason, she had taken a liking to Hannah when they had bonded over a mutual enemy during their first year at secondary school and had refused to leave her side since. Which was also why Hannah normally hid information like this from MJ, because she was the only person she was truly afraid to push away.

'I'm sorry... I shouldn't have bothered you, I just...' began Hannah, before pulling herself together. She decided she just had to be honest. MJ was entitled to the truth so she could get out before she was dragged down with her. 'There was just so much blood. I only meant to remove some, you know, stuff, which didn't look so good, and I somehow lost the grip on my scalpel and nicked a big vein. I just got scared. I get it if you're done with me now. It's alright.'

'Have you lost the plot completely? As if I'm ever leaving! Fuck off. And that scalpel better get in the bin if you know what's good for you', barked MJ in her sternest voice. 'Also, how about shooting me a text or a phone call before you go around boiling bunnies in your little hermit homestead? I'm too young for my hair to turn grey just yet.'

Hannah could hear the concern and love in MJ's voice and wanted to cry. Since they lived miles apart from each other, it was a little too easy for both of them to forget the fact that the other existed. They had a long chat, during which Hannah got MJ up to speed on her treatment – she even told her about what Kim had done – to which MJ simply replied 'That *bitch*. At least *I* had the decency to contact someone that I knew wouldn't report it to anyone else. I just needed to know that you were breathing when you stopped messaging me back.'

After their talk, Hannah went to the bathroom to clean herself up, only to discover a couple of cuts so deep they probably needed stitches, but she cleaned them as well as she could and stuck closing strips over the gaping lacerations, hoping they'd stick together a bit better once the bleeding stopped. Right now, it looked like she'd been mauled by Maugrim of the White Witch' secret police, but she still had a day of work to get through before she could leave the house. Luckily it was still early, just gone six, so she had plenty of time to have a vat of coffee and a powernap before she had to get herself into work mode. Although, apart from the slight blood loss, she was actually feeling rather fresh already. She obviously wasn't fit to drive or anything, but she was more than capable of doing her work, that today would largely consist of editing sound bites for a campaign and the aforementioned videos for her colleague. She'd become quite the functional mess, hadn't she?

She could feel herself starting to spiral again so she forced herself to try to see some positives. She was lucky to have a friend like MJ, that actually cared enough to let herself go through this kind of agony for her. Hannah had always thought of herself as being that kind of friend to most people herself, but she'd never really realised that someone would bother being there for her in the same way. Then again, MJ was one of the few people that had tried getting to know her, and even though they had lived miles apart for most of their adult lives and only saw each other every few years, they were never not there for each other – for the highs *and* the lows. And, instead of feeling guilty about being the needy friend this time, Hannah felt lucky to have someone to talk to. Particularly because that friend was MJ, who had no trouble giving her a piece of her mind when Hannah needed someone to shake some sense into her, and at the same time wouldn't judge or criticise her. So, in her time of feeling utterly worthless, she made a promise to MJ that she wouldn't give in to the darkness so willingly the next time it came for her. She figured it would be easier for her to hold herself accountable if she made the promise to someone she cared about.

Hannah decided to forgo her nap and instead started on her caffeine binge straight away. She felt that she needed to make herself useful somehow, so she got around to making a few lists to make sense of the chaos that her brain seemed so overwhelmed by. Little by little, she was figuring out some of the things she could more or less easily work out to make the road ahead a bit less bumpy. By the time 8am came around, Hannah was five coffees in and ready to get cracking in the office department as well. And that she did. She didn't even stop for lunch, and when one of her aforementioned colleagues that would treat her as their own personal secretary asked her to set up a fundraising platform for them, she did so without even flinching and had it set up and ready within the hour. She might be on her way out, but she would at least make them remember her as someone who kept their promise and delivered both quickly and expertly. She also knew by now that her colleague would take all credit for the work she did unless she Cc'd someone on their chain of emails, so she copied in the rest of their team upon delivery, with the excuse of wanting to let them all know she could help if they, too, had similar requests – she figured it couldn't hurt.

The added work resulting from the demonstrative CCing kept her busy throughout the day, so she clocked out at 4pm, knowing she could leave an hour early tomorrow, having skipped lunch today. And she was likely to do the same tomorrow, as she was going to the office so she could leave her laptop there over the weekend. Despite the fact that it was the first good thing to have happened all week – and it was already Thursday – Hannah was quite pleased that something good had happened at all. Now, all she had to do was fix the rest of her life. She figured you can never go wrong with a workout and dragged her body down the stairs to see what *YouTube* had in store for her, only to be confronted with her watch history from last night. She flinched and blinked and quickly turned on the voice search. *No wonder I went a bit mad with the knife*, she thought, silently hoping the landlord hadn't been home to hear her no doubt wailing along to the *Dreamgirls* soundtrack.

She pulled out her yoga mat and started the warm-up sequence to the 60-minute HIIT session that promised to "increase metabolism and make you see God" – or any equivalent deity – by the end of video. Hannah felt like a decent HIIT session could be as good an exorcism as any, so she went ahead with it despite the blatant religious propaganda.

A full hour later, Hannah was pouring with perspiration and could feel a blister developing between her butt cheeks due to one too many butterfly sit-ups, but so far, no sign of any deities – Christian or otherwise. The sweat was really starting to sting her battle wounds, though, so she dropped the stretch in favour of a much-needed full-body cleanse.

Hannah yelped as the soap and hot water poured into the wound on her right thigh, which was now un-secured by strips. She looked down, and a gaping, still bleeding wound half an inch wide stared back at her. She quickly finished scouring herself and rinsed her wounds out with an antiseptic, dried herself off as well as she could, whilst holding a cotton ball to the gash until she could place fresh strips on to close it back up. *Never again*, Hannah decided. If she got an infection and had to go to A&E, she'd be absolutely mortified.

Half an hour later, she found herself once again sitting in complete darkness on her sofa, contemplating her life and how she was still here, after all her efforts to make sure she wouldn't be over the years. Was there some hidden meaning to her existence that she had yet to be made aware of? Perhaps, in 80 years' time – if humans hadn't destroyed what was left of the world by then – she'd be an example in history books, of what you should avoid if you wanted to be a successful being.

Or could it be that she was destined for something greater, however cheesy that may sound?

Right now, all Hannah needed was a reason. A sign to show her that she shouldn't stop trying to dig her way out of her hole before the walls came tumbling down on her. She was quite desperate for a sign – any sign. Yet, her conscious mind knew better than to let her believe in anything that had still to be proven by science, so she was left feeling unintelligent and desperate.

Hannah knew that the best way to positive change was to change her own mindset, but she feared that only people of less mindpower and intelligence would be able to change themselves completely all willy nilly. She didn't want to be perceived as unintelligent. She'd been asked to join Mensa when she took the test for fun back in high school, for goodness' sake. How was she meant to carry on when there was so much evidence pointing towards the only way she would let herself believe she was deserving of happiness was to rid herself of her intellect and brainwash herself with mantras until she believed anything was possible?

She thought back on an episode of *Friends*, where Chandler had been struggling to give up smoking and had been given a tape to listen to while he slept, the guided sleep meditation mantra turning him into a 'strong, confident *woman*' seemingly overnight and shivered at the thought. Surely, happiness can't be reserved for the Forrest Gumps of the world? Hannah felt like she'd had too much to think in one sitting, so she got up to light a couple of candles and turned the TV back on. She needed the white noise to cancel out the racket in her head. Happiness was perhaps a quest better reserved for the future. Although, much the same as with love, she wasn't entirely convinced the concept of happiness was really real at all. She was starting to feel the familiar sting behind her eyelids again, as her phoned buzzed and the screen flashed. A message from MJ:

'Snap out of it.'

What was she, some sort of mind reading ninja? Either way, her messaged had worked. Hannah decided there was nothing more she could do to help her situation just now, so she texted MJ back that she loved her, made herself an absolutely massive cup of tea and curled up on her couch with a cheesy, not exactly award-winning, comedy that she managed to find on one of her streaming services. She made a mental note of having to look into cancelling some of the subscriptions she couldn't afford to make some room in her already limited budget, but that was a worry for another day. Right now, she just wanted to clock out for a few hours, with a few cheap laughs. She thanked her lucky star for MJ and their friendship – the one thing that made her feel like she wasn't entirely alone in this world.

When the movie finished an appropriate 93 minutes later, Hannah felt absolutely knackered, yet far less drained than before. She figured this was a great opportunity for her to get a proper night's sleep without having to turn to alcohol for once, so she started getting ready for bed, despite it still being relatively early. She wiped her face clean, moisturised and started brushing her teeth, as she studied her own face intently. She always found looking into the mirror so odd. It felt to her as if she was spying on a stranger through one of those two-way mirrors you always saw in 90s cop show interrogation rooms. Maybe, if she stared hard enough, the person on the other side would crack.

Hannah got lost in her own imperfections for long enough for her to forget to move her electric toothbrush and got an annoying reality check as the brush head hit a sensitive spot on the enamel. She winced, and to her horror she could see that her gums had started to bleed from the excessive oral stimulus. *Stupid, stupid, stupid,* she thought, as she rinsed her mouth out with mouthwash, spitting bloody suds into the sink. On the upside, she had been pulled from what would have become a never-ending picking session on her facial imperfections, so she quickly put all of her things back onto their respective places in the cupboard before promptly taking herself up the stairs and to bed. She only managed four *BuzzFeed* quizzes before drifting off into a dreamless void after setting her alarm, not even noticing that she dropped her phone on her own face as she fell asleep.

Hannah's phone had slid off her rather large nose as she slept, and when her alarm started blaring at 5.30, it was right next to her right ear – the incredibly loud ringing alone scaring her half to death, forcing her to jolt upright and smacking the top of her head straight into the sloped ceiling. What a delightful way to start the day!

A little shaken, Hannah swung her legs out of the bed and onto the floor. To avoid any more harsh meetings with her surroundings, she'd better avoid snoozing today. She'd slept almost nine hours, but Hannah felt as if she hadn't slept a wink. She felt as if she weighed a thousand pounds, as she hauled her body across the floor in a fashion similar to that of Jabba the Hutt. It was a good thing she didn't have any mirrors up there, as she suspected she might resemble him physically as well.

As slowly as she was moving, she still somehow managed to trip on one of her slippers, that was lying directly in her path. Her spiritual self detached from her physical body, and she watched on from above as she fell awkwardly towards the stairs in slow motion, her forehead missing the railing by a quarter inch. Luckily, she was still too tired to even contemplate bracing herself for the fall, so she ended up sort of half-sliding, half-tumbling down five or six steps without getting hurt, her spiritual self being pulled back into her body just in time for her to notice how dusty the steps were.

Hannah lay on the stairs for a minute or two, wondering what the meaning of this was, but as the Gods refused to provide her with an answer, she finally peeled her face off them, sat herself upright and skidded down the remaining steps on her bum, like a toddler. She didn't fancy another fall just yet. As she went to put the kettle on for her first of many cups of black tar, she flipped her day-by-day calendar to today's date; it was the 12th of April. Her eyes were drawn to the massive fir outside her window, at the same time as the first rays of sunshine came over the hill in the distance. The branch closest to her house, which had been heavy with snow just yesterday, was now slick and dripping with wet. Finally, a sign of spring! This pleased Hannah to such an extent that she almost danced her way to the bathroom to get her face ready for work. She could hear birds singing. Hell, she could practically hear the ground thawing. This winter had been so cold, dark and long, it was almost as if she'd given up on spring ever coming this year. She'd forgotten how much lighter she felt when she was exposed to proper daylight. Maybe there was a way for her to turn things around after all?

Her windowless bathroom was a sordid, little room, but the few seconds of sunlight and birdsong was enough to keep Hannah's mood afloat for the full 15 minutes she was in there, which was the longest she's been in a good mood without alcohol in a long time. As she emerged from her bathroom, though, the sun had disappeared behind the clouds again. But now, instead of it sending her directly back into the pit, Hannah knew that she would see the sun again. Spring was coming, light was coming, and she would have time to build herself back up before she had to face the shiny, happy faces of summer. She let out a sigh so immense she realised she must have been holding her breath for quite a while, and at the same time she felt a little less bloated, a little less like the aforementioned Hutt, and like she could get through the day without everything being such a massive, fucking task. Right there and then, she decided she was going to stop drinking for a bit. Just until she felt like she was in control of herself again. It might seem a little weird to make that sort of commitment just before the weekend, but to Hannah it was actually easier to do it when everyone else would go out drinking, rather than on a Monday or Tuesday. Plus, she loved going for a run on an early Saturday morning and feeling smug when she encountered people on an obvious walk of shame on her way. Even more, she revelled in logging her activities on *Strava*, knowing that more than a few of her followers would be hungover and thus impressed with her being out and about so early.

Yes, we can all agree this can seem very pathetic, but we will let her have this one. At least she's not hurting anyone – least of all herself – by indulging in this narcissistic behaviour.

As if she'd already accomplished something by simply making a good decision for herself, Hannah felt a little lighter, a bit more like herself – or the person she knew she *could* be. This spurred her on to down her now tepid coffee, do a quick mini workout and have a shower before sitting down at her desk with a fresh coffee and a bowl of oatmeal and berries, a full 15 minutes before she was due to clock in. For the first time in yonks, she felt as if she could take on the world – or at least her team of colleagues – and she actually looked forward to getting started. So, when no one else logged on until 90 minutes later, it felt a little anticlimactic. But, apart from that, Hannah had been able to finish her editing work during that first hour, so she could now see some of her bigger projects wrapping up instead of just being added to. The relief she felt was incredible, and just for a moment, she thought that maybe she wasn't entirely beyond help after all.

Another Friday meant that there wouldn't be much chat or interruptions from her team, so Hannah was able to make a huge dent in her previously assumed unsurmountable pile of tasks – and she was enjoying herself as she ticked her boxes on the task management system, one by one. By the end of the workday, there was very little left of things for Hannah to dread doing. In fact, the remaining tasks assigned to her now were all the sort of stuff she would do for fun, such as designing posters, editing photos and optimising the team's web pages. She was actually looking forward to going in on Monday, which was also a good thing, as she hadn't been able to go in today and leave the laptop like she'd initially planned. For once, she felt oddly optimistic and ready for a weekend in detox mode.

As she was wrapping up for the day, Hannah found herself looking forward to taking some time off the booze as well. She knew better than to make any forever promises to herself, but she had gone a couple of years without any alcohol in the past – albeit during quarantine, but let's not dwell on that – and she'd quite enjoyed it. In many ways, that time had been one of the better ones in Hannah's adult life. She'd never been fitter of felt better mentally than during that time period, much thanks to working out every day and being forced to avoid people she normally dreaded seeing, and she thought eliminating her social lubricant might help her prioritise who to spend her time with a lot better going forward. It's funny how being forced to choose which five out of your friends you want to stay in contact with for an indefinite amount of time makes you think, eh?

After a quick omelette with spinach and mushrooms for dinner, Hannah decided she'd go the rest of the day without eating and spent most of her evening updating her budget. She figured that if she was able to make a few adjustments, she could manage to get ahead of the bills every month, instead of having to dip into her savings a week before payday. Cutting back on the alcohol would obviously also free up a big chunk of her funds, but she wanted to see if she had any monthlies that could be culled. And, to her surprise, she found quite a few things she could do without. Even the loss of her phone turned into something positive – her old phone didn't have 5G, so she was able to shave a whole 30 percent off her bill by downsizing her subscription to fit her Android's lack of bells and whistles. And by keeping tabs on special offers in her local shop, she found that she could slice her spend on the weekly food shop in half, if not more. Thoughts of numbers and economy would normally make Hannah's skin crawl, but as she was constantly finding new ways to not only spend less, but actually be able to put something back into her savings as well, she found a strange sense of solace in filling in her spreadsheet. By the time she was done, the sun was slowly disappearing behind the hills, so Hannah made the most of the last rays of the setting sun by cleaning the flat. *One less thing to do tomorrow and more time for me to focus on what makes me happy*, she thought.

When Hannah slung herself onto the couch around 9.30, facemask on and cup of tea in hand, she decided to play a few games of solitaire, rather than turning the TV on. This had been her ritual back when she had volunteered abroad for two weeks one summer, where there was no Wi-Fi or phone signal, and she had never felt more rested. Being away from all of that unnatural blue light probably helped her find her way back to a more natural circadian rhythm as well, seeing as she'd been able to sleep through until morning.

Hannah came to the conclusion that she could save a few pennies by cancelling her streaming services. She wasn't about to put her TV on eBay, but she figured she could limit her screentime to her DVD collection for the time being.

An added bonus to starting her fast before 5 was that she would have to go to bed before she started feeling hungry again, so Hannah was fast asleep by 10.08. Still, a dreamless sort of sleep, but when Hannah woke up seven hours later, she was ready to kickstart her Saturday off with a run. And after that, she decided she would start looking for a new flat. She was desperate for a new beginning and no longer tethered down by a slowly increasing stack of bills. It was time to take control.

The weekend was over before she knew it, but rather than feeling despondent by the Monday looming on the horizon, Hannah made the most of her Sunday.

She was going through her clothes to see if she could part with some of her old stuff – some of it had never even been worn. When she was going through her things, she also came across loads of stuff she'd forgotten she had, like an old gaming console, two recyclable laptops, a hardly used keyboard and a few LPs, still in their original packaging. She decided to put some of the items for sale online, to see if someone else could make use of them – the clothes, of which most had never been worn, went straight to the donation bins down the street.

For some reason, Hannah felt the need to get "office clothes" whenever she'd get a new job, seemingly forgetting that she felt like resembled the late, great Dame Edna walking around in such a get-up – mind you, the Dame had pulled it off with all of the poise Hannah herself was lacking. She decided right there and then not to waste any more money on forcing herself to be something she was not. Surely, any person that was good at their job should be respected for the work they put in and not for their impeccable taste in blazers and pink (!) vest tops. Had they made it out of the closet, it might have been a different thing altogether, but alas, they were destined for greater things.

Hannah figured Sunday would be the perfect day for her to have a movie night – to make the most of the remainder of her streaming time – so she decided to forgo her recently adopted solitaire ritual for two back-to-back romcoms. She did however turn her phone off for her little screening session, so that she could get the full theatre experience, but felt slightly robbed due to the fact that she didn't have any barbecue seasoned popcorn. Not that she could have had any due to her fasting, but she made a mental note to split the session in two next time, so that she could have a matinee with snacks.

When the last movie finished about half ten, Hannah turned her phone back on to set her alarm – ignoring the buzzing of missed notifications – and took herself upstairs to bed, fully expecting to fall asleep before her head hit the pillow.

She woke up in a pool of sweat just after 3am. It felt as if she was getting a fever, and with the duvet sticking to her like clingfilm, Hannah struggled to get back to sleep. She contemplated going downstairs to have a shower, but instead kept her eyes closed, willing herself to go back to sleep. When her alarm went off a mere two hours later, she had just managed to drift off and she felt like absolute dogshit. *How can one have her day ruined before even getting out of bed?* Hannah wondered, as she slid out of her too high bed and onto the floor. There was no chance of snoozing today. She had to look somewhat presentable for the billion Monday meetings, and if she wanted to get anything done after work, she really couldn't be late and having to flex the missing hour – she needed the few hours amassed last week to cover her doctor's appointments, as she was sure she would get booked in by her psychologist this week. And there was no chance she would be able to get on anyone's good side if she stayed at home for another day. Although the fever was worrying her slightly, Hannah would only make matters worse for herself if she kept thinking about it. Onwards and upwards, she thought, and put the kettle on for her first cup of coffee as she went to get ready.

Three coffees later, and all the caffeine had done was make her bowels tie themselves into a painful knot before emptying themselves violently and repeatedly, so Hannah was now sat on her toilet as her carefully applied makeup had begun to melt down her face. Great. Weren't women meant to be delicate flowers, all smiles and fluttering of eyelashes, and not some sort of faecal matter flinging device resembling a downward-facing M1917 Browning machine gun?

As she dragged her now rather sore derrière off of the plastic toilet seat, she was feeling pretty weak and realised that fasting until lunchtime would become a bit of a struggle and that she should really eat something to avoid snapping at any of her well-meaning coworkers. The deserving ones somehow never found themselves at the receiving end of Hannah's tantrums, so she didn't want to scare away any more of the meek minority. If they were indeed to inherit the earth, she'd like to be allowed to stay for a bit when they did. And so she packed an emergency stash of walnuts she could safely eat without triggering another round of rat-a-tat-tats, reapplied her makeup and headed for the door in hopes of catching the train she would now struggle to get to in time due to having spent the previous 16 minutes on the can.

Hannah had sprinted down the hills to catch her train, but the initial relief of having gotten to the station on time was quickly overshadowed by heavy perspiration soaking through her clothes. Over the last couple of days, the signs of spring had overtaken the tundra-like climate and knocked the ice out of the air, replacing it with what now felt like a full-on heatwave to poor Hannah. Would she ever learn to relax?

Finally at the office, she found she was the first one to arrive. She entered the alarm code – which, weirdly, she could still remember after all her time away, when she wouldn't switch her phone off in sheer fear of not being able to remember her own pin half the time – and headed straight for the biscuit drawer in the kitchen area, absolutely famished from all the running around. There was two thirds of a packet of chocolate chip cookies left from last week, and she scoffed the lot.

Luckily, Hannah had packed for going to the gym after work, so after her binge, she popped into the toilets to give her sweaty brow a good wipe and reapply her makeup for the second time this morning. She also managed to give herself a sink shower before her sweaty armpits started to stink. Relieved to still be alone in the large open-plan space, she claimed one of the desks in the very back, giving her a great view of anyone coming out of the lift and eliminating the chance of anyone being able to sit behind her. An added bonus was the fact that this would only serve as a base in between meetings once the others started pouring in, so she wouldn't be so bothered by everyone's post-weekend chatter, and at the same time it would look as though she wasn't hiding in the quiet zone, like she normally did. She even got to enjoy working in silence for a full 47 minutes before the first shoal of millennial slackers started squeezing their bespectacled selves out of the lift, and Hannah couldn't help but feeling pleased with herself. What a way to start the workweek!

As more and more people turned up, Hannah could feel her fever coming back and her head was starting to pound. She had no time for this, so she popped a few painkillers – of which she always had a stash in her little employee locker – on the way to her first meeting. It didn't seem to relieve any of her symptoms, though, so she made a note to grab a few more on her way to the next one. Or maybe she just needed some coffee? After all, she'd shat out what she'd had earlier this morning. This turned out to be a futile thought, as there was no time for either coffee nor drugs before the next meeting, as the former ran over – all because her team couldn't agree on a single thing. She could feel a cold sweat start to develop but tried to ignore it as best she could. On to the next meeting, and the next. By lunchtime she was starting to feel sick, but since all she'd had to eat today was refined sugar, she wasn't the least bit surprised. It was lunchtime already and, since she didn't have another meeting for 45 minutes, she was contemplating going down to the cafeteria when Rebecca out of nowhere interrupted her thinking by grabbing her arm.

'Lunch? We're heading downstairs now if you want to join us?'

Unable to come up with any excuses, Hannah smiled and agreed. In fact, she was glad someone had bothered to invite her along at all.

The cafeteria was heaving. Apparently, all the other offices in the building had decided to go to lunch at the same time today, so when a few people from Rebecca's team waved them over to their table, they each squeezed in at the end, only for Hannah to realise that she'd sat down next to Drew.

Shit. Anyone but you.

She said a quick 'hi' to everyone before turning her focus to the plate in front of her. She picked at the quinoa, prawn and feta salad she'd assembled at the salad bar, now regretting she hadn't picked something she could eat through a straw.

The conversation at their table was already flowing, as they were all talking about the remarkably successful quiz night they'd all attended. Everyone but her. Hannah tried to tune out their incessant chatting about the hilarious time they'd all had, but it only seemed to amplify their voices. And their chewing. And loud breathing between bites. Even though she was sat at the very end of the table, Hannah felt trapped. She tried putting some of her salad blend on her fork, but most of it spilled back onto her plate, whilst the rest fell down her top as she missed her own mouth with the fork and hit herself in the cheek. At this rate, she'd never be able to finish her lunch in time for the next meeting, but instead of making an excuse and taking the rest of her meal up to the office, she stayed. And with every piece of food that made it into her mouth, she felt smaller and smaller, just so insignificant.

Luckily, most of them had already finished their food and headed upstairs about five minutes after Rebecca and Hannah had sat down, and then a few stragglers joined them, so that Hannah wouldn't have to participate in any conversation – i.e. awkward silence – with just her and Becs. Drew had yet to acknowledge her and left the table without even looking at her. Although relieved she didn't have to talk to him, Hannah couldn't wait for the day to end after that. Just two more meetings to go. If only this headache could sod off.

Hannah made it to the gym after work, seeing as she already had her kit with her, but her heart wasn't in it. What was normally a welcome release became a struggle, and she could feel herself half-arsing every exercise. She had also decided to take her laptop with her, as she wasn't too keen on going in the next day. She knew she was setting herself up for a guilt trip, but she didn't think she could stomach another day like today so soon.

Sure enough, Hannah ended up not sleeping very well that night and was barely able to open her eyes when her alarm went off. Several snoozes later, it was too late for her to make it to work on time, so she stayed where she was and worked from home. Although she eventually ventured into the office on Thursday, she had to force herself and she was struggling to stay awake at her desk. She didn't sleep well at all that whole week, still feverish and not feeling well, and when Friday came along, she booked an appointment with her GP before work to have herself checked out.

On the train on her way to work, Hannah was lost in thought. Her doctor had concluded that stress was the reason behind her fever and suggested another sick leave was in order. Hannah had of course protested, seeing as she only had just over a month left before she could go on her annual leave, so they agreed that she would call her psychologist to set up an appointment for next week. *Have I really become so ill that I've developed an allergy to working in an office?*

Hannah was distraught. She could feel her neck starting to twitch and her head hitting the train window as a result. Maybe it was the universe, trying to bang some sense into her? All she wanted to do was scream, but seeing as she didn't have time to spend all weekend locked up in a psychiatric ward, she didn't succumb to the urge. Instead, she turned the volume up on her headphones and dug her nails into her wrist whilst staring out the window, trying to pretend she wasn't just another oxygen thief so undesirable even her own family didn't want anything to do with her.

Normally a stair-climbing gal, Hannah opted for the lift up to the fourth-floor office. She just didn't have the energy. Also, she was coming in an hour later than her usual time, courtesy of her doctor's appointment, and would now have to stay late as well. No doubt she'd be the last one to leave, as the few people that did come in on a Friday always knocked off early, despite the fact that they arrived at the same time as she did today. But they had families. Friends. Parties to go to. People who loved them. So, they were worth a lot more to this world than she was. Hannah was doomed to spend her days feeling as if she was being punished for choosing not to force her existence on any unsuspecting fellow humanoids. A forced loneliness for someone so grateful for silence and solitude. Hannah let out a deep sigh as she exited the lift, only to crash into one of the girls from HR.

'Hi! How are we this morning? Oh, you look knackered! Are you alright?'

Hannah blinked and cleared her throat.

'No, I'm not, actually. I'm not alright at all and I really don't know where I'll go from here.'

Wait, what?! Hannah couldn't believe what she'd just said. Clearly her filter had gone completely now, and the HR person just stared at her, willing this uncomfortable situation to just go away.

'Alright, then! Must dash. Ta-rah!' she trilled and walked away.

'Fuck me', Hannah whispered to herself, realising her GP might be right about needing to take some time off.

The remainder of the day really dragged on, but at least most people were "working" from home – most of them didn't realise the 'active' icon on the work chat switched to 'unavailable' after five minutes of inactivity – so Hannah was able to work in peace. And, since she had a feeling she might not be coming back for a little while, she got a LOT done. She had lunch at her desk and didn't look up much, but every time she did, she could see how her coworkers were smiling at each other, discussing their plans for the weekend and acting like they were so much more than just colleagues. This really irked Hannah, as it made her feel left out and just plain sad. As she'd foreseen, the last few people left just after three, leaving Hannah to her own devices – and the cookie drawer. 47 minutes and two and a half packets of self-harm in form of refined sugar later, Hannah decided it was time to call it.

'Fuck this shit o'clock', she sighed. She put her things in her bag, left her laptop in her tiny locker, took her phone charger, entered her alarm code and left for the 3.55 train.

When she arrived at the station, her train had been cancelled, and she instantly regretted not having checked the app in advance. There was another train due in a few minutes, but living so far away, this seemingly minor inconvenience would eat a sizeable chunk out of her downtime, as she would now have to switch trains halfway. Either way, walking the 16 miles home was not an option today, so she got on when it arrived.

Knowing she had at least an hour left of her journey home, she logged onto Facebook to check if she'd missed any birthdays lately. As she typed her last greeting and was about to log off again, the screen on her phone flashed with the notification 'Friend request Accepted'. What friend request? Huh? Shit, the last time she had been on the app was when she'd last had a drink... this could be anyone. But who? Afraid of what she might find, yet knowing she had to check, Hannah tapped her finger on the bell-shaped symbol in the top right corner of the screen.

Chapter 6: May – The only way is up?

Hannah fought against her urge to pinch her own eyes shut, although the request had been approved, so it couldn't be that bad. Right?

Jon Milton. Of all people! Jon's family had owned one of the holiday homes near her Nan's house when Hannah was little, and they'd spent pretty much every summer together growing up, even though he was a good four years older than her. Since there was no Facebook – or Internet, for that matter – in the early noughties, they'd lost touch when he went to college and stopped spending his summers with his parents. Hannah figured she must have had one of her more nostalgic moments when she'd added him, because she hadn't thought of him in at least ten years, if not more. How odd. She decided it'd be rude to delete him as a friend mere seconds after he'd accepted the request, so she was about to log off again when another notification popped up. Then another, and another; "Jon Milton liked your photo."

Apparently, Jon was suffering from severe finger cramps, because her phone vibrated with five more notifications in quick succession. This creeped her out a bit, so she quickly logged off and tried to take her mind off all of the stupid photos she'd been tagged in, or indeed uploaded herself, over the course of her social media career. But she couldn't stop her mind from wandering, though, only this time it went to a time of innocence and joy and summers spent by the sea, her parents too busy with family to constantly criticise her every move. And her beloved granddad had still been alive. All of a sudden, she didn't mind so much that drunk Hannah had been off Facebook stalking old skeletons. This one might even be a fortuitous event. Who knew?

Her phone vibrated again, a message this time. It was from Jon!

'Hi Hannah, so sorry it took me so long to see your friend request! I've just had a lot of personal stuff going on lately, so I haven't really been on here. How have you been? I can see you've still got that cheeky look in your eye! Lol. You look lovely in your photos. Jon'

It didn't take long for Hannah to reply. She found herself quite eager to see what adult Jon was like, and judging by the photos, he wasn't doing too badly for himself. The Jon she'd known back in the day was a skinny, lanky and slightly awkward kid, but by the looks of things, he had really grown into a more rugged and solid version of himself, and at the same time his eyes and infectious warm smile were the exact same. She felt a flutter in the pit of her stomach. What if he'd been "the one" all along? Now that they were both grown, the four-year age gap was no longer as perverse as it would have been when she had been eleven and he fifteen. Hannah explained to Jon that she'd only been back a couple of years after having spent a decade abroad and that she had come across his profile on Facebook (pretending not to be aware of the obvious *how*, seeing as they had no friends in common) and how she'd been curious to know if he still remembered her.

She remembered why she'd added him as well now. She'd actually been stalking his older brother, who used to be super-duper hot, when Jon came up in the search, but she chose not to divulge that particular piece of information. She'd discovered that Jon, too, had spent some time abroad and had thought maybe they would have something in common still. And, since they already knew each other, she wouldn't have to be afraid of him asking too many questions about her childhood, of which she remembered very little. So, here they were.

They kept messaging back and forth for the remainder of Hannah's journey, Hannah nearly missing her stop because she was so engrossed in their conversation. She caught a glimpse of her own reflection in the train window as she was getting off and could hardly recognise herself; she was grinning from ear to ear. Not even the hill of doom could rock her sudden good mood. The conversation flowed so naturally there wasn't even room for awkward pauses or time for any overthinking. Hannah felt like their friendship was back to what it had been back then, as if no time at all had gone by. As if he'd read her mind, Jon messaged her asking if she'd be allowed to come out and play 'one of these days'. Just like old times. Hannah giggled to herself as she was walking along the garden path towards her little red house, even saying hello to the landlord that was doing some gardening just outside Hannah's living room window – something that would normally irritate Hannah, and in most cases even ruin her day. But not today.

Thanks to the welcome sensation of being a kid again, with far less worries than today, Hannah was able to shut all the noise out. She found herself in a little bobble with Jon, their conversation shifting between reminiscing about them going out in the boat to camp on one of the islands in the bay as kids and what they had both been up to over the two decades that had passed since they'd last seen each other. Hannah was also surprised to find that Jon wanted to know about her interests instead of spending the time just telling her about himself, as would be the norm in most interactions Hannah had with other people. She'd gotten to a point where she didn't even have to ask now – most days people approached her and just started talking about themselves. Yet, she also found that right now, with Jon, she wouldn't have minded if he did only talk about himself, because this time, she was genuinely interested.

One of the very first things he mentioned was that he had four (!) children. He said he wanted to be 'completely upfront and honest' with her, so if that were to put her off, he would see himself out. In any other event, Hannah would have been bothered by this, but this time, she thought nothing of it. In fact, she found herself appreciating his honesty. There appeared to be some ongoing drama with one of the kids' mothers, as they had very recently decided to part ways and were still living together. Again, he reiterated, he just wanted everything to be out in the open.

How refreshing! Hannah thought. And then she told him that she thought it was exactly that; refreshing. It was bizarre, really. It felt like they had nothing to hide from one another and that they could be completely honest; warts and all.

Hmm. Might be a bit soon to mention the HPV, though.

They kept messaging for a good half hour after Hannah got home, but as life was starting to happen on his end – having to make dinner for the kids and walk the dog – they wrapped up, but not before they'd agreed to stay in touch over the weekend.

'I'll just leave you with this. I'm so happy you're back in my life – it feels like it's meant to be', Jon wrote in his last message, adding a link to the Brandi Carlisle song *The Story*.

Normally, this sort of behaviour would've made Hannah gag, but right now she thought she felt something rather divine. Like Jon said, she felt a bit like this was meant to be. She felt as if she was a tween again, having met a boy who liked her back. Instead of succumbing to her normal behaviour of making this whole scenario into something negative, Hannah found herself logging back in on Facebook and looking through his profile pictures, happy he was still the same Jon she'd known all those years ago – still *her* Jon. She even listened to the song he had sent her over and over, even though it really wasn't her cup of tea.

She thought to herself, how wonderful that he'd chosen today of all days to reach out to her. When she went to bed a few hours later, she was thinking about sending him a goodnight message when her phone buzzed with a message. Him again:

'Sleep well, lovely. Can't wait to chat to you tomorrow. Xxx'

The last somewhat "real" relationship that Hannah had had had been with her then married boss, so Hannah was normally quite trepidatious when it

came to romantic entanglements, but since Jon had
been upfront with her right off the bat, she felt like it
was safe for her to let her guard down. The story of how
she got into a nearly four-year long relationship with a
married man will remain a tale for another day, but let's
just say she had a history of falling for the wrong – and
more often than not someone else's – man. Although it's
important to mention that she never went after them,
she did give in pretty darn easily once they started
showing her some attention – for which she was still
constantly flogging herself. Either way, Jon might be in
an awkward position, but he was SINGLE, and he
thought she was 'lovely'. So, Hannah allowed herself to
relish in the somewhat unfamiliar warm feeling that
was appearing to have started a thaw in her aortic
region. And then, another miracle happened. Another
message from Jon:

'I should probably get your number, by the way,
as I plan on using it quite a bit in the near future. Xxxx'

He wanted her number! Ever since the birth of
instant messaging, Hannah had seen text messaging
and phone calls as something you only did with the
people you really, truly wanted to be part of your life
and/or you actually respected. If you were prepared to
spend your minutes on someone, it meant – to Hannah,
at least – that you were invested. So, she gladly sent him
her number, not even slightly nauseated by the four
kisses, and added a 'sleep well, handsome xxx'. Less
than a minute later, she received a text message,
consisting of a single heart emoji. And Hannah swooned
herself off to sleep.

She woke up the next morning, shocked that she'd slept through the night, to a lovely text from Jon:

'Just wanted to wish you a lovely day. Might get the kids to go over to some friends later so I can give you a call. Xxxx'

Normally, she'd react to the fact that he just assumed that she wouldn't be busy, but she let it fly. He had kids and she didn't. And she was curious of what he sounded like now, all grown up. She texted him back to say that she was going for a run and was hoping he'd be free to call her later. And then, since she told him that she was going for a run, she got dressed, went downstairs, splashed some water on her face and headed out the door and into the morning sunshine. It was going to be a glorious Saturday.

Hannah took the route that led her down to the water, so that she could take in the scenery and at the same time avoid most of the traffic. She felt a lot lighter than she had done in a while, and while she ran, she could see quite a few spring flowers already starting to pop up in place of the dirty snow and ice that was now all but gone from the trails. She enjoyed the slightly meditative thump-thump noise coming from where her shoes met the asphalt and the sensation of the soles rolling over bits of gravel, and could feel herself relaxing and letting her mind wander freely more and more with every step she took. As she moved closer to the sea, the salty air crept up her nostrils, the smell reminiscent of summers spent with Jon and their friends, their skin a nutty brown, freckles across her own nose and worries safely stowed away back home for the summer.

It was weird how the restraints of social construct and stigma seemed to escape them once they were out of their respective counties, Hannah reflected as she ran. Although neither of them had been "cool kids" in school, Jon had been a proper nerd, now that she looked back, as in one of those geeks that would play Dungeons & Dragons and even *dress up* for it. Hannah had been more of a loner, largely keeping to herself and spending what little free time she had, outside of sports teams and marching band, on playing her guitar and listening to bands like *Nirvana*, *Soundgarden* and *Metallica*. She hadn't really changed much in that department, although she'd discovered other, arguably more artistically diverse, bands as she grew older. Still, she had always thought of Jon as "cool", perhaps because he was older, or maybe because he had already had a group of other holiday pals when she got to the age where they started bumping into each other on the beach. And so, by hanging out with him, she had sort of become one of the cool kids by association. Or perhaps – and far more likely – it was their mutual lack of social belonging that drew them to each other in the first place. Regardless, they had made lasting impressions on one another, and Hannah only had fond memories of Jon now. She also discovered that the fact that he felt the same way about her as she did for him made her feel like she had even the tiniest bit of value in this world, and that was something she sorely needed to feel right now. And, since they had always just been friends, there were no dirty connotations to the innocent nature of their relationship – which, incidentally, also was something she needed; for something to not have been dirtied by sexual or indeed romantic advances. Which was perhaps also why she was seeing him in such a romanticised way now. She needed to find some memories that were imprinted by pure innocence, in contrast to all of the darkness that was already inhabiting her mind.

Hannah quickly checked her phone for the time, only to find her tracking app telling her she'd already run five miles. She was surprised that she didn't feel the least bit tired and kept on going, whilst at the same time being mindful of the fact that she should probably start turning back soon, in case Jon was to call.

Despite the hordes of people that had been littering the streets due to the rather lovely weather, Hannah was still in an uplifted state as she put her key into the lock of her door. Not in her usual hurry to get out of sight of the landlord's peering gaze, she even stopped to stretch out her calves on her little veranda before she ventured back into her house, now warm from baking in the generous sunlight while she had been running.

Not having to live in constant fear of being unable to pay the electric bill over the next few months was also a welcome prospect – the warmer temperatures eliminated the need to put the heating on – so Hannah was grateful she had something to look forward to, other than darkness and living in a state of perpetual ruin. She quickly undressed, chucked all of her washing in her washer-dryer and headed to the baña for a quick shower. *Wow, it felt nice to feel good!*

After her shower, Hannah went on to clean her flat. This, of course, didn't take very long, as her house was tiny, but it always seemed like such an unsurmountable task until it was done – or if she was procrastinating. Today, however, she cleaned every nook and cranny, so that she would be free for when the call from Jon came. Sure enough, not more than a few minutes after she'd sat down on the sofa, the phone rang. Realising that she would have no idea at all what he would sound like now, Hannah hesitated for a second before shaking off the feeling of uncertainty. It was *her* Jon. It wouldn't matter.

'Hi! It's me! How are you? How weird is this?' came Jon's voice through the ether.

And it really did sound like the Jon Hannah had spent all of her childhood summers with, his voice made distinct by a certain raspy quality – almost as if he was a little hoarse – and by being slightly higher pitched than most other men's, gentle and disarming, yet somehow still quite masculine due to the raspiness.

After they had started talking, it was almost as if they couldn't make themselves stop – or at least that was true in Jon's case. He talked and talked – which, honestly, Hannah didn't mind, for once. She took it as a sign of him trusting her and that their connection really *was* real. So, she was quite happy to let him steer the conversation. He told her about his first wife, with whom he had the three first children, and who had left him when she found out she'd rather date a woman at her work. They had shared custody of the kids, who spent alternating weeks between mum and her Mrs and him and his current/former partner, their child and her child from a previous relationship. He said he was aware this might be a lot to all of a sudden become a part of and that he understood if she didn't want anything to do with him. But Hannah, who was of course listening intently, insisted that this was no issue for her and that it sounded like he really needed to talk about it and that he should continue doing so.

Happy to oblige, he did. He told her about his years abroad, where he'd gone to film school and how nothing had come of it, how he was the only one out of his siblings that hadn't become a doctor and how he was a huge appointment to his dad and how he could never be good enough for his mum. He talked about how he always tried so hard at everything and that nothing ever really came to fruition and that the reason for that had always been due to someone else standing in his way, causing him to fail. He was now working as a teacher, in order to be able to provide for his families, but of course he didn't know for how long he would be kept on, as he didn't have the proper qualification to teach.

He stopped for reassurance from Hannah every so often, making sure that he wasn't talking her ear off. And every time, she assured him he wasn't. So, naturally, he kept going. About two and a half hours later, Hannah could hear voices in the background.

'Oh, it's the kids! I can't believe it's that time already. Time has just flown by!' exclaimed Jon. 'I've got to go. When do I get to talk to you again? Can I call you once they're in bed?'

'Of course!' Hannah replied. 'Just go do your dad thing and we can talk later.'

'I'll call you later!'

Hannah sat in silence for a bit after they had hung up. It was so strange to listen to someone she knew only as a child now talk about what was going on in their adult life. She could almost picture him surrounded by his family now, cooking for them and asking them about their collective day. And here she was, sitting in the darkness, contemplating someone else's life. But it was rather nice having to focus on someone else's stuff for once, instead of dealing with the endless evaluative work up at the psychiatric hospital and not knowing what was next. And it made her feel needed, trusted and wanted, which was now presenting a welcome distraction, instead of just another issue to deal with. After all, she didn't have to do anything to improve his situation, all she needed to do was sit and listen, and maybe offer up some advice. No, this wasn't too bad at all. And he was going to call again this evening, so she was sure it would be her turn to vent soon enough.

Hannah got up to turn the lights on, made herself something to eat and put the telly on, awaiting Jon's call.

Jon called just after nine. It took a minute for Hannah, who had fallen asleep on the sofa, to register that the buzzing from her phone wasn't part of her dream, but when she eventually picked up, they picked up right where they had left off mere hours earlier. He said he was calling from his garden shed, so as not to raise any suspicion among the kids. This irked her somewhat, having been kept a secret before, and so she said that there wasn't really any reason for keeping anything from anyone, as surely a grown man should be allowed to have a catch-up with an old friend.

Because, at this stage – even though they may both be hoping for something more down the lane – they were just friends.

Also, weren't the kids supposed to be in bed, anyway? Hannah thought to herself.

And then she said it out loud, showing him that she wasn't interested in keeping any secrets herself, and reiterating her need for everything to be out in the open, due to her previous experiences. She'd already told him about her relationship with her former boss when they were messaging, so he already knew how she felt about stuff like this. She also pointed out that his eldest child was a teenager, and it would probably be best for their relationship if he were honest with her, as she was sure to figure things out anyway.

Pleased that Jon seemed to understand where she was coming from – and that he was even agreeing with her – she swept the whole thing under her mental rug, deciding to not take this as a red flag and moved on.

It quickly became clear that the reason Jon wanted to talk to her again so soon was that he had discovered that he had so much more to talk about, and he praised her for being such a good listener. He said that he never talked liked this with anyone, but now, he felt as if he could tell her about anything and everything. He trusted her and cared for her and wanted her to know everything about him. And he couldn't believe he was talking to someone so beautiful and cool. So much cooler than him.

Not used to receiving compliments – or if she did, she'd never believed them to be genuine – Hannah was flattered and could feel herself blushing. Which, of course, she told him, and they both laughed. It really was nice to talk to someone without having to filter their words or reactions.

They talked for a while, but it soon became time for Jon to head back in, as he couldn't really leave the two-year-old unsupervised for too long, which Hannah fully approved of. They each said their goodbyes and hung up, but true to form Jon texted her within seconds:

'Is it weird that I miss talking to you already? LOL. Xxxx'

'YES. Now go look after your children', she typed back, before texting again, without hesitation and slightly afraid she'd put him off with her bluntness:

'Is it weird that I miss listening to you? Haha xxx'

'I want to see you. Or is that too soon? I can wait, of course, if it's too soon. I just want to see your smile. I can do Saturday two weeks from now. Xxxx'

Hannah's heart jumped at this last message, but she took it to be a good sign and typed back that she was free and would actually love to meet him in the flesh. He offered to come to her, as he had a car, which seemed logical enough to Hannah. Also, if he was driving, she wouldn't have to worry about them ending up drinking, which was a bonus. And, although she'd been the one to insist that they were 'just friends', she was quite excited at the prospect of a date with this man that she felt she had so much history with, and good, untainted memories of. Her phone buzzed with a new message:

'My face hurts from smiling. I love this. Us. Sleep tight, my lovely. Xxxx'

Hannah smiled and texted back:
'Same. Haha. Sleep well and we'll speak again soon. Xxx'
'Tomorrow too soon?' Jon replied. Followed by another four kisses.

What was this strange sensation? Was this what love felt like? Hannah really hadn't the slightest idea, but based on that alone, she took it to be just that. Ah, to be falling in love with a childhood friend. It'd be like something straight out of one of those cheesy romcoms she watched, but she welcomed it with open arms. Didn't they say that love happened when you were least expecting it? Maybe she had to start believing in that now, too.

She chuckled to herself and decided it was time for bed. After all, she'd fallen asleep once already, and seeing as they'd chatted for almost an hour, she'd better get to it if she wanted to be well-rested for when Jon called again tomorrow. And maybe he'd tell the kids about her tomorrow as well? She was sure he would. Although, a lot could happen overnight with kids, so she'd understand if the time hadn't been right as well. She didn't want to set herself up for failure in that regard. It would all work out. After all, it was *her* Jon.

Hannah woke up early the next day, but she hadn't slept too well, so she was anxious to go for a run to get rid of the anxious feeling she'd get when her sleep pattern was disrupted, and also collect her thoughts. But she didn't want to head out in case it made her seem rude if it would make her miss a text or call from Jon, so she decided she'd wait for him to message her before heading out. The sun was out in full force again, so she was looking forward to some pavement pounding meditation in the warm embrace of the sunshine.

Jon messaged her around 11. Hannah had already been up for five hours already, but since she didn't know when she'd be able to go for her run, she hadn't had breakfast yet. Jon said there were some issues with his ex that he had to sort out, but he would love it if they could talk after – he'd probably need someone to talk to after that.

Although slightly disappointed that she hadn't just gone about her day when she'd had the chance, Hannah didn't want to seem pushy in asking him when she could expect him to call, so she just said that she was about to go for a run anyway, so she would have plenty of time for him later on, trying to convince both of them that this was really a good thing.

Hannah's stomach was growling now. She realised she would have to eat something before her run, so she made herself a massive bowl of porridge with flaxseed, which she polished off within minutes. Not daring to hang about for her standard 90 minutes before a run, and despite the fact that it was now overcast, she left the house just half an hour after finishing her meal. When she was just over halfway into her 12k, the food had started to wreak havoc on her already sensitive intestinal system, and, as if that wasn't enough, a massive drop of rain plopped onto her forehead with a loud, wet sound that was audible even over the music she had blaring through her headphones.

Although her headphones were sweat resistant, Hannah always feared that she'd be electrocuted if she went running in the rain with them on, so she sped up, her now pregnant looking belly guiding the way and pushing her through the torrential rain like the bow of an icebreaker in front of her. She was turning onto her street just as her playlist ever so fittingly skipped to *Thunder* – by legendary boyband East 17 – lightning ripping through the sky like a very skinny horseman of the apocalypse. The ground shook with the clap of thunder that followed it, and Hannah realised her house must be right in the eye of the storm. Legging it up the hill, whilst simultaneously trying to keep her breakfast from escaping the inside of her body, she whispered a quiet prayer to whichever deity was willing to listen:

'Please, please, please let me make it home without any accidents today…please!'

By some miracle, Hannah made it through the door just in time – the seat of the toilet hadn't even kissed the slick skin of her behind before the entire universe – or so it felt like – started pouring out of her, with such force she was afraid she'd suffer a prolapse. Sweating profusely, just as much – if not more – from the ongoing bowel movement as from the jog, Hannah was afraid to check if her phone had survived the apocalyptic weather. Although, the music was still playing, so at least she knew that the Bluetooth was still working.

She pulled her mobile from her damp running belt, only to discover she'd missed a message from Jon, from about 20 minutes ago. He had just texted to say, 'this might take a while', so she texted back apologising for the delay in replying and that it was totally fine and that she had just gotten back from her run anyway.

Every time she'd been late in replying to any of her ex's texts, he'd accuse her of fucking someone else, so she didn't want Jon to suspect her of that as well. Although, he was being very short with her now, not adding a hundred kisses to every message, so she was afraid that she'd done something wrong. She probably shouldn't have gone for that run after all – even the weather had started punishing her for her ignorance! She desperately wanted to redeem herself but had no idea how – or why, for that matter – so she simply texted him:

'I'll be here when you're free. Can't wait to hear your voice again. Xxxx'

Adding the last 'x' felt excessive and wrong, but Hannah couldn't stand the thought of losing Jon to something so stupid as not having been on top of her texting game. But as she was getting ready for her post faecal Rorschach shower, she received another message from Jon:

'Xxxx'

Maybe there was still hope.

Although Hannah had preferred it if Jon would've given her a time for when she could expect him to phone her, she was relieved when she saw his name flash across her phone screen a few hours later. She didn't know why, but she'd half-expected him to sound different now, but when he said 'hello', she could hear the smile in his voice. She'd worried for nothing.

This time, they talked without interruptions from the outside world. He was taking his dog for a walk, and she was on her sofa, just thinking about what it might be like to walk alongside him. Weirdly enough, at that instant he exclaimed:

'If you were here right now, I'd be holding your hand'.

Hannah, who was of the opinion that handholding was one of the most intimate gestures known to man, instantly blushed and felt the old butterflies starting to flutter in her stomach again.

When they'd talked for a while, Jon did confess that he and his ex, the one he was living with, hadn't told the kids yet that they had split up, and the issue earlier that day had been about that. He explained that she'd already gotten a job somewhere else and that she would have to relocate for it, but they just hadn't found the right time to break it to them. He very much wanted to continue sharing the responsibility for their mutual child, so he didn't want to do anything to upset her and jeopardise that, even if it had been her that had decided to leave. 'At least to begin with,' he was quick to add. 'Now I just want her out of here so that I can begin my life. Maybe with you?'

Hannah harrumphed at this ridiculous notion, but she wasn't deterred:

'What would that be like, do you think?' she asked. 'Us, together, I mean.'

This question prompted Jon to paint Hannah a vivid picture of his hopes and dreams of becoming the owner of a small farm, right around the corner from his parents' summer home – Hannah remembered the place well. It was a dilapidated old wooden house, white with a blue door and window frames, with a massive, blue barn and a large field, which attracted tick infested deer all year long. It was old, but very charming, and the barn especially had tonnes of potential for keeping livestock, or even building an art studio, or a flat for letting out to holiday makers. Hell, with the size of the thing, you could probably accommodate all three. He said he wanted to add a greenhouse and that his dream was to become completely self-reliant on his own produce and to reduce his carbon footprint and save money in the long term. The farm had been for sale for a while and he had asked his dad to put in a good word for him, as he was relying on him – and to a certain extent his mum – to get the deal he wanted.

Hannah, who wouldn't dream of asking her own parents for such a thing, was astonished that a grown man would need his parents to do the talking for him, but she knew that her family dynamic was quite different from that of others and assumed this might be normal behaviour for most people. Either way, it did sound like it had the potential to become a great home for him and the kids, so she was more than happy to support his decision. He sounded so happy when he was talking about it, so she wasn't about to piss all over his dreams with questioning logistics, swapping school district for three kids and at the same time uprooting them from their lives and separating them from their friends and siblings. What did she know? Maybe they were miserable where they were now? It was none of her business, so Hannah was just enjoying listening to Jon talking about it in such an enthusiastic way.

Her train of thought was interrupted by Jon changing the topic:

'There's something else I've been thinking about a lot as well.'

'Yeah? What might that be?'

'You, silly. I get to see you in less than two weeks.'

This put Hannah's worried brain to rest for now, replacing the worry with giddy excitement, and when they hung up that evening, Hannah felt hopeful. So hopeful, in fact, that she decided to go to work tomorrow after all. Now that she had Jon back in her life, she wouldn't have to worry so much about Drew.

The next week was filled with incessant texting and evening phone calls. Jon had to go away with his family on the weekend – which was why, it turned out, he couldn't come to see her sooner. But they kept in touch with texts throughout, and he sent her photos documenting their trip for her to see. 'If only you were here', he'd texted.

On the following Monday, Hannah had a doctor's appointment, during which they decided that she should cut back on her hours to make space for treatment, effective immediately. It would make the remaining weeks before her holiday more tolerable as well, and the psychiatric hospital shut over the summer, so she wouldn't be able to see Andrea should something happen. Although her mood had lifted since Jon rejoined her life, she agreed that this was a good plan. She didn't have enough to fill her days with at work as it was – having finished everything on her to-do list a little while back – so she might as well only be there when she had actual shit to take care of, so they agreed that three days a week would be more than enough. Hannah's boss was not very hard to convince – she genuinely wanted Hannah to get better, and most of her colleagues had started taking their annual leave now anyway, so there wouldn't be any last-minute campaigns to facilitate or press releases to send out for quite some time.

Relieved to have such an understanding boss, and a little sad to be rid of her, Hannah texted Jon the news. He didn't reply for a while, which was unlike him, but she figured he might be in the middle of a lecture – he was working after all. And when he did reply, he did so with the following:

'The kids will be at their mum's on Thursday. Fancy an early visit??? Xxxx'

'YES, PLEASE xxx' Hannah texted back, suddenly giddy and sweaty at the same time, but that didn't matter. She was finally getting to see him after all these years, and in just two more days!

Hannah's next two days were filled with hospital appointments and exercise, so when Thursday finally arrived, she had to go to work to fill her quota, so Hannah had very little time to self-sabotage before he was due to arrive. Just before she was about to clock out, Jon messaged her asking for her address. She gave it to him, adding that she was looking at a 90-minute commute before she was home. He replied:

'Perfect. Am just about to drop the kids off. Will text you when I'm on my way. Xxxx'

Hannah was still on the train when her phone buzzed again:

'Maps tells me I'll be seeing you in 42 minutes. Can't wait. Xxxx'

Hannah took the hill in long strides when she got off the train. She didn't want to become a sweaty mess, but she needed at least ten minutes to get herself ready before he got there. She got home with 15 minutes to spare, so she managed to calm herself a little bit, before topping up her makeup and grabbing a quick sink shower and mouth rinse. As she was spitting her mouthwash out into her sink, she heard a knock at the door. She didn't even have time to start worrying or thinking about how she felt. This was it – on the other side of her front door was the potential beginning of the rest of her life.

Part 3: Summer

Chapter 7: June – The meaning of 'no'

Hannah was at a loss for words. Standing in front of her was Jon from 25 years ago, exactly the same, except now he had grown a beard. He literally had not changed a bit, as in not even grown an inch since mid-puberty, so he was a good five inches shorter than her very average and not at all tall 5ft 4inch stature, which now felt massive compared to his 5ft 2. But she told herself *'No. Don't be heightist'*. (Probably not a word, but Hannah figured, if you could be ageist, you could be heightist as well.)

Jon didn't seem to mind one bit that a giantess was stood before him. In fact, he was grinning from ear to ear, becoming visibly moved and simply said:

'Can I give you a hug?' his voice thick with emotion.

Something in Hannah wanted to slam the door in his face and bolt the door, yet there was something about his sweet, hopeful, wee face that made her resign and let herself be embraced by this strange man child. Although, she felt rather uncomfortable standing out there in the open like this, for the whole world to see, so she invited him in.

Once they had sat down – and the height difference was no longer so palpable – Hannah found herself letting her guard down. He really was that same person she used to know, and now he was here in front of her, fully grown. (Not as grown as she'd like, but beggars can't be choosers.)

Jon admitted he was a little nervous and asked for something to drink, so Hannah got up to get him a glass of water. When she came back, he'd settled into her couch, propping himself up on her cushions. *What, was he nesting?* Hannah thought to herself, yet she sort of liked that he seemed to feel like he belonged there, with her. Even if she herself did not.

She gave him the water and sat back down, and they started talking again, and they didn't stop until he all of a sudden demanded something to eat as well. He'd been too nervous to eat all day, so now he was famished, he explained. He was known to get sudden drops in his blood sugar levels, so he had to eat something every so often, lest he faint.

Going against her better judgement, Hannah promptly got up and made him the two boiled eggs he'd requested. She wasn't used to this sort of demanding behaviour from a fellow adult, so she just did as she was asked. Maybe this was normal relationship behaviour these days? She wouldn't know, as she had been avoiding them for the past decade (bar the fling with her married man, but that was hardly a standard relationship).

When the eggs were boiled, Hannah sat and watched him eat in silence. His tiny belly again full, Jon had enough energy to start talking again. He did have a very disarming way about him, and before long, Hannah was feeling very empathetic towards him and the stories he told her, in which he was more often than not posing as the victim. This applied to his experience with studying abroad – which he again reminded her had resulted in a project that had never really come to fruition – his first wife that had left him for another woman, and his parents looking down on him for not choosing the path they had wanted for him. He spoke of his experiences in such a way that Hannah couldn't help but feel bad for him. It made her want to give him a hug and make his pain go away, so she sat and she listened intently, for as long as he needed.

'Gosh, I feel like I've talked and talked for hours!' Jon suddenly exclaimed, cheerfully.

'Oh, I don't mind,' Hannah said, half-truthfully. 'I think maybe you've been needing to talk about things, maybe to gain some perspective? It can sometimes be nice to talk to an impartial party.'

'Yeah, I think you're right. I really did need this. I think maybe all I needed was to have you back in my life', Jon beamed. 'And since we've known each other all our lives, I know you can see my side of the story as well. I needed someone to be on my team for once and I'm so glad it's you. I need you.'

Hannah liked being needed, so she nodded and smiled, not really saying anything. Jon then started reminiscing about the old days, when they had been running around the forest paths, or when they would go fishing on his little dinghy.

'I always thought you were so pretty', he said, dreamily, his voice growing thick again.

Pretty? Hannah thought. *That's a little pervy for a 15-year-old to think about a child.* But she didn't want

him to leave, so she kept that to herself. She was sure
he didn't mean it that way.

'What do you think the guys would say if they
saw us now? They were always jealous of our
relationship back then', Jon chuckled.
Hannah laughed as well. That was just bizarre,
as she'd been the annoying kid that had always been
running after the older boys, wanting to play with them.
Then, Jon brought up the farm again, and this
Hannah was really interested in, as she thought it would
be good for him to have a project to focus on.

'Maybe I'll build a little flat for you on the
property, so you can come live there too?' he said, with
hope in his voice.
Hannah naturally thought he was joking, yet she
could see it happening. She could probably be able to
afford renting it off him from time to time when she
wanted to get away from the city. It was close to her
sister and nephews as well, so that was a bonus.

'Yeah, that would be lovely, actually', she said.
'Then you could use the rent money to pay off the
mortgage'.

Jon seemed thrilled with this response. He
checked his watch and realised it was almost time for
him to go.

'God, I don't want to leave you', he said after he
had put his shoes back on. 'But I have to go pick up the
kids. Do you think I could get a hug for the road?'

'Of course!' she exclaimed, and once again found herself in the warmest embrace. For such a little person, he sure was a good hugger. She hadn't been touched in so long, she was actually enjoying it, and when they finally let go of each other, they both had tears in their eyes.

'Right, I'd better be off', Jon said as he opened the door. 'It has been so lovely seeing you. I can't wait for the weekend'.

And then he started down the garden path, towards his car.

Hannah leaned back on the wall next to the door for support after she'd closed the door behind him. It was like she'd had her breath knocked out of her. But before she'd had the chance to analyse it, a knock came at the door. She opened up, and it was him:

'I was sitting in my car, and I just couldn't make myself turn the key in the ignition. I had to see you one more time', Jon said, and threw his arms around her once more. Like out of a fucking romcom.

'Oh, wow', he said as he pulled away, a single tear running down his face. 'Just wow. This was a lot. Right, I'll be off for real now. I'll call you later.'

And then he went, again, leaving Hannah flustered and struggling with emotions she couldn't quite place.

Before Hannah had the chance to think much about anything, a message came from Kim:

'Hey, any chance you'd be up for a walk on Saturday? The weather's supposed to be lovely and I'd love to see you'.

Already in a weird, and forgiving, mood, Hannah accepted and agreed to meet Kim at the park Saturday morning, as she had her visitor coming over that evening. She needed to talk to someone about this Jon business as well, so she figured it could be a nice chance for them to have a catch-up, without having to discuss such dark matters.

When Saturday came along, Hannah was in a rather good mood, despite the fact that she'd be spending the weekend socialising, for the most part. Jon had suggested they have a few drinks that evening and offered to bring his own homebrew, and although Hannah was reluctant to drink these days, she felt that what Jon and she had was a safe space where she wouldn't go completely off the rails. She had started to look forward to her walk with Kim as well, as she was afraid she'd judged her too soon this time, when maybe she should have given her the benefit of the doubt. She must have meant well, right? It was Hannah's own fault that she had let herself get hurt – she knew very well that people couldn't be trusted. After all, this was exactly why she didn't tell anyone *anything*. So, when Kim and she met at the bus stop near the park, Hannah smiled at her old pal:

'Hey', she said, as if nothing had happened. 'How have you been?'

But then Kim surprised her by saying that she was more interested in hearing about what was going on in Hannah's life, so – deciding this was a safe topic, one that didn't reveal anything about her inner workings – Hannah simply said:

'I've met someone.'
'What?!' shrieked Kim. 'That's great news! Who is he? Do I know him?'
'No. Well, I suppose it would be wrong to say that I've *met* him in that respect. I mean, I have met him, but that was 40 years ago. I've always kind of known him, but then we lost touch somewhere along the line. But now we've found our way back to each other. I know, it's disgusting. I'd want to punch myself in the face if I were you.'
'No, not at all', Kim said. 'You look so happy. I love this for you.'

So, Hannah told Kim about how it all started and how he was coming over to hers that evening. She left out the parts where he'd been the only one really talking and how she'd wanted to slam the door in his face, as she felt that that didn't really matter now. It wasn't a sexual thing for her, it was more of a spiritual connection of sorts. And everything just felt so easy and familiar with him, since they'd known each other forever. And Kim surprised her by saying she thought it was romantic! Now, that was a word Hannah had never thought she'd hear coming out of Kim's mouth, so she started laughing and told her exactly that.

'Well, maybe we've both gone a bit soft', Kim said, smiling.

They kept the conversation light this time, mainly talking about work stuff and their upcoming holidays, for which Hannah still didn't have any plans. She made a note of doing something about that as soon as possible. Kim hated beach holidays, so she'd opted for a tour of the UK's most visited art museums – which sounded to Hannah like her worst nightmare, and she was glad she didn't have to go with her. When their walk ended back where they'd first met, they awkwardly hugged each other goodbye and promised it wouldn't be long until they'd see each other again, before jumping on their respective buses that were going in opposite directions.

Hannah felt relaxed about this evening, so when she got home, she fixed herself something to eat before jumping in the shower. As there was no pressure for anything to happen, she didn't have to worry about a whole grooming regime, so she left her unwaxed nether region un-pampered and legs stubbly. They'd agreed that Jon would stay over, as they'd be drinking, but he had offered to take the couch. No pressure at all. So, when the knock came at the door, Hannah opened with a smile, ready for one of his long hugs.

Jon handed her a sixpack of his own IPA, which she put in her tiny fridge for later, saying she was looking forward to tasting it. They went to sit on her large L-shaped couch, and Jon pulled one of her legs onto his lap and started massaging her foot as he was telling her about his week and his upcoming excursion with the school.

'The entire class is coming', he said. 'Twenty-six teenagers, for a fortnight!'

They both had a chuckle at that. Again, Hannah was relieved she didn't have to go, so she said so as well.

After he'd talked and rubbed her foot for a good thirty minutes, Hannah started thinking about the beer in the fridge. Wasn't it time they crack those bad boys open? But she kept her mouth shut, as she didn't want Jon to think she was some sort of raging alcoholic. And they were enjoying each other's company after all, so why add alcohol to that?

As Jon urged her to give him her other foot for him to rub, she accidentally rubbed it against something hard in his trouser area. Good grief, he had a full-on erection going on, and all they'd talked about had been his school trip. *Ick!* Hannah thought to herself, not sure if she thought the cause of the raging boner had been the foot rub was any better.

'Oh, sorry about that', Jon said, his voice changing a bit, 'I've thought about you all day and now that I'm finally here, touching you, you just make it impossible for me to stop myself. You make me so horny.'

What the fuck??

Hannah didn't know what to do. She really wanted to pull her foot out of his grip, but she was afraid she might kick him in the nuts. (She'd done this to someone before, when she was a teenager, and she still felt bad thinking about the excruciating pain the boy had experienced, from just a tap of her knee).

'You're funny', she laughed, nervously. She'd told him on the phone that she wasn't ready for anything sexual, so this was a bit much for her. Only minutes earlier, she had been thinking about what it might be like to kiss him, but that thought had now become something she'd rather not explore any further. She decided she'd let him keep rubbing her foot, after all he'd driven all this way to see her, but that would be it. And, since they hadn't had anything to drink yet, there was a chance that he'd decide to go home and leave her there all alone, and she didn't know if she wanted that either. It was as if she couldn't trust herself with this boy now. She tried to tell herself that she knew him. She must have just misheard him. There was nothing remotely rapey about this lovely boy that so clearly just wanted someone to love him.

But then he started rubbing her foot against his crotch.

'Sorry, this is a little too much for me, Jon. I'm not ready for this. Sorry', she said, to make him stop. She had no idea why she'd apologised twice, but she didn't want him to feel bad. She'd probably sent off some signal that he'd misinterpreted. After all, she hadn't pulled her foot back.

'Don't worry about it,' Jon said, clearly flustered now, with his erection pushing against his khakis. (Also, Hannah didn't date men who wore fucking *khakis*). He went to adjust himself, before nonchalantly and seemingly unperturbed continuing his monologue.

Surely, this was just a misunderstanding, Hannah thought to herself and tried to shake off her nagging feeling of similar past experiences with boys she'd seen as just pals as just that. Hannah suggested they watch a movie, to somehow manipulate the mood a little, but Jon wanted to keep talking, so she let him have his way, although she now felt rather on edge. She could feel herself starting to get tired. Jon had arrived at 8, and since he'd already talked non-stop for about two hours, it was nearing her bedtime. She yawned.

'God, I'm so sorry! I didn't realise I was so tired', she said, genuinely surprised at her own body's sudden outburst.

But Jon didn't take it in any negative way. He said he was starting to get tired as well. 'Far too tired to be getting behind the wheel, though', he added. 'We can go to bed if you'd like?'

Erm...bed? Did we not agree that you would sleep on the sofa?

Too tired to argue – not that she would ever argue anything in her own defence – Hannah agreed that they might as well go to bed. 'But clothes stay on. Hands on top of the duvet!' she said, half-jokingly, but with a very serious undertone.

He said he wouldn't want it any other way. All he wanted was to lay beside her and pretend to look up at the stars, 'like when we were kids, like we talked about on the phone. I just need to hold your hand for a bit'.

This last utterance of Jon's melted her heart a little bit, showing her that he was still the same Jon she knew. *Her* Jon. So, they headed for bed.

Hannah woke up to the sound of a soft yet hoarse groan, and the feeling of something pushing against her from behind and a hand pulling at her knickers.

'Come on, babe, ohh, you're so wet for me', Jon's voice came from behind her, and then, with the sharp sting of an unwelcome thrust, she could feel him inside her. Shocked speechless, she just lay there, unable to move, as tears welled up in her eyes. She wanted to scream.

'Oh, yeah, baby, I knew you wanted me too, fuck me hard', Jon breathed into her ear, making it moist with spit.

'Ow, you're hurting me!' she was finally able to gasp. 'Please stop, you're too big!'

The half-truth seemed pleasing enough to Jon, who finally pulled out of her, but he didn't stop groaning. He simply took his hands off her and placed them both around the shaft of his penis, tugging at it as if he was trying to make it perform some sort of trick and finished himself off whilst looking at her, breathing heavily and groaning loudly in her ear.

Afraid to move, all Hannah could do was try to find out what on earth she must have done in her sleep, to make him think that this was something she wanted. The shame – and simultaneous relief – she felt when he came, with a deafening roar, was soul shattering. Yet, it wasn't the first time something like this had happened to her. She must have done something to him in her sleep. It was the only explanation.

As Hannah went to pull her trousers and knickers back up – she must have kicked them off in her sleep, surely, as she'd kept them on last night – Jon was saying that he had to get a move on. One of his kids had messaged him in the early hours, asking him to come pick him up. He was wiping his cum off of his belly with one of Hannah's pillowcases as he was chatting away.

Again, the shame Hannah felt was unbearable, but she was relieved that he was leaving so soon. On his way out the door, Jon turned towards her, kissing her hard on the mouth, before saying 'I love you. Call you later.'

Hannah felt sick to her stomach and went to scrub herself clean in the shower, yet no matter how hard or long she scrubbed, the feeling of being fully clean never came. Her skin red raw from scrubbing with her hemp loofah, she stepped out of the shower, anxious to cover up her own dirty body. If this was 'love', she wanted none of it.

As the minutes started ticking away, the beer that he'd left in the fridge started calling her name. Wanting – and needing – to retain her sober streak, Hannah decided to go for a run, despite knowing that she would have to take another shower and deal with touching her body again. It would be worth it if it meant she would be able to clear her head just a little bit. Right now, she couldn't focus on anything, other than trying to repress the memory of this morning's awakening by engaging in her destructive pattern of compulsive rituals, so Hannah strapped on her running shoes and headed out, but opting for the forest route, rather than her favourite seaside one, not wanting to ruin it for her future self.

It was slightly colder this morning, and Hannah could feel the smell of rain on the air. The cold air felt harsh, but soothing, on her naked face as she pushed her body along, just a little faster than she was comfortable with, to tire herself out enough for her to disconnect, *Carmina Burana: O Fortuna* blaring through her in-ears as she went. She hadn't run very far before she could feel a niggle starting to act up in her right hamstring. She really didn't have time for this right now!

Luckily, this pain was almost immediately cancelled out by the feeling of sweat seeping into the fresh abrasions now covering her torso. But Hannah didn't mind. In fact, she embraced the physical pain and favoured it to the psychological pain she'd have to deal with otherwise. This was the sort of cleansing she was after, so she stepped up her pace even more, taking advantage of the downhill slope that had appeared before her. Hannah pushed and pushed herself, her pace slowly increasing for every mile she ran, the intensity of her classical music playlist further spurring her on. It was starting to rain again, first a gentle drizzle, which quickly developed into a hard rain. Hannah could feel herself starting to let go, and she could feel the tears she'd been holding back finally streaming down her face, her chest contracting with deep sobs.

In the rain, no one can see my tears.

Hannah was on a forest trail now. She had no idea how far she'd run; all she knew was that the trail was gentler on her legs than the asphalt she was used to, and there was no one around in the bad weather. This encouraged her to pick up the pace even more, her sobs now fewer and farther between. Hannah felt as if she were completely alone in the world, but this was a welcome and maybe even sought after solitude in her case, meaning she could look like shit and no one would be there to judge her – a sense of freedom Hannah truly cherished.

Curious to see how far she'd run, Hannah checked her tracking app, to find that she'd already left behind her a good eight miles in just over 70 minutes. Looking at the numbers, she could feel the tiredness in her legs making itself known and realised she should turn around and head back before she collapsed on the trail. She wouldn't want any children or animals to have to come across her bruised, filthy, decomposing body once the skies cleared.

Now that Hannah had started noticing her aches and pains, it became impossible to ignore the familiar throbbing on the front of her lower legs – she really could do without the tendonitis, so she slowed her pace just a little and stayed on the trail just a little bit further, instead of heading back onto the paved road where she'd entered the forest.

Distracted by the dull pain, Hannah didn't see the branch in the middle of the trail, and as her left toe got caught on the piece of rotting birchwood, she once again floated out of her physical body, only to hover above herself as she saw herself being thrown through the air, arms flailing wildly. Only this time, she somehow managed to pull her leg loose before hitting the ground and throwing the right leg in front of her, returning again to a trot along the trail, although this time it became impossible to distract herself from the pain coming from her hamstring, as she'd overloaded it in her attempt to save herself from faceplanting.

'Motherfucking fuck!' Hannah heard herself scream over the Vivaldi track currently playing. Suddenly fearful that someone may have heard her – although there was still no trace of any other humans around – Hannah legged it, constantly on the lookout for a way to get back on the road and some more familiar surroundings. If she was lucky, maybe she'd be able to catch a bus going in the direction of her house.

As we already know, Hannah was not a very fortunate person, and so no buses passed her on the way back. The few cars that did go by didn't seem to see her dragging her leg behind her, and some even drove straight into the puddles that had gathered along the road, spraying her with filthy rainwater. Covered now, in mud, filth, grime and sweat, as she was incapable of getting out of the way of the spray quickly enough to avoid it, Hannah tried as best she could to numb herself from the pain in her leg and braced herself for the last few miles. She knew that if she were to stop now, even just to walk, she wouldn't be able to go on for much longer.

As she started on the last hill that led her onto her street, the pain seemed to have subsided somewhat, a welcome sensation of which Hannah took advantage, and she was able to schlep herself up, onwards and onto the garden path. It was only when she was trying to fit her key into the lock that she realised her hands were shaking so violently from exhaustion that she had to hold her arm still with her left hand in order to actually find the slot for the key to fit into. She finally managed to get the door open, and as she stepped across the threshold – wrong leg first – she discovered the leg had lost all its ability to keep her upright, and it buckled beneath her – heaving her into the kitchenette and onto the tiled floor, in a messy heap of once human flesh. Unable to deal with this, Hannah dragged herself across the floor, towards the bathroom and poured herself into the shower, where she sat – still in her running gear – on the floor as warm water poured over her. Hannah's shoulders started to shake, her chest again contracting, and loud, violent sobs escaped her lips as she wept. Warm, salty tears sprung from her now closed eyes, as it dawned on her that she would probably be unable to go for another run any time soon.

The fear of another extortionate electric bill was what got Hannah out of the shower in the end. She peeled off the layers of clothing and examined her still throbbing hamstring in her handheld mirror. The skin on the back of her leg had turned a bright purple, and for someone who doesn't normally bruise easily, it was a bit disturbing, to say the least. Hannah tried and failed to put weight on her leg, realising she was unable to walk as well. She decided she would have to see a physical therapist to get some advice on how to recover, but as that would require walking – and for it to be a weekday – Hannah wrapped herself in a towel for now, pulling an oversized hoodie over her head, sat down on the floor and proceeded to scoot her way into the living room and onto the couch, where she would sit until her empty stomach started growling. On the bright side, though, Hannah's initial want for alcohol had completely evaporated.

After she had fixed herself something to eat, Hannah tried as best she could to keep herself busy by looking for physios in her area. Most of the ones that would be covered by her health insurance had long waiting lists, but she emailed a few of them in desperation, hoping some of them would have a last-minute cancellation. Knowing she would have to try to get herself into the office for tomorrow's meeting bonanza, Hannah decided to order some pain pills for same-day delivery. Although absolutely extortionate, and funded by her rapidly diminishing savings, it would be worth it. She also looked online to see if she could find any workout routines that would help her in her recovery. She had put her phone in don't disturb mode – there was no one in the world she wanted to face talking to right now anyway – so there were no distractions for the rest of the day. When evening came, Hannah – now filled to the brim with ibuprofen – was so knackered that she fell asleep on the sofa, laptop open in front of her. She stirred awake sometime around 11 and contemplated going upstairs to bed, but her leg quickly reminded her that climbing any stairs was not an option – regardless, she couldn't stomach the prospect of a night in those sheets either, so she would be better off staying where she was. She turned her laptop off and set her alarm before falling back into a dreamless, exhaustion-fuelled slumber.

Hannah woke up before her alarm went off on Monday morning. Filled with the existential dread of having overslept – and completely forgetting about her leg – she jumped up and onto the floor, only for her bad leg to give way beneath her. Hannah yelped in pain and sat back down, reaching for her pills and at the same time checking the time. Exhaling with relief, she discovered that she had another hour before she *had* to be up, and so she popped the pills and allowed herself a 20-minute snooze while the painkillers got to work. She wouldn't exactly call this getting up on the right foot, but it was so much better than many other scenarios. Half an hour later, she'd managed to drag herself upstairs to get dressed and ready for work. She shuddered at the sight of the scene of yesterday morning's crime and made a mental note to burn the sheets later. Now all she needed to do was get to work and through the day.

After Hannah had managed to limp her way to the train, and from the train to the office, she was already exhausted, but she took comfort in the fact that it only seemed to really, really hurt when she was moving and not when she was resting, so she found a desk near the meeting rooms to eliminate any excess movement. During the first meeting of the day, it was announced that the 10 o'clock meeting had been cancelled because so many had already taken their annual leave, so Hannah was left with a bit of breathing space that, quite frankly, for a Monday, was like being gifted a bit of extra life. Needless to say, this was a huge relief.

Although, just after 10, her phone started ringing. It was Jon. She was dreading talking to him again after yesterday, but since he was calling when he knew that she was supposed to be in a meeting, it had to be some sort of emergency, so she picked up:

'Hello?' she said, her voice a little unsteady.

'Hannah! Do you know what? I'm just so HAPPY!' Jon shrieked on the other end of the call.

'Excuse me?'

'Oh. Maybe you didn't hear me properly, I'm in the car. Hang on.'

She could hear him fiddling about with the radio in the background.

'OK. Can you hear me better now?' he asked.

'Yeah, I can hear you. What's going on? Is everything alright? I'm at work', she said, slightly irritated now.

'Oh, I'm just so happy! I couldn't wait to tell you. I'm so happy we're in love! I think I'm going to tell the kids about the ex and I splitting. I'm so happy I could cry!'

And then, he actually started *sobbing*.

'Erm, Jon. I'm at work and this doesn't sound very urgent. I'm supposed to be in a meeting right now and I need to go. Are you sure everything's alright?' Hannah asked. Even after what happened yesterday, she still had compassion for the guy – he sounded unstable, judging by his bizarre course of action.

'I'm great! Never better, actually, and it's all because of you!' he exclaimed. 'It's always work, work, work with you, isn't it', he added, the last part almost as an accusation. 'I'll let you go and carry on with your *important* business, then,' he said, half-mockingly, half-laughing.

'Right. Bye', said Hannah and hung up before he could say anything else to piss her off. What had she gotten herself into with this guy? Why had she even answered the call to begin with? She shoved her phone in her bag – she didn't need it for the rest of the day anyway, and she really wasn't up for any more surprise calls. She felt utterly disgusting now. And tired. So goddamned tired that she was unable to do a single thing, so she just stared blankly at her laptop screen until it was time for the next meeting, realising slowly that her friend, the perpetual fever, had returned.

The only thing that kept Hannah awake for the duration of the rest of the day's meetings, were the constant flashbacks from yesterday. Every time she started to relax and focus on the tasks at hand – BOOM – she was back in the bed, feeling Jon's breath on her ear whilst he was forcing his way inside her. If any of the other meeting attendees were unfortunate enough to possess mindreading capabilities, Hannah felt truly sorry for them. For herself, she just felt apathy. It felt very clear to her that the universe wanted her gone. Just when things were starting to look up, life was there to knock her back on her ass. Did she really deserve this? She also felt guilty for not being able to contribute properly in any of the meetings, although the marketing team had announced that they would soon be on the lookout for a new web editor – Hannah's dream job. She made a mental note to at least check out the listing, but she wasn't sure why she would.

As Hannah was wrapping up for the day, she received a message from her boss. She wanted to know when Hannah would be in this week so that they could plan around her sick leave. Hannah, who didn't really feel like coming back at all this week, took out her phone to check her calendar for treatment appointments, only to discover that one of the physio clinics had emailed her back saying they were able to squeeze her in tomorrow morning. Finally, some good news! She messaged her boss back to say she could do Wednesday and Friday and started mentally prepping herself for the limp-along towards the commuter train. Now knowing that she wouldn't be going into work tomorrow at all, she also booked an appointment with her GP to see if she'd give her something for the pain, but she took her laptop with her, just in case she'd be in equal amounts of pain two days from now.

 After the strenuous trek home for work, Hannah didn't much feel like climbing the stairs to change her sheets, but upstairs was also where most of her clothes lived, so if she wanted to see them again, she would have to deal with the other mess as well. She grabbed a bin bag, dropped her phone in it, put the bag between her teeth and sat down on the third step and proceeded to tricep-dip her way to the top, dragging her aching, useless limb in front of her. 'At least my arms will be in great shape by the time I'm back on both feet again,' Hannah chuckled darkly to herself.

 When she got upstairs, the whole room reeked of bodily fluids, the hot air trapped under the low ceiling not helping matters much. Hannah opened the windows on both sides of the loft to let some fresh air in before stripping her bed of sheets laden with sadness, regret and a single, dried out bloodstain. Again, the flashbacks took over and she fell to the floor, clutching her arms around her legs and rocking back and forth, like that would make the memories go away somehow.

Then she realised, she wasn't alone. Not really. She pulled her phone out of her front pocket and phoned MJ.

She didn't tell MJ what had happened. Not at first. It was all a blur, anyway, and it *could* have been a misunderstanding. All she needed right now was to hear MJ's voice and have a laugh. So, when MJ picked up after the first ring, they just had a normal chat. Hannah told her friend about her stupid injury, and MJ told Hannah about one of her Tinder meetups going awry and they both laughed at each other's terrible sense of judgement. It was really lovely to just have a normal chat with someone. It also gave Hannah the space to gain some perspective, and so she decided to tell MJ about what had happened. Well, not about him entering her, but she did tell her about the part where he started wanking next to her. She obviously told her everything leading up to it as well, but MJ was adamant that he'd had no right to do what he had done – especially after Hannah had told him that nothing was going to happen:

'It doesn't matter what you do or say in your sleep, Hannah. No means no. Setting boundaries should be enough. Honestly!'

Just hearing her friend say the words out loud was an enormous weight lifted off Hannah's shoulders. She decided enough was enough, and that he really wasn't the Jon she used to know anymore. *Her* Jon.

'I should really have a talk with him, shouldn't I? she half-asked. 'I mean, I don't want anything to do with him anymore, but he knows where I live now, so I want to end it properly. He can come and get his IPAs, but that's it.'

'Do what you need to do', said MJ. 'But you call me straight after', she added, reassuringly.

And that's how Hannah, who feared conflict more than most, broke her first barrier towards becoming a more self-assured version of herself. She realised she needed MJ as a crutch, but she was glad to have the support, and so should we be.

She called Jon, but he didn't pick up. When she thought about it, they had only ever talked when it suited him, so she shouldn't be surprised. Either way, she was eager to get this over and done with, so she sent him a rather lengthy text about how this wasn't working out for her, 'in case he wondered why she had called'. He messaged back straight away, that it was 'fair enough'. Which, quite frankly, Hannah found odd, as he'd declared his love for her less than 36 hours ago, but she let it slide. Then he asked her if he could call her if he needed to talk, and that's when she had enough. She told him 'No, and it would be nice if you could come and get your beer as well, as you know I don't like having alcohol in the house.' To that, he simply replied that she could keep it, and that's when she realised that he hadn't listened to a single word she'd said. Not now and not since they started talking again. So, she blocked his number and deleted him as a friend on social media.

She was a little sad that it had gotten as far as it had, yet she knew that she probably wouldn't have been able to pull out if it hadn't. It was the story of her life, really. But she decided now to sever that particular storyline and begin a new, healthier, one.

Hannah started her Tuesday with a series of appointments, beginning with her meeting with her new physical therapist, who concluded that she had indeed overloaded her hamstring and that she would need to start on a recovery programme involving supervised strength training twice a week. Everything was covered by insurance, so this basically meant that Hannah got two free PT sessions every week for six weeks. She was so happy she could cry, as she hadn't been able to afford going to a proper gym with decent equipment for so long. So, maybe this injury had been more than just a painful wakeup call. Her therapist was fresh out of college but incredibly knowledgeable despite their young age, and Hannah felt as if she'd won the lottery when she walked out of there. She even got a recommendation for her to give to her GP, so that she'd be put on the appropriate meds to take during the course of the recovery training.

At her GP's, she was prescribed heavy duty painkillers, and they discussed the return of Hannah's physical symptoms, i.e. the perpetual fever situation. The doctor diagnosed her with burnout in addition to her complex PTSD diagnosis and advised that she continue working three days a week until her annual leave started, 'and maybe you should start thinking about going away somewhere, if you can justify making such an investment? I think a change of scenery would do you a lot of good'. Her GP really wanted to see her getting well, she'd made that very clear on multiple occasions, so Hannah took her advice seriously. Hannah also thought that going away on holiday might give her the strength she needed to recover properly as well, and then returning to work full-time afterwards and start fighting for her job back, or maybe she'd even have the energy to apply for that job that had become available as well...Hannah's head was spinning.

Both of the two first appointments of the day had gone really, really well for her, so on the way to her next one – an emergency check-up with her psychologist, Hannah emailed the head of marketing, saying that she would like to throw her hat in the ring for the open position and attached her resume, proving she had the qualifications and work experience needed to do the work. Once that was done, she booked herself a holiday on one of the last-minute booking apps, for which she paid with her special "for travel" savings account, one she'd sworn she wouldn't touch before it had enough money in it for her to go away for at least a week. And now, it seemed, it did.

Hannah felt accomplished and relieved entering her therapist's office, only to find that her therapist wasn't very happy that she'd applied for yet another job. 'I don't want you to go back to work for at least a year', she said. 'Maybe even two. We've got a lot of work yet to do here'. Hannah agreed, of course, but her fear of having her funds run out and not getting paid sick leave scared the shit out of her. But she said she would 'probably withdraw her application, if they'll even consider it'. She mostly said that to reassure Andrea, though. She *would* need another job, and soon.

After their session, Hannah found that the head of marketing had replied. They would *love* for her to interview for the position! Pleased with having impressed the head, Hannah went home to get some rest. She popped two painkillers, plopped onto her couch and slept clean through to midday the next day.

The next few weeks, all Hannah did was prep for her interview. There was nothing else to do around the office, so she was free to work on the case presented to her – and due to her injury, she had an excuse to work from home as well, meaning no one could really see what she was doing.

She wasn't allowed to run, or even walk, for the time being, so between her physio appointments and working on the case, there was nothing really happening in Hannah's life worth mentioning. She wasn't drinking – she didn't dare drink whilst on the meds anyway – but she didn't feel the urge either, and it did her a world of good in the calories spared alone.

Little by little, she was getting better, and by the end of the second week, she was able to walk slowly and cycle without pain. Just in time for her sunny beach holiday that was now just two short weeks away. She'd have her interview with the marketing team two days before she left, and she was starting to feel well prepared for both.

Hannah's psych treatment had also been upped over the last fortnight, with two double sessions a week, which was a real lifesaver for Hannah, who would normally self-medicate and keep her emotions in check by running. At least now she was able to hit the trails with her bike, but it wasn't the same – it didn't give her the same level of total exhaustion and surrender as running did. Either way, things were going well, so when Hannah accidentally ran into an old flame on her way home from work one day, she actually stopped to say hello. (It's not like she could outrun him if he came after her anyway.)

She hadn't seen him in a decade, and even though he bore the unfortunate moniker of Jon, she eagerly accepted when he invited her to come along to a gig that same week. And knowing she wouldn't be pre-drinking by herself beforehand, like she would normally do – the beer still in her fridge all but forgotten – she knew that she would be able to remember her evening for once. Maybe she would even have a drink? She would be off the meds by then anyway. She gave him her new number and told him she was looking forward to it – which she was. She hadn't told him she wasn't drinking at the moment – they weren't *that* close anyway – but she was sure it wouldn't be an issue.

When the day of the gig finally arrived, she'd been off the pain meds for a couple of days already and she was feeling great. They were on the guest list for the gig, meaning she didn't have to worry about money for the ticket either, just like the olden days. Although, she would definitely get a t-shirt or something from the merchandise stand as a small 'thank you'. She was meeting Jon – and we shall call him Irish from here on out, as he hails from the Dublin suburb Shankill – at a bar around the corner from the gig. He was stood outside waiting for her as she arrived, looking handsome as ever, in his black jeans, band tee and sunglasses. Apart from the beard, he looked the complete opposite of the other Jon, who was wispy, ginger and very short. Irish was, like herself, an obvious gymgoer, strong and broad-shouldered, with dark brown, curly hair and brown eyes. And then there was the accent, of course. *Nothing wrong with a bit o' Irish*, Hannah thought with a smile. They gave each other a hug hello, both of them lingering slightly before they headed into the forgiving darkness of the airconditioned pub.

Irish and Hannah had a lovely time catching up, so much so, in fact, that they were both chatting so much, the only time they were able to shut up was when the band was playing. Hannah didn't end up drinking, as she was working the next day, so she'd been able to both behave herself *and* remember the entire evening. As luck would have it, Irish wasn't local anymore either – he'd moved back to Ireland – so he was staying in a hostel in the centre of town. As they hugged each other goodbye, he asked if he could see her again the next day. He was only in town for a few days and wanted to make the most of it, and since tomorrow was Friday, maybe they could have a drink? If it hadn't been for fear of messing up her recovery, Hannah would have skipped home in the warm summer evening.

Irish and Hannah ended up having quite a few drinks the next day. Due to the current ongoing heatwave, they'd started off with a boozy slushie – a specialty drink at the venue they'd been at – and of course hilarity ensued. Or so he told her the next day. Either way, by the end of the night, they'd decided that it was a waste for Irish to spend his money on accommodation, when he could just as easily stay with her, so they jumped in a taxi and ended up in bed together. They ended up having sex the next morning, and then he stayed with her until she had to leave for work on Monday – he had a suitcase chock a block of duty-free booze that needed drinking, so sobriety was out the window. But they had fun until she had to kick him out and go back to her real life. It had been like they had been in their own little bubble, and it was exactly what she needed. Even her therapist agreed it was a good thing when Hannah told her about what had happened the following Tuesday. She didn't recount the exact amounts of alcoholic units consumed, obviously, but she decided it was unimportant on this occasion. Although, it appeared she was back to drinking again.

This was also the last week before her holiday, but the interview that she'd had scheduled for Friday had been pushed until when they'd all be back in the office again. Hannah didn't really mind. She would be going on holiday for the first time in years, and so she decided to focus on that instead. She happily clocked out Friday afternoon, leaving her laptop and work behind for the next three weeks.

She stayed in touch with Irish via text, and they talked about meeting up again next time he'd be in town. It was almost like having an imaginary boyfriend – one that didn't really exist but kept her out of trouble regardless.

Hannah headed for the airport at stupid o'clock on Saturday morning, only to discover her flight was delayed by three hours, so she sat in the airport lounge, reading one of the many books she'd brought, while at the same time trying to convince herself that this wasn't one of the universe's cruel jokes directed at her. (Of course it was directed at her and only her, and not at the other two hundred passengers that were in the same boat, so to speak.) So, when the boarding call finally came, Hannah pushed her way to the front of the queue and half-ran to get to her seat. Once they were up in the air, she ordered herself two mini bottles of wine. Because why not, right? It was a four-hour flight and she.was.on.holibobs.

Chapter 8: July – The Great Escape and demi-fresh starts

Even though Hannah's flight had been delayed, there was still quite a bit of daylight remaining by the time they landed in sunny Spain. The warmth enveloping her entire body as she stepped off the plane made her almost giddy with excitement. The wine had all but knocked her out, so Hannah had slept the whole way there and was feeling rather refreshed from the flight. As she walked onto the coach taking her to the adults only hotel she'd booked, she felt as if she really *was* on holiday.

The hotel coach had a guide, who offered fun and curious facts throughout the journey, so Hannah was for once enjoying switching off her wireless headphones, as she gazed out the bus window at the various historic sites they passed along the way. Having booked the trip last minute to accommodate her steadily diminishing bank balance, she knew very little about the resort town she was going to and was eager to learn. She'd tried to learn some Spanish using one of the language learning apps, but the free version she'd opted for wasn't too reliable, so Hannah did what she could to soak up some of the culture. Although quite bare and desert-like, the landscape was stunning, with expansive sand dunes stretching out towards the sea on the left side of the bus, and rolling hills, studded with palm trees and tiny, colourful brick houses, on the right – it was really quite picturesque, and she felt a surge of happiness taking it all in. Her first holiday in years, where she knew she'd have a job to go back to after her time off. For now, at least. It was actually wonderful, and she did not take for granted that she had been able to go.

She didn't really know what to expect when it came to the hotel she'd booked, so when she'd pulled her suitcase from the hold of the coach, she walked up the sleek marble stairs towards the entrance with some trepidation. All she knew was that they had an age limit and a gym, so she was surprised to be welcomed with a complimentary glass of traditional sparkling white wine at check-in. The second surprise came when she motioned to leave her now empty glass on the bar to go find her room, when she discovered that the barman was topping her up:

'It's free! You are on holiday. You have to enjoy yourself!' he said in a strong Spanish accent and smiling warmly.

Who was she to go against his wishes? So, Hannah stayed for another two complimentary glasses before heading into the lift that would take her up to her room on the third floor.

Hannah struggled to get her key card to work on the digitised lock, but as the door finally clicked open, she was astonished by what she could see on the other side of it; this was a *suite* – the size of the downstairs of her house – not a *room*. She stepped into the little hallway, from which she could see all the way through the open plan space to her own, private balcony looking over the town to the right and the sea to the left. Once she stepped onto it, she could see that she had a good overview of the hotel pools and garden as well. Should she wish to use the communal areas, she would be able to check if they were too crowded before heading there. This was excellent news for a closeted introvert as herself. Not having to deal with people was the dream.

Her suite was equipped with a small kitchenette with a full-sized fridge, a hob and a microwave, so that she would be able to cook her own meals and save on trips to restaurants – or just avoid the sheer agony of having to dine alone, completely surrounded by couples and families, altogether. Everything, including the kitchen utensils, looked brand new. As she was checking out the lounge area, she discovered a complimentary bottle of the same sparkling wine she'd had downstairs, along with a handwritten card wishing her a magical holiday, on the coffee table. The joy she felt at that moment was almost overwhelming and she was beaming from ear to ear. And then she noticed her bed. A massive king-sized bed, just for her, bedded with crisp, clean linen, and towels, oddly enough shaped like a birdlike creature from the cretaceous era, but this might be the sparkling wine playing a trick on Hannah's *Jurassic Park* obsessed mind. She *had* watched it at the very impressionable age of 10.

Hannah had kept the bathroom for last, for some reason, so as she pulled the sliding door open, her eyes widened with wonder – this room was bigger than her kitchenette at home! It had a large rainfall shower, double vanities and a golden throne for her wees and poopsies. She giggled to herself, again fuelled by the sparkling delight she'd felt earlier. Fittingly, it was a very childlike, careless sort of joy that Hannah felt in that moment, and as she washed the grime of the journey off of her face, she looked into her own eyes and smiled at her own reflection, completely succumbing to the present moment. She unpacked, put her duty-free shopping of peanut and chocolate sweeties and sparkling rosé in the fridge, quickly changed into her shorts and bikini top and brought one of her books and her complimentary wine to the balcony to enjoy the last rays of the sun before it set. *Life is good*, she thought, as she could hear waves crashing on the beaches in the distance and seagulls squawking above, reminding her of what summer used to feel like, in a much more carefree time of her life.

Halfway into her first bottle of wine, Hannah picked up her phone to put on some tunes. In an uncharacteristically good mood, she proceeded to snap a series of selfies, as she was curious to see what this happiness business would look like from an outside point of view. Pleased with what she could see through her rosé-tinted glasses, she posted some of them on Instagram, and then she messaged one to Irish, not even over-thinking it a little bit. She couldn't help but think that, if this was what it was like to be on holiday, she should have gone much sooner.

Now, a girl can't live off of sweeties and wine alone, and Hannah was starting to feel a bit peckish, just around the time the sun had set for the day. She decided to indulge in some room service. She soon discovered that this service was limited to pick-up only, so she sheepishly took her now rather tipsy self downstairs – after having changed into a dress for the clearly important occasion – to the food pick-up area adjacent to the hotel bar. This was how she discovered they had live music at the hotel, so after she'd devoured her burger like an exceptionally ravenous rhino, she took her dolled-up self back down to join in on the festivities. By that point, she must have had about three bottles of wine to herself, and having spent the past few hours in the blasting sunshine, they had all collectively gone straight to her head. When Hannah woke up in her suite the next morning, she had absolutely no idea how she had gotten there, but she could vividly remember herself heckling the performers, singing along and trying to dance with a few unwilling strangers in the crowd. And... had she got up on stage and flashed the crowd as well? Granted, there wasn't much to flash – *Maxim* wasn't going to come knocking on her door anytime soon – but, regardless, some people might take offence to a forty-year-old woman showing that much skin completely unsolicited. Needless to say, the anxiety was real. How had she even found her way back to her room in that state?

Hannah had a quick rinse in the shower, trying to wash off some of the shame, before venturing out to get stuff for breakfast from the nearby corner shop, being extra careful to not draw any attention to herself as she snuck out of the lift in the reception area, like a special agent from the seventies. Gah...she figured she'd might as well start day drinking after the mid-morning fitness class she'd booked herself onto at some point during the night, just to deal with any oncoming anxiety before it was able to fully manifest.

Hannah was delighted to discover that the fitness class wound up really clearing her head, and even more pleasantly surprised that it didn't cause her hamstring injury to flare up. *I'm cured!* Hannah thought triumphantly, to herself. And instead of opting for more wine in the shade on her balcony, she took a quick shower and put on her bikini and shorts, before filling the small rucksack she'd brought with a towel, something to read, plenty of water and some snacks before strapping on her trainers and heading for the nearest beach in a light jog in the blasting heat. Nothing quite cures a hangover like a dip in the sea.

Hannah spent the two-mile trek familiarising herself with the neighbourhood surrounding her hotel. It didn't seem super touristy, she was happy to discover, and was full of cute little restaurants, shops and brown and peach coloured brick houses. It was only when she got closer to the beach promenade that the high-rise hotels and obvious tourist shops and signs with translations in English and Scandinavian languages started popping up. But apparently July was off-season for the tourist crowd, so the beaches were filled with local holidaymakers and shift workers, working on their respective tans and surfing skills.

Hannah discovered the beach promenade was actually a level above sea level, so after descending a very winding set of steep stairs, walled on each side, the salty sea air and smell of coconut scented sunscreen exploded in her nostrils as she reached the sand. As far as her eyes could see were brightly coloured parasols and sun loungers, crisp blue skies and golden sands. Again, Hannah felt a blast of happiness and was completely unable to stop herself from smiling. She walked along the beach for a bit, looking for the perfect spot where she wouldn't be in anyone's way, greeting passersby with a nod and sometimes even an '¡Hola!'. She decided to work on her Spanish some more when she got back to her room, in case she wound up having to talk to someone. She eventually found a secluded spot right next to a breakwater, on which several elderly men sat fishing, smoking rollies and drinking from tiny bottles of what she assumed to be an alcoholic beverage of some sort. This, too, brought a smile to her face. Everything seemed to be so calm here. She'd read a book once, about the general differences in societies based on location and climate, and it appeared people living in warmer regions had a more relaxed approach to life than those hailing from the northernmost part of the northern hemisphere. Hannah was of the opinion that any falsifiable theory was a good one, and she found this particular theory to correspond with her own experiences from travelling. Not that it mattered right now. She was just grateful to be travelling and experiencing something new at all. She laid her towel out on the beach, kicked off her trainers, dropped her shorts and rucksack and sprinted out into the waves, diving into the surf just before the water reached the top of her thighs.

Blissful as her first dip in the sea in years had been, she didn't stay in for long. Terrified of what may lurk in the depths, she always failed to swim out particularly far, so she was back on her towel within ten minutes, feeling refreshed. She patted dry her extremities and began the impossible task of putting on sunscreen without ending up with massive handprints on the harder to reach areas. She managed to do a semi decent job of it but stopped once she started getting sand everywhere and laid down on her front, fishing her book out of the rucksack. *This really is the life*, she thought, for probably the second time in her entire existence. And with that thought, she got her phone out from her rucksack as well, to book herself onto a few more of those fitness classes and snapping a photo of the beach and water in front of her, which she posted to her Instagram stories before turning it off and putting it away again for a short digital detox. Gone – for now – was the shame for having made a complete fool of herself in the hotel bar on her first night of her first proper holiday, ever.

Mid-first chapter of her book, Hannah wished she'd set a timer for how long she'd been on her front, as she wanted to make sure the sun got to every inch of her body for an even tan, but she decided to keep the time by the number of pages read. She was a pretty consistent reader, after all, so she turned onto her back once she'd finished the chapter, only to fall asleep with her book on her face. She couldn't have been asleep for very long, as the sun hadn't moved that far from where it had been when she nodded off – or had it? Either way, she was now super warm and sticky and decided another dip was in order. This time, she took her time wading through the shallows. The water felt a little cooler on her skin now than the first time, but that wasn't very strange, nor was it entirely unwelcome, as she'd now been baking and sweating in the midday sun for God knows how long.

She walked until the water reached her hips this time, before she slowly submerged her entire body in the water, holding her breath and keeping her eyes shut before kicking her legs forcefully on the seabed and shooting out of the surf like a flesh torpedo. One of the best things about being in the water was definitely that feeling of weightlessness, she thought. That was, however, when Hannah realised she really needed a wee, and in a very childish manner, she swam away from the shore – and other people – to release the contents of her bladder into the salty water. The tide seemed to be on its way out, so she was sure it'd be fine. Saltwater was essentially a disinfectant, right? Either way, she didn't stay in long after her public urination. She had to get back to her book and a new round of SPF50. Burning on the first day would be a bit daft for a grown woman.

As far as the saying of famous last words go, the following event was probably pretty much what had happened when the phrase was invented in the first place. Sure enough, after just a few hours in the sun, Hannah discovered she'd turned an unflattering shade of bright red – and even purple in some places – when she got back to her room to have dinner, so she soaked herself from head to toe in aloe gel and after sun to soothe her now very tight skin. She stood in front of the mirror for a good while just poking herself to determine how bad the burn was. After every poke left a white mark that didn't turn red again for a good 15 seconds, she determined her case was pretty bad, so she went again to the nearby corner shop – which seemed to have absolutely everything, from chewing gum, foodstuffs and wine to beach clothing, over the counter pharmacy meds and condoms – and stocked up on antihistamines, SPF60, more aloe gel and some tequila, snacks and margarita mix. As she should probably stay out of the sun tomorrow, there was nothing standing in the way of her having a little cocktail party to herself this evening.

Despite her little booze fest, Hannah didn't get drunk that evening. Instead, she practiced her Spanish, made herself a nice Greek salad and read a few chapters of her book, whilst listening to music and taking her time with her drinks, mixing them with fizzy water to make them last longer. She figured, as she was only staying a week and her leg was in better shape, that she should make the most of it.

So, over the next few days, and once her burns were a little less severe, Hannah got into a bit of a routine. She woke up around seven, had a coffee and some breakfast, went to the 10am HIIT session in the gym, headed back to her room for a light lunch and then a quick jog to the beach, where she'd spend her afternoons reading and swimming, all the while enjoying the fact that there was nothing that she *had* to do; no deadlines, no places to be, no friends to carry.

Around 3pm, she'd head back to the hotel and sit in the sun on her balcony, letting herself get lost in her reading some more and sipping her sparkling rosé. She made herself a nice, healthy salad every evening and, despite her alcohol intake, didn't feel as stuffed or bloated as she normally would after dinner. She was aware that she was drinking a lot, but she felt like getting it out of her system, and she never got smashed and she never blacked out once – which, strangely enough, was completely new for Hannah.

It seemed the open sea swimming did a good job of fuelling the continued recovery of her hamstring as well, so a few days into her holiday, she was confident enough to go for a very slow 5k jog. Even her Spanish had improved, despite the app's attempt at only teaching her phrases such as 'the women are eating a strawberry'. (Several women, and just the one strawberry? This seemed a very unlikely scenario to Hannah's brain.) She found herself being able to hold very short conversations with the staff at the corner shop after just a few days – mainly about the weather and how many bags she needed, but she felt like she was doing something to embrace the culture and integrate, other than just contributing to the economy. It made her feel better about holidaying in one of those resort towns most people seemed to go to because they knew they wouldn't have to learn the language and could find items you'd find in your local Sainsbury's in every shop.

Hannah had also noticed one other person that would go to the same fitness classes as her, an Irish guy that was probably a good ten years or so younger than her, and they'd started greeting one another and helping each other out in the gym. She'd found a sense of community here that she hadn't realised she'd been missing at home. This other person and the instructor had both kept complimenting her on her technique and strength, and although she'd been embarrassed and brushed off their words of encouragement at first, she had now given herself permission to revel in it instead. Of course, she'd reply by the same token – they were both in great shape – but nothing seemed forced and there was nothing about the situation that made her feel uncomfortable or made her think she made *them* feel uncomfortable. It was simply a bunch of nice people being nice where niceness was very much deserved.

The Irish boy had introduced himself as Patrick. He lived in Dublin and was here by himself, just like her. He was a genuinely nice guy and they quickly struck up a friendship, their conversations light and short and mainly about exercise. It was nice to have a gym buddy, Hannah thought, but it didn't seem like either of them had any need to see each other outside of the gym. He was very much the sculpted, attractive type anyway –

and far too young for her – so not really her type. And her loyalties lay with another Irishman at the moment anyway, so there was no chance of her doing anything to sabotage herself. Another new thing for her.

Every evening, as she sat watching the setting sun from her balcony, she was very mindful of the fact that this was the best she'd felt in longer than she could remember, maybe even ever, so she savoured every moment. Every time a gentle breeze carried the refreshing whiff of salty ocean air up to her balcony, every time she got a smile from the cashier at the shop for bothering to learn how to speak their language – hopefully without butchering it too much – and every time she was able to enjoy a meal without thinking about how it made her feel disgusting afterward, because she was taking her time with it. And every time the sun caressed her now evenly tanned skin. She loved the way her skin smelled when it had been in the sun all day – maybe she was a closeted cannibal and quite fancied some human style barbecue – and she loved waking up every morning knowing there was not even the slightest chance of rain, or even clouds, on the horizon. Nothing could stop her from carrying out her newly adopted routine and she absolutely adored it. For someone who up until that point had reduced love and adoration to an empty concept, this was quite the radical thought, and Hannah laughed with compassion at her old, grumpy self for being unable to let the light in. She loved this happier version of herself.

Although it was a bit like observing herself from outside of her body, she liked what she saw in the mirror. Her tan made her look so much healthier, a little slimmer and tighter, and it complimented her dark eyes, which would change colour depending on how the light hit them. They sparkled with happiness, her pupils wide from taking in the beauty surrounding her. Her teeth looked a little whiter with the contrasting darker skin – even her hair looked shinier somehow. Was this who she was now? One of those shiny, happy people? If that were the case, she sure didn't mind.

Another thing that helped Hannah's mood was putting her phone in flight mode whenever she didn't need to use it for tracking her runs (in case she'd get lost along the way). That way, she could focus solely on what made her happy, which was mainly working out, reading and immersing herself in music. *This truly was the life.*

As the days went on, Hannah started feeling a bit anxious that her wonderful holiday was coming to an end, so she tried calming her mind with the only form of meditation she knew – running. So she took her trainers and went exploring and ended up discovering that the beach promenade stretched on for miles and miles, taking her past a couple of other resort towns, a protected nature reserve with some spectacular sand dunes (and a nudist area, that popped up with no warning), as well as a few pristine, untouched by tourists, volcanic rock pebbly beaches, and several golf courses. Since there was so much to see, apart from the parts where she'd rather close her eyes and leg it, keeping an eye on the mesmerising and ever-changing scenery – and the blasting heat – kept her pace down, keeping her from overloading her hamstring. Running in the 38 degree heat was in and of itself no small feat either, thought Hannah, and so she allowed herself the sense of accomplishment that came with it.

She was glad she'd brought the running belt with the small water bottles on it, as she reached for one of them to pour the contents over her boiling head. The water was already more than lukewarm, of course, but she needed to cool her reddening scalp before she had a heatstroke.

She'd stopped at a little clifftop plateau off the promenade, with a rope and wood railing and a view of the entire coastline towards where her hotel was. She leaned herself on the railing as she took in the vista. *God, it's so beautiful here*, she thought, not even minding that she was pouring with sweat as people were strolling past her. She looked down towards the bottom of the cliff, where waves were crashing against enormous wet rocks that had been there for longer than the promenade itself, or even this town. It made Hannah reflect on just how short and fleeting a human life could be, and in that moment she decided she would take whatever measures she needed to not only get herself back on track, but to create for herself a sustainable future, inviting enough for her to stick to a new and improved routine. She had two days left in this island paradise, so she'd make the most of the freedom before going back home, but made a note to start looking for flats the second she stepped off the plane – she had to get out of that house *now*. She'd made what once was an oasis into her own prison and there was just too much toxicity in the walls for her to stay. Also, her landlord had a bust of their own ass hanging on their living room wall, which was in Hannah's direct eyeline every time she opened her front door, and if it were up to her, she'd rather not see that thing again.

Hannah had swung by the beach for a quick dip before heading back to her room, so by the time she got back to the hotel, it was almost time for her early dinner. She decided to celebrate her new course of action and give a toast to herself for creating a future filled with good experiences and sustainable decisions by cracking open a bottle of bubbly. Again, she took her time with the wine, not wanting to cheat herself out of a single second of her time here.

The next day began in much the same way as the previous one, although after their mid-morning workout, Patrick approached her and mentioned he'd seen her running the day before and that he'd been curious to do the same but hadn't yet dared to venture out of the airconditioned comfort of the hotel gym to do so. Hannah surprised herself by inviting him along to her last morning run the next day, and he accepted with a smile.

She left the gym in an even better mood than she had been in when she arrived and went off in search of some lunchtime paella to make the most of her last full day.

As it turns out, paella isn't something you can just order at a restaurant, as it takes hours to prepare. Slightly disappointed to learn this, Hannah decided to take this extremely lightly as it in fact meant that she wouldn't have to suffer through any restaurant crowds, so she took a final trip to the corner shop to get stuff for dinner, along with an absolutely massive banana flavoured ice lolly to inspire one last long run after dinner later on. Her schedule slightly delayed by this miniscule bump in the road, Hannah decided to go to the beach one last time as well, bringing along her usual beach kit, as well as a canned mojito. She could feel herself growing increasingly anxious about making arrangements for tomorrow's departure, so she needed to take her mind off it for a little while. There wasn't much she could do anyway; other than finish packing. Everything else was sorted, as the coach would pick her up and take her and her luggage to the airport the next day.

She decided the best thing for her to do was enjoy the last bit of sunshine, maybe have another wee in the sea and spend so much time treading on the scorching sand that she would make herself slightly sick of it so that she wouldn't be so sad leaving it.

Having finished all three of the books she'd brought, Hannah stayed on the beach for as long as she could stomach just lying on the beach for the sole purpose of, seemingly, getting bed ulcers. How did people do that without going absolutely bonkers? Or maybe this was another symptom of her disorder, and that all normal people were capable of such a task. Hannah hadn't the slightest clue, so she got up, shook the sand out of her towel and left the beach behind for the last time. Feeling all of a sudden nostalgic, she turned around before climbing the stairs and gave the beach a mental wave goodbye as if to say; *So long, new friend. You have served me well.*

With no real need to practice her newfound language skills, Hannah made herself her final dinner and had it on the balcony, before heading out for her last longer run, where she bid the beach promenade the same adieu as she did the beach.

Hannah didn't have much to do when she got back to her room. She'd already packed everything she wouldn't be needing for tomorrow, so she was all set there. She'd made plans to meet Patrick at 9am the next morning – the coach pick-up was at 1pm – so Hannah watched a movie after the sun set, accompanied by her last bottle of wine and leftover margarita, and took herself promptly to bed after the film had finished.

Not entirely convinced that Patrick would show up, Hannah made her way down to the lobby the next morning. But it turned out she hadn't needed to worry, as he was already there waiting for her.

Hannah had picked a route she knew to be almost exactly five kilometres long, so they jogged along at a comfortable pace, spending their time getting to know each other better, chatting about their respective lives outside of the island. Despite the fact that there was a ten-year age difference, they found they had quite a bit in common, so when they got back to the hotel and the time came for them to say their goodbyes, Hannah almost wanted to hug him. Instead, she waved awkwardly and said she hoped they'd see each other again, to which he agreed enthusiastically.

Back in her room, Hannah had just enough time to grab a shower and change into her travel clothes before getting the rest of her things together and checking that everything had been properly switched off – at least twice, as anxiety was starting to rear its ugly head yet again – before going back downstairs to check out and wait for the airport shuttle. Minutes before the bus was due to arrive, she could heard a familiar voice behind her; it was Patrick – probably on his way to the beach, as he was carrying a towel.

'I'm so glad I caught you!' he beamed. 'I just wanted to check if you were on social media at all? If you want to stay in touch, I'll give you my handle so you can add me. If you'd like, of course.'

She said that of course she wanted to keep in touch with him and added him on the spot. In that same moment the bus arrived, so she said:

'I hope you have a great day at the beach! Can't say that I don't envy you.'

To which he replied:

'Oh, I'm not going to the beach. I was coming out here to see if you were still around and then I'm heading to the pool.'

The pool was in the opposite direction, so Hannah smiled brightly, cherishing the fact that this lovely young person had gone out of their way just to stay in touch with her, and she was still smiling as the massive tourist transportation device was pulling out of the parking lot and headed for the airport. She could hardly believe this short, yet somehow lifechanging, week was almost over.

Safely strapped into her seat on her homebound flight, Hannah struggled to relax. The plane was full of screaming children and tired parents, which made it very difficult for her to concentrate on what was going on on the tiny screen in front of her. Yet, she somehow managed to shut herself off just enough to fall asleep, and when Hannah opened her eyes again, the plane was on solid ground and the spell had been broken. She switched her phone back on and was met with a torrent of texts, emails and missed calls – most of which were work related. She was already regretting leaving her perfect holiday, and now she was being pulled back to reality far too soon. There was however a message from Irish as well, asking if she'd be free around mid-

October, as he would be free to go away for a few days. Although that was a good three months from now, it would be nice to have something to look forward to, so she told him she'd reserve the date for him.

Hannah had another two weeks of holiday left, so she let the autoreply take care of the work emails and pretended to ignore the calls. One of the texts was from her sister, though, inviting her to come stay for a couple of days during the last week of her holiday, so Hannah gleefully replied that she'd be delighted to come. She wouldn't let a chance to see the boys pass her by, especially now that she was feeling like a functioning human being for once.

As promised, the first thing she did once she got home and had unpacked was starting to look for a new flat. The rent on most places was extortionate, though, so she had almost given up when she came across one that was calling her name. She phoned the agent straight away and booked herself onto a viewing. It wouldn't be available until October, so that would give her time to stay at her current place until her lease ran out, meaning she would get her deposit back, which at this time would be sorely needed – especially as there would be a two-week overlap between the places. Having moved every eighteen months or so for the past twenty years, it was also quite the luxury to have three whole months to do the packing properly and take her time to dispose of any belongings no longer needed, plus having two weeks to move stuff across without having to hire a car more than once. She was going to get that flat and that was the end of it. She immediately emailed her landlord to say that she would be leaving, adding a mental 'so mote it be', as if to back her decision up with magick.

Hannah spent the next few weeks in an alcohol detox, mainly exercising with her physio and manifesting her desire for the new flat. The viewing was booked for the day she was leaving to go see her sister and the kids, so she needed it to go well. She purposely stayed logged out of her work email and work chat app and only kept an eye on her personal email in case there was any news from the letting agent. Her days were largely controlled by compulsive rituals, but for Hannah, this was a necessary evil. Her psychologist would be back from her annual leave soon as well, so they could discuss and tackle her coping mechanisms together.

On the last Friday of the month, Hannah eagerly followed Google Map's instructions to a high-rise building, right next to a tube station that would cut Hannah's travel time to anywhere in the city by at least 70 percent. She tried to keep her excitement in check by drawing and holding her breath for a few seconds before ringing the doorbell. An unfamiliar voice answered, directing her to take the lift to the second floor. A lift! Another added moving bonus.

As she stepped through what she was hoping would be her future front door, she discovered that the space was tiny. Without the furniture in the photos from the listing, it looked even smaller, but she refused to let it throw her off. Her vivid imagination could make her see where everything would go for it to become her own little oasis. She also noticed a spacious furnished patio leading onto a large communal roof terrace that looked onto the forest behind the building – i.e. there would be no traffic noise bothering her, and there was actual double-glazing on both the windows *and* the door leading out to the patio. The windows and glass door were framed by dark grey blackout curtains, keeping the sun out for those long summer nights. The kitchenette was separated from the combined living/sleeping area by a wall, making it absolutely microscopic, however it was furnished with a very large fridge-freezer and had more than enough cupboard space for Hannah's belongings. There were also two large dressers for her clothes and bedding out in the small closed-off hallway between the kitchenette and the front door. Hannah noticed there was a room she hadn't seen yet and realised that the bathroom must be behind the closed door in the hall. When she opened it, she could have squealed with joy. In stark contrast to her current silverfish and termite infested crapper, she was now standing in a pristine, modern bathroom suite, with a large rainfall shower, a proper sink with a mirror and spacious cabinets, as well as a wall-hung toilet and a washer/dryer. Honestly, she would have submitted her flat application for the bathroom facilities alone.

There was one other person arriving at the viewing just as Hannah was about to approach the agent, so she thanked him for showing her the flat and told him she was very interested. All of two seconds after she heard the door closing behind her, she sent him an email reiterating her interest in the flat. To her surprise, she didn't have to wait long before he got back to her, saying it was hers if she wanted it and for her to submit the necessary details for the letting agency to run their standard background checks. If everything went smoothly, they'd be ready to have her and the owner sign the contract on the coming Monday.

Hannah was delighted, to say the least. She'd gotten it! The flat was hers! Not for a few months, still, but she got it! She went back to her old home to pick up her overnight bag and headed straight for the train to her sister's. She texted her to share the good news and got a cheerful message back that they were thrilled for her and would be waiting for her at the station when she arrived.

Hannah sunk back in her seat on the train and listened to music and solved sudoku puzzles for the entire two-hour journey, whilst all along smiling to herself as if she had a wonderful secret only she knew about. And as if that wasn't enough, the sheer joy on her nephews' faces when they saw her coming towards them was enough to melt even the coldest of hearts. They both ran towards her, flinging their chubby little arms around her and let her carry them both to the car, screaming 'AUNTIE HANNAH!!' with unadulterated glee. Life was good, yet again.

Chapter 9: August – A new routine

Hannah's weekend with her sisters' family had been an absolute delight. Exhausting, but delightful, nonetheless. The weather had been spectacular, so they had taken the kids to a nearby amusement park, and when they got back to their house, Hannah had been their own personal jungle gym for the duration of the weekend.

On the train home, however, she felt the need to mentally prepare for the coming week and got the distinct feeling that things were about to take a turn for the worse. Having to deal with going back to work and the emails she'd ignored for the past few weeks was too intimidating a prospect and she could feel the familiar anxious feeling slowly creeping up her spine and taking hold of her cerebral cortex, shutting out all the light that had penetrated it during her time away.

As Hannah approached the office the following Monday, she was not in very high spirits about returning to work. Her time off had been fantastic, but it had left her yearning for the holidays not taken over the past decade, and she felt rather drained just by thinking about it. She realised that, had she looked after herself better instead of jumping from one project to the next without taking the time to breathe in between, she would probably have been a more harmonious person today. She tried reminding herself that you can't change the past, but she couldn't quite let it go, and so she turned up for work in a somewhat dishevelled and unrested state, only to discover that her interview, with the presentation of her case, had been scheduled for the next day – one of her sick days.

Ah, so that's why they had tried to get in touch with her.

Today was an ordinary Monday, so it was near impossible to get anything done with all the meetings, making room only for lunch, and by the time lunch rolled around, Hannah was too tired from the people pleasing to do much else than refuelling her power bank. There was no way she'd have the energy to go over her case presentation before tomorrow, so she decided to just wing it when the time came. If she was truly cut out for the job, she would nail the interview without much prep.

Apparently the moon was in retrograde or something, because it felt to Hannah as if everything she tried to get through was akin to wading in a shark infested sea of thick molasses, so when the last meeting of the day finally came to a close and Hannah's boss asked to see her for a quick catch-up, Hannah's patience – and filter – was gone. But of course she agreed. What sort of idiot would turn down their boss on the first day back from holiday, and with a possible new job hanging in the balance, right?

It turned out Hannah's boss had just wanted to see how Hannah was coping and check if she needed anything to help the remainder of her contract run smoothly. Hannah appreciated the gesture and felt like her boss was genuinely concerned about her wellbeing, so she let her guard down and let her in on specifics about her treatment, as well as adding that she was frustrated over the fact that her psychologist didn't want her to return to work for at least another year. These one-on-one sessions were normally bound by a mutual non-disclosure agreement, so she felt confident that what they discussed would remain between the two of them. Ultimately, Hannah left the office feeling like she had the support of her current boss and hopeful that she would nail tomorrow's interview so that she could start focussing on becoming part of the marketing team after a very short hiatus between contracts.

In order to get some sleep before tomorrow's interview – although not absolutely vital, as it was the only thing on Tuesday's agenda – Hannah went for a quick jog to clear her head when she got home. After her run, she scrolled through her personal emails, where she found the agent had emailed the contract for her to sign. Done. She then shoved some tomato soup and dry bread in her gob, before surrendering to her evil spirit infested bedchambers, where she would spend the night in a constant cold sweat, tossing and turning with no chance of getting some much-needed kip before she had to get up and head for the office for her ten o'clock interview.

Hannah hadn't told anyone about the interview, so she was delighted to find that it was taking place in one of the off-site meeting rooms on the first floor of the building, instead of on her company's designated floor. This meant that she didn't have to work too hard to come and go completely unseen by anyone who might raise questions as to why she was there on her day off.

Hannah actually quite liked and admired the members of the marketing team, and she was particularly delighted to see that she would be presenting her case to the Digital Marketing Director, rather than the Head of Marketing, as Hannah knew that her expertise was specific to what Hannah would be presenting, and therefore the best person to call her out on any bullshit. Hannah wanted the job, she really did, but only if she was the best candidate. So, she went in guns blazing.

45 minutes later, it was all over. Hannah looked around the room to try and read everyone's faces for any indication of failure on her own part but found none. Eventually, they all started getting up to shake her hand, and the DMD just said, 'Wow. I didn't know that you had the background to pull this off. Thank you! You're the last one to present, so we'll just have to discuss amongst ourselves and get back to you by the end of the week. But I have to admit that this just might go in your favour. Thanks so much for taking the time out to do this.'

Hannah left the office with a smile playing on her lips. If she got this, it would be a gigantic financial burden lifted off her shoulders, and she would be doing what she'd actually gone to Uni to specialise in, so she crossed her fingers in hope that this would be one of many things that would play out to her benefit.

A couple of hours later, as Hannah was trying to rest her overworked and under-rested brain on her sofa, her phone vibrated with an email notification. It was the Head of Marketing:

'Hi Hannah

Just received news that you really impressed the team with your presentation. Congratulations!

I would love it if we could set up a meeting with HR to discuss this further, as I would like to do a second interview to see if you're really the best fit for the team.

Regards,

Mrs Camilla F. Jones
Head of Marketing'

Erm… right. That was a bit formal for an email between colleagues. So, she had to do the bit of the interview she had been told wasn't needed as she was already working there now? Hannah thought this was a bit odd, yet she replied that she would be 'more than happy' for them to set it up at a time that suited them. She really did want that job, after all.

Hannah was happy she'd been given a chance to present, but now she had an aching feeling that someone was trying to take that chance away from her. Needless to say, the chance of her getting settled enough to take a nap was now blown, so she opted for a HIIT workout before heading to her physio appointment for some semi-heavy lifting that would hopefully help her take the edge off.

The workout helped, like it almost always did, so when she came home from training, Hannah kept herself busy by putting some of her belongings in boxes for the move, and at the same time contemplating setting fire to that disgusting bed that was no longer fit for its main purpose of sleeping. She could feel her body starting to ache with a fever, so she popped a couple painkillers to keep herself going until it was time for bed. Yet, when the appropriate time for sleep finally came, a proper rest managed to mostly evade her again, if not completely.

Hannah felt as if her skull was packed with glass wool, making the inside of her skull itch like hell, as she was trying to stay awake on her commute to work. Having been unable to sleep more than a minute here and there throughout the course of the night, she wasn't exactly in the best of moods. By the time she arrived at the office, she felt as if a thunderous dark cloud was hanging over her head, slowly bearing down on her, making her suffocate with its intense mugginess. She was the first one to arrive, as per, but not even that could brighten her morning today.

Hannah sat down at her favourite spot in the back of the room, knowing that this was where the marketing team would normally gather as well. She felt like she had an in with them now and was anxious to become part of their group, so she spent the first hour of work trying to better her mood by working on her old team's webpages until people started showing up. She'd even popped by the nice café near the train station to pick up croissants for Rebecca and the Art Director, which she'd placed on the desks they would normally use. She did this not to butter anyone up, but to remind the ones that she'd had a good report with before her little breakdown that she was back to being there for them.

Lost in work, and in a slightly better mood, when the stragglers starting to come in through the lift at the far end of the room, Hannah realised she was looking forward to seeing the joy on her coworkers faces when they discovered their little "gifts". She'd also taken time to write them little notes (not signing them, of course), praising each of their unique qualities, so she kept her head down and pretended not to see them as they sat down at their respective desks. Then, the squeals came:

'OHMYGOWHODIDTHIS?! That's so nicccceeeee!' shouted Rebecca. She was looking around her in disbelief until she spotted Hannah trying to inconspicuously keep her head down behind her computer monitor. 'Hannah! I know this can only be your doing. Was it you? I can't believe it, it's like you knew I'd have the munchies. LOL!'

Even despite Rebecca's incredible faux-pas of spelling out the abbreviation where it certainly wasn't needed – and she wasn't laughing, just shrieking happily – Hannah couldn't help but smile at her. She was quite sweet, really, despite her millennial grandeur, and Hannah really liked her. Also, if they were to be team buddies in the very near future, Hannah didn't see her very visible reaction as a bad thing.

Just a millisecond later, the AD had a very similar reaction to her own orange peel and marmalade croissant – her favourite. Of course, Hannah knew this as she'd spent hours listening to the office chatter for almost a year now, instead of participating in it, but said nothing of it:

'I just thought you guys deserved a mid-week pick-me-up', she smiled and got back to her work.

In an oddly good mood now, albeit still in a fragile state, Hannah didn't let herself be put off by the email she received two minutes after the Head of Marketing had arrived. Hannah knew she'd arrived, because she had positioned herself exactly two desks across from Hannah, yet still found it appropriate to send an email instead of walking the three extra feet to acknowledge her.

She wanted to know if 1pm would be a good time for their interview and Hannah agreed. Might as well get it out of the way. She had some proofreading to do before their meeting, so between that and lunch with Rebecca and the AD (whose name was actually Allison), Hannah was able to fill her time with constructive things rather than pulling out her own hair over something she had no control over. Although, as she made her way towards the small interview room, she felt like the prisoner from *The Green Mile*, a voice shouting 'dead woman walking' in the back of her mind.

Hannah didn't have to wait long before the real reason why she had been summoned for a second interview became very clear; her boss had divulged to HR how Hannah's psychologist felt about her continued employment.

'It's been brought to our attention that you might not be up for taking on this position, in regard to your mental health', the HR rep began.

'Quite frankly, I'm worried that you won't fit in too well with the team either', the Head of Marketing added. 'I mean, you haven't really made any efforts to make friends with your coworkers.'

Well, fuck me for being more interested in meeting my deadlines than socialising during working hours, Hannah thought to herself, but she didn't say anything. The two women across from her began bombarding her with observations they've made about her over the past year, to make it abundantly clear to Hannah that she did not now and would likely never be part of any team at that place if it were up to them.

Furthermore, they had noticed she didn't dress the same way as the rest of them did, she didn't come from the same socioeconomic background as them (i.e. her financially poor upbringing somehow made it impossible for her to have any value, despite having a Master's degree), and these things added to a long list of stuff that heavily outweighed the fact that she had turned out to have been the top candidate for the position, based on her presentation alone.

At that moment, Hannah was overwhelmed by her own reaction to the situation, that to her felt like the ultimate betrayal from her boss had led to this blatant attack of criticism. The fact that they were sat opposite her in the way that they did, arms folded across their chests, did very little to help the situation. Finally, something good had come along, only for it to be pulled away from her faster than it had taken her to wrap her head around being qualified and encouraged to apply and subsequently becoming considered for her dream job. This was just so unfair! Not only for her, but if she was the best candidate, why on earth would they turn her down?

Hannah said nothing. All she could do was fight back the tears at this point. She blinked quickly to get rid of the excess moisture filling her lower eyelids.

'If we're being completely honest', Hannah heard the HR person say, 'you've never fit in here, which beckons the question as to why you've now applied for *another* position with us.'

Without hesitation, the department head added, in a tone that indicated the opposite of what she was about to utter:

'We're going to have to hold off on employing anyone and advertise the position again in the autumn. You're obviously welcome to reapply, should you feel up for it, but it might be in your best interest to focus on your mental health for the time being.'

A pregnant silence manifested in the room, as the verbal bombardment had finally ceased. It appeared the time had come for Hannah to speak. She cleared her throat audibly, trying to regain control of her trembling body, not wanting her voice to sound as unsteady as she herself now felt:

'When I first heard about the position being advertised, I couldn't believe it', she said. 'It's what I've wanted to do professionally ever since before I got my Master's, and I wrote my thesis on the main task of this job. I fully agree that I never fit in on my own team, but that was never the point of my role there. I was meant to be the bridge between departments and establish a new pattern of communication, something I think we can agree that I succeeded in. My personality should be irrelevant in that aspect.'

As she uttered the last few words, her voice broke, and she knew that she had to accept defeat. She couldn't hold the tears back for much longer. As she felt a teardrop escaping her right eye, she got up, thanked the women for the opportunity and for being honest with her and apologised for having wasted their time. Hannah let herself out of the room and quickly escaped behind the door of the disabled toilets opposite. The door securely locked, her back against the door, Hannah's knees buckled, and she fell slowly to the floor, sobbing quietly. There was no way she was applying for another position there again. When there were no tears left to cry, quite possibly due to dehydration, Hannah scraped herself off the bathroom floor, dusted off her bum and went straight back to her desk, not even acknowledging her colleagues, where she emailed her boss saying she'd be working from home for her remaining hours of the week. As she was leaving the office, she pulled out her phone to make an emergency appointment with her psychologist. Maybe taking a year "off" wouldn't be such a bad thing after all.

With almost all of the tasks of her project now completed, and no real reason or ambition left in her to try to prove herself at work, Hannah found herself taking advantage of being able to work from home. She started taking more online courses during work hours – the reasoning behind this was that they were for the most part work-related and on the company's own course portal – and worked out during her lunch breaks, not really caring if she was late coming back by a minute or ten. She even took toilet breaks outside of her allotted lunch hour now, which was new for her.

She'd made a habit of crossing out the remaining days on her calendar, just to have something to signify the end of her workday – and to some extent what had started to feel like a prison sentence. Knowing no one wanted her there made her feel extra paranoid. She didn't really talk to anyone outside of the online meetings and she wouldn't have wanted it any other way. Hannah realised that she was pulling away from all social interactions in her life outside of work as well, but she found that most of her so-called friendships were mainly acquaintances with whom she endured one-way conversations where she was on the receiving end, and she had no time for other people's problems anymore. If she were to stand a chance to live the rest of her life in a way that would make *her* happy, she would have to start by rebranding herself to her own subconscious.

Hannah knew that she would only continue to attract the people and energies that she thought she deserved and that she would have to change her own mindset in order for her to be able to attract the good things she ultimately wanted. This required very little input from members of the public and all of that from the mental health professionals involved with her treatment, as well as plenty of effort and goodwill from herself. Hannah 2.0 was a work in progress, but the road to recovery would no doubt prove to be strenuous. She would need all the strength she could muster, and in order to avoid self-sabotage, she would have to control her use of rituals and substances that would only make her feel worse about herself. She wanted to feel that she was worthy of a change for the better, and doing that was only possible if she was able to convince herself that she really was. Because who was she doing it for, if not for herself?

The psychiatric hospital's summer closure had finally ended and Hannah's treatment was back in full swing, so she had sessions twice weekly, yet she felt as if they were doing very little to improve her situation; it was all about testing her for different diagnoses and filling in forms to document the degree of various symptoms. This whole process was exhausting and, for a while, made matters worse.

All Hannah wanted was to talk. To purge herself of all of the mess that was threatening to spill out during any moment of temporary weakness. It was a terrifying prospect, to say the least. Her fear that all their work was going out the window for every second wasted on another one of those forms she'd filled out countless times before intensified her sometimes crippling OCD, and there were times where she couldn't get down the stairs before having touched the banister just so before she was able to go down them and then back up to repeat the process at least twice. And then twice again. Everything had to be done in pairs, or else she would lose all sense of equilibrium, and the sense of something "bad" happening followed her around like a shadow.

Whenever she went to the shop, she would have to get two of every item and then return to the same shop the same day to repeat. If she hadn't been forced to get two of them, she would have bought herself one of those step tracking watches. One. Such a dirty number. Yet, she had no idea why.

The most annoying thing about her obsessive-compulsive disorder was that she realised it made no sense. She was well aware over the fact that she had no magical powers to control the universe. If she did, wouldn't she have used them to her benefit instead? Hannah also knew that her stopping herself from switching the stove on and off one more time after she'd finished cooking didn't make her gay, or make the Hague blow up, or give her HIV, yet she had no explanation for the horrible feeling she'd get if she didn't. It was that same feeling you get when you've done something terrible by accident – say, you've hit an animal with your car or said something detrimental about a friend – and it would come out of nowhere. It got worse whenever she needed to feel like she had some control over what was happening in her life, she knew that much, but why the logical go-to for her brain was to enforce this sort of tyrannical regime on her was lost on her. Maybe she had gotten so used to being knocked down by her parents and teachers when she was little that she at one point had started flogging herself to feel like *she* was controlling the abuse.

Either way, the OCD made her treatment feel even more tiring than it needed to be, when just trying to escape her house to get there became its own little project. But she had lived with this condition for as long as she could remember, so she didn't even start to think that this would possibly need treatment as well at some point, and that the comorbidity that it was had become just as much of a symptom of her mental struggles as anything else. She was so sick of this introspective analysis. Wasn't that meant to be someone else's job, after all?

She soon had to stop taking the online add-on courses as well, as some of them didn't allow her to take the certification qualification quiz more than once and failing it on purpose the first time affected her overall score. This meant she was running out of things to do at work, so the remaining days were really dragging out.

At home, Hannah had almost finished packing everything she didn't use on a daily basis and her living room and the large space between her bed and her home office were filled with boxes. How on earth had she accumulated so much new stuff in the short space since her last move?

Summer was drawing to a close, and so was her contract. Her 41st birthday was coming up shortly after

and she would be forty-fucking-one and fucking
unemployed like the loser that she was. She was
incapable of taking her own life and she had no money
to speak of. Where would she even get the money to pay
rent if her health insurance claim wasn't paid out in
time? Hannah thought about spending what was left of
her savings on scratch cards or the lottery but decided
against it. The one thing she did have was her
psychologist, so Hannah figured she'd spent all of her
good luck on her. Because she was truly excellent. Dr
Andrea seemed to care and do everything in her power
to see to it that Hannah's case was thoroughly evaluated
so that she wouldn't have to go through it all again. But
Hannah felt as if an invisible clock had started ticking
somewhere and that time was running out. It was as if
the sun had started setting on her life, and she had only
just begun to live it. And she wasn't ready for it to end
now.

Hannah was sitting at her desk, just looking
absentmindedly at her own hands when her phone
vibrated. Hannah didn't bother with checking it at first,
as she assumed it was a team chat notification and kept
staring down at her hands. Her skin was dry and
swollen around the joints of her fingers, as if the last
few weeks had shrivelled her up completely. Her eyes
got caught on the scar she had on her right middle
finger, where her mother had scratched her so violently
her nails cut deep into the skin and tore so many layers
off you could see the white of bone shining through,
leaving a permanent, still visible, thick, purplish white
indentation that resembled a fly zipper made from
human flesh 30 years later. Why had she scratched her?
The then nine-year-old Hannah had beaten her at a card

game. Luckily, you don't need to go to A&E for stitches when your mum's a psychiatric nurse and you've got superglue in the house.

In an attempt to shake off the awkward memory, Hannah tore her eyes away from her fingers and looked towards her phone. She really should check it, it could be important, so she entered her pass code and prepared herself for the nagging she was sure was awaiting her, but then she saw the notification. It wasn't the work chat at all; in fact it was a message from Irish!

She'd almost forgot about him in the midst of everything that had been going on, and herself trying as best she could to dig herself a deeper hole for her to shrivel up and die in...and here he was, offering a welcome distraction from becoming utterly consumed by the nothing, not unlike Artax in *The Neverending Story.* She wondered for a second if she should be concerned that she hadn't spent a single thought on him, but chose to ignore the feeling that it was a bit too 'out of sight out of mind' for this to be something real from her side.

'Hey lovely, I'm just over in Ulster, visiting the abbey ruins. Made me think of me and you doing very naughty things in the cemetery on the way back to yours last time we saw each other'

Then followed two photos of the ruins, a video of himself talking to the camera about the origin of the historic ruins and three more messages about why he was there and how much fun they had had the last time they were together.

Hannah had no recollection of doing anything 'naughty' near someone's final resting place, yet she wouldn't put it past her drunken self. It wouldn't have been the first time she'd had someone say that back to her. Oddly enough. Yet, she wasn't particularly keen on dwelling on it, as she was sure this was the autobahn to eternal damnation should she recall having initiated such behaviour, so she therefore tried to slip in a response before he sent another message with more historical facts she couldn't care less about:

'Hey! Lovely to hear from you 😊 Ulster looks fab. Wouldn't have minded the guide either. Haha. Hope life is treating you well'.

Hannah wasn't expecting a reply, as she hadn't really asked him any questions, but about a minute later she received another video from him, where he said that he loved the compliment and that he'd been working out a lot, so he felt he looked like he was in good shape for his age.

Hannah thought that was a bit weird, but she thought to herself that maybe he was too embarrassed to put something like that in writing at that was the reason he sent a video to reply instead. And, since they were old friends, it wasn't really that weird. It would be very different had this been a dating scenario, she thought. If that had been the case, she would likely have gotten to greet her breakfast a second time that morning. But they were just old friends having a laugh. And it was nice to have a pal that shared her passion for working out. Kim, who had to take beta blockers to control her food intake and was allergic to any other form of physical movement other than walking her dog, almost attacked her if she so much as mentioned going to the gym. And, as if he'd read her mind, Irish messaged back:

'I know how you're into your fitness stuff as well. I guess that's something we've got in common 😊'

Hannah smiled to herself. Working from home and not seeing other people for extended periods of time could quite easily make her forget that she had people in her life worth staying in touch with and she was grateful for the interruption, even if it was in the middle of the workday.

She wondered then what *he* did for work, seeing as he could be fucking about in Ulster in the middle of the day, but she supposed he might be on holiday. And she also felt that after more than fifteen years of friendship, it was a little late to ask about what the other did for a living. Hannah switched jobs all the time, so she was used to having to explain what she was up to every so often, but most people her age had been in the same line of work for as long as she'd known them. She knew he did something creative for bands that he was able to do from home if he needed to. She wasn't too fussed about the details and didn't want to cock up by asking him about something he'd probably talked about a million times. At least he wasn't a musician, like most of their mutual friends, and that was all that mattered. She could not deal with another one of those right now, as somehow trying to avoid them in the past had only seemed to attract them, much in the same way that cats tend to follow people who don't care for them. Unfortunately for Hannah, this particular vein of

reverse psychology only worked on musicians –
particularly bass players – and married men, and not if
you tried to persuade someone suitable into looking
your way. *'Hey, wait a minute'*, a voice in her head spat
at her. *'I thought we weren't talking about dating here'*?

Hannah had issues with dating. A profound
disdain, I suppose you could call it. So, if she could
avoid it, she did. This had unfortunately resulted in a
history of one night stands so large in number that
Hannah had stopped counting once she hit triple digits.

She had once kept track using a spreadsheet on
her computer, but when her ex had found out about it,
she felt forced to delete it so that he wouldn't be able to
hold it over her. And, just to be clear, she only kept the
spreadsheet so that she would be able to notify previous
partners should something come up in her bloodwork.
It wasn't as if it had been anything she had been proud
of. Still very much wasn't to this day. Especially as she
couldn't remember the last time she had had sex sober,
and many of the one night stands she had found out
about by picking up evidence from off the floor, such as
a used condom or blood-stained knickers. There were
far too many of these sexual encounters she had
absolutely no recollection of, some of which she knew
of only because she could feel that someone had been
inside her.

She'd once been pulled aside by airport security,
as they had found a condom floating around inside of
her on the X-ray. Another proud moment for the books.
Hannah would have much rather have been suspected
of trafficking drugs than carrying around a boner
poncho she had no idea how had gotten in there. Or,
indeed, whose membrum un-virile it had fallen off of. I

suppose you could call it a case of 'vas *deference'*. Giving birth to the rather foul-smelling thing whilst, unsuspectingly, having a relaxing pee a couple of weeks later was also an experience she'd be glad to rid herself of. But at least there was evidence of precautions having been taken for once. Although, if it had fallen off and ventured off on a tour of her uterus, they were probably both undeserving of any standing ovations for having practiced safe sex.

For a rather foul-mouthed lady, Hannah was in fact a tad frigid, if not completely, and she didn't even bring up the subject of sex when sober, so it was only when she had been drinking that she was confident enough to act on her urges, so to speak. Because she did have those, and quite overwhelmingly so. But, as it turned out, she lacked the backbone to insist on condom use whenever she had succeeded in attracting a willing male, so she had spent years being constantly worried about her own health in that department too. Yet another form of self-harm, she was now discovering. She had no idea how she would go about it if Irish expected her to do anything sober. But who knew if he would be that keen once he did see her in daylight and without the beer goggles. It was silly to worry about things that probably wouldn't come to fruition.

Hannah was rudely interrupted during her trip down memory lane by a loud 'ping!' from her laptop. Shit, she'd forgotten about the 2.15 team meeting. She must have missed the fifteen-minute warning as this was the five minute one, so she sprinted down the stairs to put some makeup on and came panting back up with a few seconds to spare. She definitely needed a run after work to feel like she'd at least accomplished *something* today, she thought to herself as she tried putting on a not entirely disinterested face for the camera and entered the "lobby" for the digital meeting.

Of course, the meeting ran over due to bickering between her colleagues. Why was she even surprised? They had quarrelled and shouted over each other for a good 20 minutes before her boss had managed to get a word in, and what she had to say only gave them more fuel for the fire. Hannah couldn't help but rolling her eyes so aggressively over their trivial arguments it had given her a headache. Hannah had started working extra early so that she could in good conscience slam her laptop shut at 3, but when the meeting was finally over it was closer to 4 and the previously blue skies and sunshine had been replaced by clouds heavy with rain and gale force winds. God, how she hated working with these people.

To Hannah's relief, she could feel the frustration from being faced with losing her job lifting. The stress this was causing her just wasn't worth the financial stability. And if her psychologist and GP were right in thinking she would be entitled to financial aid from the government, she'd happily take it instead of jumping straight into the next best thing.

Right now, she didn't think she'd be able to do her dream job with dream colleagues just because she was so mentally unstable, vulnerable and goddamned knackered. The fact that she'd been looking forward to her last day since pretty much her second month there should have been enough of a deterrent. This place and these people were completely and utterly *not* for her. She did *not* fit in, nor did she want to, and that was the end of it. Hannah was done with putting everyone else's wellbeing above her own, and when she slammed her laptop shut a few minutes later, she made a promise to herself that she would do her absolute best to walk away from that job, knowing that she had completed what she was hired to do, with an excellent reference from her boss, and after that she would try to take her time finding the right job for herself – not one that she would have to force herself to fit into. Only two days remained of August, and then she'd have three weeks before she could kiss this job goodbye for good. She would not let this place become her downfall.

Part 4: Autumn

Chapter 10: September – Can't shake this feeling

Hannah embarked on her last three weeks at work by being physically at the office, with her head held high. Who knew who out of these people she'd be likely to bump into ever again, but she'd be damned if she didn't go out without leaving a very impressive mark on them all. Hell, she'd even make a point of smiling her way through every pointless meeting she'd had to sit in on – if only just to prove to the marketing head that she was capable of doing so.

Every minute outside of meetings Hannah spent by dividing her time between tweaking her department's webpages and improving their visibility and earning those course certificates she had initially abandoned. She was dead set on making every second count, both in her own case and in that of the company, even if it did take every little bit of what was left in her – she did after all have a dedicated team of mental health professionals who were ready to help her put her Humpty Dumpty self back together by the end of it, if she did end up cracking into a million pieces by the end of it. Hannah wondered for a minute if this sudden motivational surge was a sign she was getting back to her former self, but as the days went past, she'd grow increasingly tired, with no energy left for anything but work. She hardly slept as it was, and now she was down to four hours a night on a good night. Even sobriety had stopped reaping any benefits, it seemed, as the stress of Hannah's situation caused her to gain weight, despite her strict workout regimen. But she kept telling herself she could keep anything up for three weeks. Compared to the year she'd been there, it was nothing! But soon enough, she started comparing it to anal – at first it was both difficult and painful, then just painful, and then you'd spend the rest of the time wondering if you'd accidentally emptied your bowels.

The courses Hannah was taking weren't really doing much to improve her station either. None of the course videos seemed to make any impression on her, and she more often than not found herself getting infuriated with the speakers' lack of ability to control their bodies' production of saliva and unnecessary heavy breathing and swallowing directly into the mic. The least they could have done was to edit out all of the excessive noise in post-production, but here they were, torturing her by triggering her misophonia every chance they got. In many cases, she'd have to replay the videos several times, just to wrap her head around what was being said. She soon discovered that the subtitling function was a dead end as the subtitling software, too, had trouble figuring out what was being said with all the excess noise. This, in turn, had Hannah cheating on the quizzes, just so she could earn the certificates without losing the plot completely and chucking her laptop out the window every time she watched a video. Hence, she wasted a tonne of time forcing herself to sit through these ridiculous videos and still learning nothing and then adding certificates to her résumé without having anything of any real substance to show for the time spent. The cheating of course added to her anxiety by giving her conscience a run for her money, even if the only one she was truly cheating by going about it this way was herself, but she didn't have the energy to try to make herself more tolerant to noise and shoddy workmanship of video producers. But her way of dealing with this was soon sending signals of feeling disrespected to her subconscious, which largely overshadowed the short-lived joy she took from making necessary amendments and vastly improving the traffic to the webpages she was working on. It was mostly backend work anyway, so no one could see just how much she had done, other than by looking at the statistics only she and the web developer had access to. Which made for a very undercelebrated venture for Hannah. And as she wasn't much for holding a parade in her own honour for her ability to do her own job, no one would ever know, unless someone else would let her team know how much she had actually done. In an office where most people were patted on the back just for showing up, Hannah desperately longed for some acknowledgement. This, of course, never came.

Hannah was sat in the open-plan office, rapidly turning into a husk of a human being and trying to remind herself that she only had a handful of days left, when a notification on her screen caught her attention. It was an invitation to a production meeting set to the week after her last day. Thinking she'd been added by mistake, she chose to ignore it at first, but then someone started allocating tasks for her to do, both in preparation of the meeting and for the project itself, so she was forced to respond. She messaged the meeting organiser directly:

'Hey, I just received your meeting invitation so wanted to remind you that I will no longer be here at that date, my last day is on the 18th. Probably best to reallocate those tasks. 😊'

Hannah didn't have to wait long for a reply:

'What? You're leaving???'
'Yes. I thought everyone knew. My position is only temporary.'
'Yeah, initially, but then I thought we'd decided to change it to a fixed position, or at least extend your contract? This has certainly thrown a spanner in my works!'

Hannah caught herself smiling at this response to her leaving. Here she was thinking no one cared she would no longer be there by the end of the month, as the office always made a big deal about organising leaving dos, even for interns, and no one had even mentioned her departure. At least someone seemed to care, and the fact that it had been the UX specialist, who normally disliked most people, made it extra heartwarming.

Over the next couple of days, quite a few people approached her to express their shock of her leaving, many of them adding that they would really miss having her around the office, as she had been someone they had been able to count on for support, positive reinforcement and a motivational work ethic. None of them were people from her own team, but this was no surprise to Hannah, yet she couldn't help but thinking that the lack of support from her own peers was what had made her feel like such an outsider since the very beginning. In the end, having to be the one to constantly explain and defend their erratic behaviours to other teams from which they required support to carry out certain brand related campaigns, had become increasingly difficult, as she couldn't in any good conscience vouch for the way they continued to treat people outside their department.

A big chunk of her job had been to better communication between teams, and she had found the other teams to be so open to this that she felt as she was constantly being kicked in the face by her own team colleagues when she'd started a dialogue and they used the opportunity to bulldoze the 'other side' with demands and hostile accusations of uncooperativeness, their excuse behind their behaviour being that 'they've never been interested in helping us before'. Hannah thought it was very odd to demand change when you weren't inclined to believe it to be possible when it did come around once you had put in the work. She also suspected the possibility that the other teams had been open to helping them even before she'd started interfering, but that they in fact used her more human approach to further their own agenda rather than actually cooperating.

Every time she'd been able to organise a meeting between departments by convincing the other teams that what they wanted to accomplish would benefit the entire organisation, her team had ended up wasting everyone's time in said meetings, criticising ways they had done things in the past and not wanting to accept anyone's input, ultimately making Hannah look like the villain. She'd been the one to set it up, after all. Yet, the members of these other teams turned out to be the ones that had enjoyed having her there, in some cases just as a buffer, but they appreciated her being there, nonetheless. This, however, largely augmented in Hannah's mind the non-reaction from her own department. Another team she had never felt as if she had been a part of. She had been nothing more than a drifting cargo ship with no direction and no lighthouse to guide her way to the shore.

On the Tuesday of her second to last week there, Hannah finally received a message from HR, asking if she wanted them to throw her a little farewell ceremony – they could 'probably book one of the smaller meeting rooms'. The fact that they contacted her about this on one of the two days a week they knew she'd be out of office was not well received by Hannah, who took this action to be just another indication of how little she was worth to the company, but she decided to passive-aggressively reply that she would like that very much. She added, too, that quite a few people had approached her asking if they would get the chance to give her a proper sendoff, so it might make sense to book the lounge. That way, people would have the chance to pop by and grab some cake if they wanted too. The HR person somewhat reluctantly agreed to this, adding that they might want her to say a few words if that was the case – as if Hannah was completely inept at stringing a couple of sentences together. Hannah resisted the urge to type back 'FUCK OFF' in capital letters and simply replied that that would be absolutely fine and that she would be honoured to be able to address such a lovely bunch of colleagues, whilst violently flipping her phone off with her left hand as she typed using her right thumb. If someone was to cut her down like the ancient tree that she was, they'd probably be able to tell her forty years from counting her growth rings, but her physical age didn't stop her from staying a defiant teen at heart.

All work chat aside, Hannah was starting to get a little antsy about the move that was now a mere month away, her synapses firing at the thought of all the money that would surely go straight down the drain with it. She would have to hire a car, as she'd long since parted ways with her beloved old Volvo, she'd have to buy all new furniture, the double rent… she was starting to wonder if it really had been necessary for her try to move out so quickly, seeing as she had no new job in sight and no reliable source of income, but then she remembered last winter's electricity costs and decided that was reason enough to not look back – not to mention the fact that she could no longer sleep in a bed where someone had forced their way inside of her. She was quite literally unable to sleep these days. And then – of course – there was the arse statue that had greeted her every morning for the past 18 months. The commute to her treatment facility. To work – for when she'd be employable again. Yup. She was definitely doing the right thing if she had any hope of reclaiming her sanity.

Back in the office Wednesday morning, Hannah was made aware that she would take care of the invitations herself if she wanted to have a farewell gathering, but her boss, that had apparently been inundated by HR with the responsibility of organising it, made a promise of cake and healthy snacks for those that would like to attend. So, as the last task of the workday, Hannah set up a public event, to which she invited everyone. She set it up around lunchtime on her very last day, when most of the few people who turned up on Fridays would venture downstairs to the cafeteria, and didn't mention anything about cake, because she only wanted people who actually wanted to spend their time with her to show up. She'd be surprised if anyone cared to turn up at all, so she didn't walk around with any delusions of a full house – nor did she prepare any speech of her own. But she loved the opportunity offered to have a ceremony that would mark her time there. To her, it signified the sort of closure she needed, without her feeling that she'd given up on her assignment, or her future. After hitting send, she packed up her laptop and left it in her locker for Friday and headed out the door with the event firmly pushed out of her mind for now.

Hannah's Thursday was filled with appointments, divided between her physio and two different specialists at "the asylum", to which she had now started referring the psychiatric hospital where she received her ongoing treatment. In order to cope with any frustration or sensitive skin brought on by her sometimes intense therapy sessions, she'd put a reminder to go for a run that evening in the calendar app on her phone. It might seem silly to anyone that didn't live inside Hannah's brain, but this helped her feel accountable. And any time spent away from any sugary foods that was currently sat in Hannah's kitchen cupboards was time well spent these days. Also, a nice long run helped with muffling the constant screaming in her head.

Hannah's appointment with the physical therapist went really well, in fact so well that they decided to wrap up her treatment with one last session two weeks later, just so she'd have time to really feel around for any remaining niggles in her hamstring. This was a huge relief to Hannah, who knew she had started running again a bit earlier than her therapist had liked her to, but as she'd managed to keep the pace down in sheer fear of any pain flaring back up again, and added onto her normal training some sorely needed resistance training, she was well on her way to stress-free running.

The psych sessions didn't go as well as the physical check-up, mainly because Hannah was pushing her own limits to get everything done at work – and with little to no sleep – to such an extent that it was eating away at her mental capacity and her ability to communicate anything in a way that made any sense. But when Dr Andrea wanted her to slow down, Hannah argued that she would only have three days left after Friday and that she desperately needed to tie up all and any loose ends if she was going to be able to put this chapter behind her without falling apart any further. She could do four days. Really. Couldn't she?

The therapy sessions had left her mind frazzled, and when her phone reminded her that she had to drag herself off of the sofa – where she was lying staring at the ceiling – and go for a run, all Hannah had wanted to do was roll onto her side and sleep, but she decided she had to do this for herself if she wanted to tire herself out enough for her to get some shuteye once the sun finally set on this sordid day.

Hannah half-stumbled into the warm sunshine at seven pm, surprised to find that it was still warm at this time. Summer was definitely a thing of the past, as mornings were now quite fresh as far as temperatures went, but now there was a smell of barbecued meats hanging in the air and fruit trees heavy with near-ripe, un-plucked offerings in every garden Hannah passed on her way, making her long for summers she'd spent sleeping these glorious days away in favour of booze-filled nights that stretched into the early hours. What if she'd taken the time to enjoy some of the daytime instead, she thought, instead of favouring the nights that she somehow managed to drink away every memory of anyway?

Hannah was currently going through the stage of sobriety where her memories would start to return, and she actually quite liked this stage, regardless of how unpleasant it may be at some instances. Because it also reminded her of the sense of belonging she'd had when she had been part of a "we", an "us", a group of people who had come together because they studied the same things at uni, or they worked together, or loved the same music. These moments past were parts of her history she had a tendency to disregard, and looking back at them now, she sometimes questioned the validity of these seemingly utopic memories, if they were in fact memories at all and not just dreams that she'd had. There was no photographic evidence to show for, as they had all been so engrossed in what they were doing that they hadn't bothered to document any of it. And some of these memories had her feeling as if she'd been watching scenes unfold from a bystander's point of view, and not a participant's.

Some of her acquaintances from that time were no longer of this earth, whilst others had settled down with spouses, some with kids, some had travelled across the world and stayed away, and others were touring with bands they'd only dreamed of ever seeing live only 15 years ago. It was odd where life took you. And, specifically to Hannah's own life, where fear took you. The concept of time was even more baffling. It appeared it still baffled her in the present, because Hannah got lost in her own philosophical trance and it kept her feet pounding the pavement for over an hour before she realised how far she was from her house and had to turn back.

When Hannah got back from her run, she was still contemplating the past as she was stretching her soon-to-be-sore limbs. Was there anything that was *meant to be*, or was that another human construct? Hannah had so many delusions drilled into her from a very early age, so she had no idea how well her intuition really worked – if there was such a thing – or if some things were just predestined and forced together by the powers of the universe. Was free will a thing? If it wasn't, Hannah could rest a little easier, knowing that her former attackers hadn't knowingly done what they did to her because they were out to harm her, but because there was another entity forcing their hands, so to speak. But, then again, the whole judicial system would be obsolete. If no one was truly guilty, why should they be punished? You can't unteach nature.

Hannah caught herself going off on a tangent. *I really should get some friends to talk to*, she concluded, and got up to wash her body clean of yet another day on this earth.

She didn't sleep very well that night either, despite her attempts at tiring herself out with a long run. Her brain had gone on an analytical rampage with this whole "meant to be" conundrum, and the harder she tried to get herself to relax, the worse it got. Of course, Hannah knew that this always got worse on the days where she had somewhere to be the next day. As if she was even capable of oversleeping! Yet, she tossed and turned until the sun started peeking through her makeshift curtains, and another day was about to be ruined. *At least I won't have this worry for a while, after next week is over and done with,* thought Hannah, as she nodded off for a full 23 minutes before her first alarm started going off.

When Hannah arrived at the office, no one was there, and so she headed straight for the cookie drawer, desperate for something to munch on. (Fun fact, her lack of sleep made her absolutely famished and uncritical as to the nutritional value of what she would use to kill the hunger pangs.) Back at her desk, with half a packet of choc chip cookies, a handful of salted almonds, six water biscuits, some sultanas and an apple for good measure, Hannah was set for the next fifteen minutes at least. She had also gathered an arsenal of drinks around her, in the shape of a moat; two double espressos, bottle of water and a ginger lemon flavoured tea, to eliminate any need to move for the next few hours. She was dead set on smashing out some sorely needed content for the website today, so that people could see that she was doing something. Hannah found that she always worked best on very few hours of sleep – probably something to do with her brain thinking it was about to die and had one last shot at redemption – so she used this to her advantage this morning. The downside to that, though, was that her tolerance for any noise coming from outside of her own head almost disappeared. So, if someone dared venture into her personal space of at least a ten feet radius this morning, they were bound to get their head chomped off. Luckily, for Hannah and her coworkers, no one turned up for a good wee while. In fact, she was alone in the office for so long she started to think that she might have forgotten about a holiday or something. Although, she was pretty sure September was lacking in red days. She'd been too busy working to check if any of them were logged on in the office chatrooms as well, so when the first few people started turning up just after 10am, she felt a sense of relief she was no longer alone. As much as she loved being the first one there, she detested being the last to leave, so at least someone else would be setting the alarm at the end of the day.

Tomorrow would be Hannah's 41st birthday, and as they were rather big on celebrations in the office, she thought they might have something arranged for her. She had always found birthday celebrations to be extremely awkward, with the singing and everything, but she wouldn't mind it this year. In fact, she would have loved for them to make her feel a bit special. It wasn't as if she'd be throwing herself a party at her shitty, little house, nor did she think any of her so-called "friends" would bother with doing anything. Especially as last year, she'd tried to organise her own 40th birthday bash, but when only two people – people that she didn't really know that well to boot – had announced their attendance on the event page by the morning of, she had cancelled the whole thing and decided to go out on her own and see where the night would take her – after she'd dried the bitter tears off her face and reapplied her makeup. She didn't want a repeat of that ever again, so she hadn't drawn any attention to the fact that the date – that had always been special to her – was coming up, as she knew that HR had notifications set in the intranet that would at least have them send out an automated message, like they did with every other employee. At least she could expect that much.

Most of the people that turned up to the office that day were very much in a pre-weekend getting shit done kind of mode, which Hannah didn't mind at all, so the remainder of the day went by without ceremony. No birthday message ticked in either, but they normally didn't send those out until after the big day should it fall on a weekend date, which in her case it did.

As Hannah had muted the chat notifications on her laptop so she could be left in peace while working, there hadn't been any interruptions all day, so the last thing she decided to do before wrapping up early was to have one last look to see if there were any fires she'd have to put out before shoving her laptop in its locker.

Hannah was stunned to find 48 messages waiting for her when she opened the app. 48! And none of them work related…these were all messages from distraught colleagues that were shocked to hear she was leaving, as they had all thought she would stay on – they had all heard how well she'd done on her presentation. Hannah didn't really know where to begin when it came to replying, but after the initial shock she started typing out heartfelt thank you messages to each and every one, saying she hoped to see them at her leaving do. For every reply she sent, she could feel the lump in her throat growing bigger and bigger – not with anger or frustration this time, but relief and genuine gratitude that so many had taken the time out to tell her that she would be missed. She struggled not to let her feelings get the best of her – she was truly touched by this unexpected reaction to her announcement – so after she'd replied to all of them, she had to sit at her desk for a few minutes and dig her nails into the thin skin on her left wrist, just to offer herself a feeling she was better equipped to handle before trusting herself to walk through the scarcely populated office without losing her composure.

'Have a nice weekend, everyone!' she half-shouted as she headed out the door and slowly descended the stairs. Was she making a mistake by letting this place go so easily? For the first time in a long time Hannah felt like having a drink, but she didn't. She'd made herself a promise that she wouldn't. If she still wanted one tomorrow, she'd have one then.

Feeling lonelier than most days at the prospect of another birthday spent in solitude, Hannah stopped by the shop on her way home. She had absolutely no intention of venturing outside her door on her birthday, only to have the happiness of others pulled down over her head like a sort of suffocating, itchy home knit jumper that never really seemed to fit her but looked great on others. But she was however intent on celebrating the day she escaped her mother's putrid womb to cheer herself up, so she went to the fancy bakery and got herself one single slice of cake – not that she really liked cake, but it wouldn't feel like a celebration without it – then to the wine shop for a few bottles of sparkling rosé that reminded her of her holiday and then to the slightly upscale supermarket where she got ingredients for a birthday pizza, with extra – and freshly picked – chanterelles, for all the mushrooms she'd denied herself when she was dating her mycophobic ex, as well as some pretty fancy pick & mix, a big block of mature cheddar and a salted pretzel the size of her head. Pleased with her loot, she started

on the hill of doom, just as her phone cut off the music
in her ears with the sound of her ringtone. She had to
stop and set her bags down before she could check who
was calling and was delighted to see MJ's number
flashing across the screen, so she picked up. Before she
could say anything, MJ squealed in her ear:

'Bee! Happy day before birthday day! I'm on the
nightshift tonight and won't be human tomorrow, so I
just wanted to catch you before I descended into
nightwatchman mode, and I couldn't *not* call you on
your birthday weekend'.

Despite her own panting under the weight of the
bags and the inhuman incline of the hill, Hannah was
glad to have company for the home stretch of her
commute. Throw in the fact that she wouldn't be forced
to have another awkward chat with the landlord – even
more awkward now that she was leaving – who would
no doubt be prancing around the garden, was an added
bonus.

They chatted for a good wee while, mostly about
absolutely nothing, which was nice. Having a light
conversation and not having to try to regurgitate
repressed memories for a change was a very welcome
event, and Hannah felt almost elated after they'd hung
up – she was lucky to have a friend like that. So, instead
of wallowing in sadness over not having anyone that
wanted to celebrate her existence with her, she now felt
like she very much had that, if only in spirit this time.
But she *did* have someone who gave a fuck. And that
someone was pretty awesome. So, Hannah squeezed in
a short workout, made herself something to eat and

half-watched a silly comedy before taking herself to bed just after 10pm. She didn't know if she was quite ready to wake up and be 41 and alone the next morning, but she decided to leave that worry for the next day. At least she wouldn't have to go to work.

Despite being knackered after a week of little to no sleep, intense therapy sessions and trying to do everything all at once for the final push at work, Hannah didn't fall asleep until closer to 1am, so when she awoke only five hours later, she tried her best to go back to sleep, but when that didn't work, she defied her own ban on going outside and went for a run. The endorphin release of the exercise turned out to be a great start to her birthday, not to mention the fact that running 12k on an empty stomach made her look pretty decent for 41 – inspiring her to leave breakfast for another couple of hours.

Hannah had contemplated turning off her phone, but hadn't gotten to it yet after her shower, so when her sister unexpectedly called as she was stood at the stove making herself an egg and bacon bagel, she picked up with a smile in her voice:

'Hell-'

And that was as far as she got before her nephews started belting out Happy Birthday at the top of their voices, so she stood there, slightly stunned, and just listened until they ran out of words.

'Happy birthday, auntie!' shouted her sister.

'Thank you!' laughed Hannah, on the verge of crying now. 'Oh, that was such a lovely surprise! Thank you!'

It turned out they'd only had time for the song, but that was more than what Hannah could've wished for at that moment. She couldn't believe they'd remembered her, knowing they were always so busy. She was deeply touched, thinking she'd lucked out with that sister of hers as well. They might have their differences, but when push came to shove, they seemed to know what to do when one needed the other.

The lovely display of affection persuaded Hannah to log on to Facebook as well, for the first time in about a week, but the heaps of notifications, generic greetings – obvious app generated suggestions – and the urge to reply to every single one started stressing her out, so Hannah ended up switching the bloody phone off anyway after a few minutes. But she was glad she'd kept it on for the two most important – to her – calls of the week. Having been able to squeeze in a run so early in the day, Hannah decided to allow herself a brunch bottle of fizz with her late breakfast bagel and some unbridled indulgence in the buffet of junk food she'd prepared for later, accompanied by a good playlist, interrupted only by viewings of a few of her favourite films.

All in all, it was a pretty good birthday, at least what she could remember of it – after the second bottle of booze, it became a bit of a blur. Having broken her one rule for today already, she'd gone to the wine shop again after she finished her first bottle, to get reinforcements. Luckily, she'd stayed in after that and been able to keep her drunken self entertained enough that she hadn't done anything she'd regretted when she woke up on her sofa well into the next day, covered in fondant icing and her *The Commitments* DVD playing on a loop on her DVD player.

Once she'd sobered up enough and had something to eat, Hannah went to work some of the excess calories off, but only managed a couple of miles before she turned back again. But she didn't beat herself up about it – as long as she'd at least done something, she was happy. She squeezed in a mini strength session with her dumbbells and called it a day before crashing out on her sofa with the pizza she'd forgot to make herself the day before. Tomorrow was the first day of her last week at work before the great nothing awaited her on the other side in the shape of the very scary unknown world of unemployment and sick leave. She didn't quite know how she felt about that now, after Friday's lovely messages, but decided to put off thinking about it until she was back in the office. Now, she just wanted to enjoy her Sunday with pizza. And maybe some leftover booze. But after she'd finished the last bottle, there would be very little of that in the coming weeks.

Hannah entered the office Monday morning, expected to be greeted with well wishes for her birthday, but no such thing happened. As she switched her laptop on, she found that HR hadn't sent out the email yet, so she reckoned that was probably why – they sometimes waited until lunchtime to do that anyway.

When lunchtime rolled around, there was still no email from HR, congratulating her on her 41st round around the sun. There had however ticked in a birthday email for Emily in the legal department, whose birthday it had been yesterday, just around 10. Had they forgotten about her? Or maybe the system didn't recognise temporary employees in the same way as the fixed position ones? Although, that would rule out the interns... so they must have gotten a notification and just not cared enough to send her a simple 'Happy Birthday'. Needless to say, this pissed Hannah off. But she wasn't going to give them the benefit of acting petty. In fact, she acted as if nothing had happened and made sure to congratulate Emily on her big day – you only turn 24 once, you know! And as Emily harped on about her friends having celebrated her the whole birthday weekend through (why the fuck were these babies entitled to a whole weekend of celebrations these days??), Hannah smiled through the bile slowly rising in her oesophagus and filling her mouth with its foul taste, and politely declined to joining them all in the lounge for some birthday cake and a song for Emily, as soon as she'd been able to swallow the worst of it. She left the office that day in a huff, allowing herself the selfishness, but at least now she knew she was right to leave permanently on Friday. A day that now couldn't come fast enough.

For the next few days, Hannah just went through the motions. Tuesday's trips to the asylum went much like her previous visits, Wednesday was just another day at her desk, yet she'd managed to finish everything but one small task she'd kept for Friday. She went for runs and worked on her resistance training, ate, showered, tried to sleep, tried to avoid falling asleep at work... Thursday was treatment day and then, finally, the Friday had arrived. Having slept all of 122 minutes that night, Hannah was feeling a little worse for wear, but she managed to slap some makeup on her tired face and get to work a whole hour before anyone else showed up. She pushed her event back to work through lunch on her last task, which she submitted at around 2pm, then transferred all of her files to her little memory bank before resetting the factory settings on her laptop and handing it back to the IT department. Just in time for her little farewell gathering. As she turned the corner that led her to the lounge area, she was astonished to find at least 30 people there, who all got up to say how much they'd enjoyed working with her. She did notice, though, that her boss and her mentor were the only ones there from their department, but she wasn't the least bit surprised. To be frank, she wouldn't have wanted the others there anyway.

It turned out to be a rather lovely gathering, with a nice speech from her boss and some healthy snacks – no cake! They'd decided to finally listen to Hannah's request to replace the office snacks with something healthy, the one time she'd wanted the cake – mainly as a reward for the attendees – and all she could do was laugh, as she bit down on a hefty stick of celery.

It appeared as if no one had expected her to really say anything, so when she finally got up and cleared her voice after disposing of her veggie platter, people looked at her in amazement, as if they couldn't believe their own eyes. Or ears. But Hannah had something nice to say about each and every one of them, and for each person she addressed, the more shocked they looked. When she had finished talking, they all came up to her to give her a hug, uttering different iterations of 'I didn't realise you were such a competent speaker. You really saw all of us here and had something unique to say about each person'. It was at that moment that Hannah felt like she'd come full circle. She'd succeeded in impressing them, if only for her way with words – the exact thing that had landed her the job in the first place. So, she left the office with her head held high, with less than a week left of her birth month – the last month of guaranteed warm weather in this part of the world – with only one thing to look forward to: the big move.

When Hannah got home that day, she laid down on her sofa, fully dressed, and slept. She slept until very late in the day the day after as well, and awoke only to grab some water, get out of her stuffy work clothes and move her zombielike self to the bed, where she slept straight through to the next day. She woke up then, to a message from Irish:

'Looks like I'm in town for a few days from the 15th. Up for an overnight guest for a few days?'

The 15th was Hannah's big move-in date. This was exactly the push she'd needed to get everything sorted so that she could rid herself of this place and start the next chapter of her life fresh, without having to look back. She decided right there and then that she would move in the second she got the keys on the 15th and welcome Irish in her new home and replied:

'Hey! Yes, very much so. I'll be in a new flat by then, with a proper bathroom. Haha. It's right next to the tube station, so much easier to get to than my old place.'

He replied two seconds later:

'I'll bring the wine, then... ;)'

Chapter 11: October – Back to square one

Another week, another countdown started, Hannah thought to herself, as she was getting ready to embark on her first week as a total and utter burden on society – jobless, friendless and penniless, but in treatment nonetheless and starting to accept that she was on the verge of becoming something other than hopeless. A few days into October now, the move – and a visit from Irish – was fast approaching. Hannah had spent the past week in the sort of haze you find yourself in when you've slept for too long, with the strange feeling in the back of your mind that you've entered an alternative reality, where nothing of what you do has any effect on the real world because it's not really real. (If you've never experienced this outside of your teenage years or under the influence of illegal drugs, I envy you.) She'd drag herself out of bed for her hospital appointments, back aching from having lain on a too soft mattress for far too many hours, squeeze in some light at-home weight training or a run after her sessions, and then she'd eat so much that she'd fall asleep on the sofa, TV forever on in the background, stir awake around 10pm – still uncomfortably full from her binge – and drag herself back up the stairs to repeat the cycle. Having had her last physio session, she no longer had to be afraid they'd put her on the scales or measure her body fat percentage, so she'd stuff her face with everything she had denied herself whilst she was there.

Self-harm with food may have begun as a less unhealthy alternative to cutting, but the more she ate, the fatter she felt and the stronger the urge to remove the accumulating flab with her scalpel became. She knew she had to nip this behaviour in the bud, but in her zombie-like state she struggled to find the meaning of anything. Although, it wasn't as numbing as being on sertraline. Which was how and why Hannah decided she needed to make this new countdown matter. Knowing from previous experience how well she could do under pressure, she was certain that she would be able to rid herself of the excess bodyweight by cutting her calories to around 1100 a day, and being unemployed would allow her to fast for 20 hours every 24 hours for the two weeks up ahead. Her reward would be a celebratory box of wine with Irish, in her new flat. Also, she wouldn't be able to go on a massive food binge whilst he was there, so the work of the two weeks wouldn't be immediately lost over the course of the weekend.

With no job to show up for, Hannah withdrew further and further into her own shell, too embarrassed to explain her situation to anyone who might ask if she bumped into them. She didn't leave the house unless she had an appointment, and she'd started doing her food shops online – although she largely relied on what was left in her freezer and cupboards for sustenance before the move, so all she really needed was fresh fruit and protein. Other than the odd message to Irish, she hadn't made any efforts to touch base with her former colleagues or acquaintances either, so she was surprised when her phone screen suddenly lit up with a message from Kim:

'Hi! How are things? It's been a while since we said we'd do something soon, so I've decided 'soon' has now arrived. LOL'

After the initial shock of the fact that someone from the outside world had attempted to contact her had somewhat subsided, Hannah replied that she was getting ready to move in a couple of weeks – forgetting if she'd told her she'd secured a new flat at all – and that it was probably not the best time to socialise, but Kim didn't give up:

'You're moving?? What's the date? If I'm free I'd love to help!'

Hannah couldn't remember the last time someone had helped her move, and now that Kim had offered, it felt wrong not to take her up on it. But knowing she'd be stressed on the day, Hannah made one final attempt to scare Kim off. She explained that the move would be on a Friday afternoon, so she'd fully expect Kim to be at work, and that she probably wouldn't be in the best of moods navigating a car she wasn't used to during peak time traffic, yet it only took Kim about 20 seconds to reply:

'I'm due an afternoon off to compensate for my overtime. Just name the time and place and I'll be there.'

And that's how Hannah got moving help for the first time since she left her parents' house, the feeling

that this new place was meant for her returning at last.
With the extra pair of hands, her chance of getting
everything sorted before Irish showed up had also
increased.

The following day, Hannah received notice of an
evaluation appointment with the trauma specialists at
her psychiatric hospital. The letter said that if she
passed this "interview", she would be eligible for the
intensive treatment programme for complex PTSD. The
interview was to take place two days before her move-in
date, and it was incredibly important to Hannah that
she got this spot, as she was desperate for some form of
treatment to actually start. She was sick of all the
paperwork and wanted to get on with things so she
could feel like more of a human being than a human-
shaped turd living off the scraps of society. Still, for
Hannah, having to go through an interview where she
had to prove to someone she didn't know or trust that
she was completely fucked in the head wasn't as
enticing as you'd might think. Quite the opposite,
actually. Especially as it meant she would have to go
through weeks of group therapy before being granted
one-on-one sessions. And group therapy had nearly
been the end of her last time she'd tried. So, she was
torn between going along with what the system thought
was appropriate and speaking up, just out of sheer fear
of being left with no treatment at all just because she'd
voiced her opinion. Luckily, she'd have an appointment
with her psychologist the day before and the Tuesday
after, so at least she'd have someone to discuss it with.
Until then, all she needed to do was prepare for her
move and stick with her new routine of sleep, fasting,

working out and eating as little as possible. She was sure she could do it. She had to.

For each day that passed, Hannah felt herself getting increasingly worried about the interview. Especially as her psychologist called in sick on the day of their appointment, and Hannah was left to her own devices. The receptionist had called her early that morning to let her know, so the first thing Hannah did was to try and calm herself the only way she knew how; she went for a run. And when that didn't seem to work, she tried to take a nap, but wound up tossing and turning until she started to feel sick. She still had a few hours left of her fast before she could eat anything and was struggling to find ways to keep herself busy. She didn't have the energy to think of anything, but at the same time she had too much energy to simply sit still, so she went for a walk, all the way down the hill of doom and into the small shopping centre near the station. As she walked through the revolving door, she felt a familiar craving starting to creep up on her, her legs now leading the way straight into the wine shop. How many calories were there in a bottle of the *Slim Zero* sparkling wine again?

With only a four-hour eating window fast approaching, Hannah powerwalked up the hill of doom like a woman possessed, three bottles of low cal fizz under her arm. She figured that, mixed with a bag of frozen mango chunks, she'd be able to stay within her daily calorie budget *and* get some nutrients in her system, not taking into account what she'd already burned off during her morning run, of course.

She popped the cork on the first bottle the second she got through the front door, downing it in long gulps, not even bothering with a glass. The second bottle, she'd mixed with mango chunks and flaxseeds, and halfway into the third one, she blacked out.

Hannah woke up on her sofa in the early hours of the 13th, feeling like utter dogshit. She'd forgotten to drink enough water yesterday, which was very unlike her, and now she was paying the price. Had she been sick? It felt as if someone had glued cottonwool to her teeth and pissed down her throat. She checked her phone for the time and discovered she had to leave for the hospital in just over an hour. Just enough time for Hannah to disinfect herself semi-properly and get rid of some of the boozy odour that was surely escaping through her pores in a cold sweat. One hour and 53 minutes later, she found herself being led into a dark room resembling a police drama interrogation room and told to sit down across from two stern-looking, middle-aged women that introduced themselves as Terri and Fiona, specialists within the field of PTSD and co-heads of the trauma unit at the hospital. Their unsmiling demeanour and aggressive body language made Hannah's hungover self squirm in her seat. She felt as if all of her madness was about to erupt with words spilling out of her like verbal diarrhoea, so when they asked her why she thought she was there and why she'd be a good candidate for the very specific treatment they offered there, the words just came pouring out of her:

'If you were my therapists, I'd probably begin by telling you about how I lost my virginity to a bar of soap. I was four years old. The soap belonged to friends of my parents, and it was their son, three years my senior, who did the deed. I can still feel the sting when I get a waft of yellow bar soap when I've lost my way and wandered too close to my local *Lush* or *Body Shop*. When my screams reached the ears of the adults upstairs, they gave me an earful about how I shouldn't provoke such behaviour. Shouted at me. At me! Again, I vas *four*. He was seven, going on eight. I'd *never* treat a child that way. But I digress. I try not to think about it', she began. 'Sorry, what was the question again?'

In her panic about having to go in for an interview to see if she'd qualify for trauma treatment, Hannah had drunk herself into a right stupor the night before, and somehow, she'd made her filter completely evaporate by letting it marinate in cheap sparkling wine. And this she made the obvious mistake of admitting to the psychiatrists on the board as well, before they'd smell it on her and had the chance to ask. At least you can't say she wasn't proactive in her actions.

'Oh, right. Trauma. Do I have any examples. Erm...there's not just the one recent episode with me, it's repeated traumas over the course of forty fucking years, of which I can recall less and less for each day that arrives, so it's not that easy to pick just the one. Who am I, Johnny bloody Mnemonic?'

They looked at her blankly, clearly missing the movie reference, like a pair of unmoved sociopaths.

'So, what I'm hearing is that you're probably experiencing severe symptoms of OCD to cope with this, right? I've had my bout of OCD when I had my first child, I know it's no picnic.'

'No, actually, that's *not* what I'm saying at all', Hannah retorted, not really shocked that one of the women had turned the focus of the conversation over to herself. Hannah wanted to scream but didn't think they'd be interested in what she had to say anyway, as they both seemed to have made up their minds.

'I've lived with my OCD for as long as I can remember, it's so ingrained in me that it can sometimes be a sort of scaffolding for me in times of not so extreme difficulty. What I am saying is that I need someone to TALK to, because I've got so much bubbling up to the surface at this point that I can't fucking hack it anymore. I'm losing control. So, I need proper therapy, someone who listens to what I've experienced as a child, or what little I can remember, so that I can purge myself of this horrible darkness that's trying to convince me to go back to wanting to kill myself again. Not group therapy, but one on one therapy. But you guys seem to be a prerequisite for me to get through so that I can be taken seriously and advance to the next level or whatever, so here I am. All I want is some help. Can you help me?'

'So, what you're saying is you're suicidal,' Terry, the one with the white lady dreads, said matter-of-factly.

'No, that's the opposite of what I am trying to communicate here', said Hannah, rather angrily, whilst trying to keep her composure. 'What's changed is that I actually *want* to live. Do you know how hard that is when no one else seems to want you to?'

'Regardless', the hippie creature from the black lagoon stated, 'we're not really sure if this place is for you. And there's the drinking problem. We'll have to

reconsider your case and get back to you. It's obviously
not difficult for us to have some empathy for you, but we
have to reevaluate now. Are you drunk still, do you
think?'

'No, I stopped drinking at around eight last night,
so I am not drunk now. I realised that I was self-
sabotaging, so I stopped. But if you feel like I'm not a
right fit for the programme, I'd quite like to know so that
I can start making some plans regarding my next course
of action.'

'Right, let's not use terms we're not really
qualified to use', spat the overgrown flowerchild
sarcastically. 'Like I said, we'll get back to you. It'll be
next week.'

'Thanks' said Hannah. 'I'll be awaiting your call.
Have a lovely rest of your weeks and thanks for taking
the time to see me.'

Hell, she was nothing if not polite, which was
more than she could say for them. They hadn't even
thrown in a courtesy 'nice to meet you' when she first
walked in. Fuck those fucking cunts. She couldn't
believe they've steered the conversation over to their
own mental problems, and then just bulldozed her
every time she tried to say something, because they had
a degree in psychology and she didn't. Also, they didn't
know that she didn't, so why assume? AND she'd
studied psychology as an extracurricular in uni, in
order to better understand her own condition, so FUCK
them. With a rusty strap-on. God, she was so frustrated
that she was almost vibrating. She tried checking the
train times on her phone, but her hands were shaking
so violently she was afraid she'd drop it, and she really

couldn't afford a new phone right now. It was difficult enough to see anyway, because of the tears welling up in her eyes. FUCK!

Luckily, for Hannah, she couldn't drown her sorrows in booze after the session, during which she'd probably spoiled her only shot at some proper treatment of her increasingly cumbersome symptoms. Jointly because she'd already spent far too much money on booze yesterday and because she'd be driving less than 48 hours from now, and she just couldn't risk anything going wrong with the move. So, instead of finding new and inventive ways of ruining her own life, Hannah went home and set about cleaning as much of her flat as possible, with her weight vest on and her playlist set to eleven.

By 4pm, Hannah had scrubbed her hands red raw, and she'd managed to pack every single thing for the move, bar the coffee, clothes and makeup she'd need for the next day – due to her fasting, she wouldn't have to worry too much about food.

The whole process was drawn out because of her constant compulsive rituals, but she somehow got through it. Hannah stood for a while just looking at her life in boxes, for the umpteenth time in the past twenty years. All that remained of hers in the now boxed up living room was her wireless speaker and some sage she'd bought on eBay yonks ago, so Hannah put on a guided meditation episode for new beginnings on her *Spotify* – not really sure if she believed in this new age stuff, but desperately wanting to believe in something – and completed the ritual by smudging the whole house with the foul-smelling, nausea-inducing sage to prevent any negative energy of hers to infect the life of the new tenant in any way.

Hannah had emptied the contents of her fridge and turned everything off and opted for takeaways for her remaining days in the house. Her rent covered the rest of the month in her old house, but she was eager to get out of there and leave the forever tainted furniture behind. She spent her last two nights in her sleeping bag on the sofa, now that there was nothing left for her to do upstairs. She felt like an unwanted guest in her own home, so when Friday finally came, Hannah got up early and went straight to get the hire car, which she packed to the brim to limit the number of trips back and forth. The letting agent had assured her she'd have access to a parking garage for the move after collecting the keys, so all she had to do before she received them was find a space outside the building, where Kim could keep an eye on the car whilst Hannah was getting the keys.

As Hannah navigated the jam-packed hire car through the half-empty shopping centre car park around the corner from her new flat, everything was set up to go off without a hitch. She had arrived with plenty of time left for getting her food shop for the weekend visit done *and* pick up her preordered items from the wine shop – and hide them away from Kim's judgemental gaze in one of the boxes already in the car – before Kim was due to arrive.

Once Hannah had put all of her bags and things in the car, she still had some time left before she was due to meet the agent and wished they'd hurry up. She was nervously jumping up and down, raring to go, when – as if she'd manifested it herself – she received a text from the agent that they had arrived early. Hannah didn't even think twice about leaving the car that contained her entire life – the car park looked pretty safe – so she snapped a quick photo of the car and texted Kim that she was getting the keys and would meet her at the car, 'no rush'. All she had needed was a bit of luck, and she was sure this was the first of many signs that this move signified a turning point in her life, as she jogged around the corner to meet the agent.

Receiving the keys also included a slightly confusing tour of the facilities of the building, including the storage space on the parking level, so Hannah was glad she had arrived early, or this would've easily set her back, but she was still in a great mood when she met up with Kim in the car park half an hour later, yet only ten minutes after their agreed upon time. But at least now she had the keys.

As they slowly drove into the underground car park of her building (or should they have chosen the one on the higher level?), something suddenly dawned on Hannah. She had accounted for everything today, apart from one very important little fact. She was fasting and had yet to eat and hadn't factored in having to deal with people, traffic or unfamiliar vehicles. And especially not a parking garage that was far too narrow and full of other cars for Hannah to feel entirely comfortable navigating. She could literally feel her shoulders coming up around her ears and Kim's incessant chatter starting to grind her gears before they had even found a place to park.

Hannah tried to ignore her own low blood sugar but was already struggling to remember where the entrance to the storage facility was. Her initial plan of action had been to put everything she wouldn't need in storage straight away, but now she couldn't find it, they would have to get everything upstairs. Luckily, there was a lift, so the panic didn't last too long, although Hannah was becoming frustrated with her own inability to remember something she learned not one hour ago. And since she was much stronger than Kim, much due to her own obsessive workout regimen, she made sure she got all the heavy boxes, the guitars, the weights, which seemed to only irk Kim, who had come to help and not just watch Hannah flex. On the bright side, though, Hannah figured this tension would allow them a break from the friendship after this.

By some miracle, the two middle-aged women managed to shift all of Hannah's things up the stairs with time to spare and they were now contemplating whether to make one last trip to the old house to pick up the three items that wouldn't fit in the car, or for Hannah to go to IKEA and pick up the bed that she'd desperately need if she didn't want her and Irish to christen her new floor in the worst possible way. Hannah had of course also neglected to tell Kim about Irish, whose arrival was the real reason they were in a hurry, but she knew how sensitive Kim could get at any mention of relationships, so Hannah didn't want to put her through that. She was however surprised to find that Kim wanted to help her pick up the bed, so they jumped back in the car, only to discover that there was very little wiggle room for them to get back out of the garage, and this was where Hannah started to unravel.

Her blood sugar now dangerously low because of the heavy lifting and general stress; her brain had stopped working. It was keeping her upright, but that was about it. It only allowed for autopilot mode, which most certainly did not include getting a whale-sized vehicle out of a trout-sized exit. They were gonna need a bigger ocean, so to speak.

But Hannah tried. God, how she tried. She drove ten inches forward and eight back for what seemed like an eternity, also noticing that the garage was starting to fill up with other cars returning from a day of work, so time was of the essence. Hannah needed to get her ass out of there ASAP, and so for the final push – trusting the motion and position sensor on the passenger side of the car to let her know if she got too close to the brick wall – she slowly let the brake pedal go, only hear the loud scraping sound of metal being torn apart by brick moments later. SHIT. Hannah's jerk reaction was to back up, which only made matters worse, and so she sped up to exit the garage. Once out, she jumped out of the car and ran back in to survey the damage, which only seemed to have befallen the hire car and not so much the building itself, so since it was a Friday afternoon, Hannah decided to call the appropriate people and fix this on Monday, so not to ruin anyone's weekend, but noticed too late out of the corner of her eye a nosy looking neighbour walking past as the garage door closed behind them and got a distinct feeling this was the kind of person that would *not* wait until a Monday to stir shit up.

But she had no time to worry about that now, she needed to get her bed and to drop poor Kim – who looked as if she'd been scarred for life – off so she could get away from this whole situation.

Although Hannah offered to take her home before heading to IKEA by herself, Kim insisted on coming, so they had a rather awkward drive there, during which Hannah apologised profusely, adding that she hadn't eaten yet that day and was now getting rather dizzy. After that Kim just glared at her and they drove in silence, picked up the bed and had a hotdog each at the gigantic warehouse before driving back in the now pouring rain with the bed. As Hannah said goodbye to Kim, she couldn't help but feel like their relationship was now broken beyond repair, as was probably her first impression with the new neighbours, whom she was discovering were in quite the huff about what had happened in the garage, so Hannah got on the phone to the board (well, she texted them) to do some damage control before it was too late. Then she returned the hire car, sent an insurance claim and poured herself a pint of red wine – of course the glasses were among the first items she'd unpacked – which she knocked back as she assembled her new furniture. Not the best start to her new tenancy.

She did manage to start putting everything together after having a wash in her wonderfully big shower, and she was beginning to feel human again when she received a text from Irish that he would be there in just over an hour, which was enough time for Hannah to dry her hair, put some makeup on and move the worst of her stuff out of the way so they wouldn't have to feel as if they were trapped in a storage unit for the weekend. When Irish finally rang the doorbell – yay, intercom – Hannah was already three sheets to the wind, in a much more welcoming mood than she had been only hours earlier and slowly getting hungry for another banger.

In the short time it took Irish to get to her flat, however, Hannah started feeling deflated, thinking again about the neighbour that had reported her incident to the board, and as Irish came through the door, she found herself uncharacteristically falling into his arms when he offered her a hug. Sensing something was up, he gently asked her what was wrong, and to her own surprise she told him everything.

She was also amazed at how caring he seemed to be and how easily he managed to calm her down just by being there, which made her think that this whole thing might be more than just an old friendship. She even thought this might be a sign that she might finally be ready for a real relationship.

The two of them agreed that the best way forward was to give the leader of the board a call to explain and apologise – that way they could go into their evening without any bad surprises, so Hannah poured Irish a large glass of wine and stepped outside to make the call. And sure enough, she felt a lot better afterwards.

It turned out the whole thing had gotten blown into proportion, and with Hannah's penchant for overanalysing, she'd made herself fret over something that really wasn't that big of a deal. And with that, the two of them descended into a red wine haze that lasted the whole weekend through. They didn't even leave the flat on Saturday, as they had everything they needed, so they spent their weekend drinking, cooking and listening to music, seemingly without a care in the world and with their phones out of reach. Although when the time passed 4pm on Sunday and Irish had made no indication of wanting to leave, Hannah, who was starting to sober up, began to feel more than a little stir-crazy. She couldn't bring herself to ask when he was planning on leaving, as she'd pretty much kicked him out the last time they'd seen each other, but something needed to happen, or she was bound to lose the plot. Or eventually use the bathroom whilst he was still there. She couldn't quite decide which was worse.

Out of the two boxes of red, two bottles of fizz and one bottle of whisky they'd had between them, there was now just a small glass or two left in the last of the boxes, and Hannah knew she couldn't take much more of being this close to another person without an alcoholic refill.

As if he'd been reading her mind, Irish suggested they go for a walk. He knew the area quite well from when he used to live there, so he'd brought his hiking gear with him. Hannah jumped at the chance of venturing outside for some fresh air – and the possible opportunity to release some of the air that had built up inside her by now as well – so they took a tour of the neighbourhood and into the forest nearby.

It was a beautiful, sunny day, so Hannah was a little surprised that they seemed to be the only ones out on a walkabout, forgetting that normal people would probably be gathering around their dining tables for their Sunday roasts around that time. Regardless, they had the forest to themselves and walked around exploring in the warm autumn sun, foraging for mushrooms and berries, all the while retaining their little bubblelike existence, even outside the flat. And, as they approached a clearing next to a little lake, Irish revealed what he'd been carrying in his little rucksack – two beers for each of them. Thus, more merriment ensued. And when they got back from their little adventure, Irish said he'd book a ticket for the midday bus the next day, as he had some work to get back to. And just as Hannah started worrying about having to share her new bed for one more night, he pulled out two backup bottles of wine from the rucksack he'd left at hers – her flat warming gift, he'd said – and the spell lasted the whole night through. Yet when they awoke the next day, neither of them seemed particularly sad it was ending.

Hannah's Monday was spent getting the rest of her shit out of the old house. She was done with that place now and, regardless of the remaining days she'd paid for, she was more than happy to leave the keys in an envelope in the mailbox she'd shared with the landlord, and at the same time ripping the sign with her name on it off it. Three return bus trips later, that chapter of her life was finally behind her.

Tuesday morning, however, Hannah was acutely reminded that there was another chapter of her life that needed some seeing to. It appeared that Kim had spotted the bags of booze among Hannah's mountain of stuff and had made another call to alert the on-call psychiatric service on Friday, who in turn had gotten in touch with her psychologist. The fact that she'd managed to ruin another one of Dr Andrea's weekends by doing something Hannah had specifically asked her not to just highlighted how little respect Kim had for her. Luckily, Hannah had told her psychologist that she was expecting a visit that weekend, so Andrea knew she hadn't been alone and therefore chose to trust her to not commit suicide over a dented hire car. They did however have to discuss Hannah's behaviour in the trauma team interview, and why she'd chosen to sabotage herself in such a way. The plan was still for them to call her to arrange a second interview, so all was not lost.

The week went by with not a word from the trauma unit. You would think that, since they were used to dealing with people that needed a little – or a lot – of coddling, they would keep their word, yet this just proved to Hannah to be another two mental health *un*professionals, who were likely in need of some mental aid themselves. She wasn't surprised, but she was more pissed off than saddened by them breaking their promise to her. After all, why make a promise when you have no intention of keeping it?

Hannah had deep cleaned the flat after Irish left, so she could make her mark on it in her own way. She'd been grateful that he'd been there on that first night when se so desperately needed the distraction, but she was now dead set on making it hers. Especially as he'd managed to somehow stain her sheets with wine, she knew she had to act quickly to avoid it marinating in her mind. She did care for the man, and it would be silly to let a few drops of booze get between them.

Their binge-heavy weekend had however managed to break up Hannah's workout routine and she was struggling to get back into it. And with no hill of doom – or driving commitments – to deter her from going to the wine shop, Hannah found herself putting quite a lot of her savings into stocking her shelves with new boxes of wine. And since it wasn't in her nature to collect anything that might have an expiration date, they didn't last long on those shelves, and she found herself having more than a glass or two most evenings. The chat from Irish mainly referring to good times had whilst imbibing such liquids, it was as if she thought she could hold on to the nice feeling of having someone around and not wanting to kill them by continuing to do what they'd done together.

The sexual innuendos and undertones of Irish's texts was also reason for Hannah to continue drinking – there was no way she could reply in any way that would be considered even slightly flirty before she'd had a drink in her. They'd talked about seeing each other again in about a months' time, so she decided to keep up the charade of herself being a normal person without any intimacy issues.

Whilst she told her psychologist everything about Irish and his better qualities, she'd failed to mention that she was unable to interact with him when she was completely sober. She didn't really know why she hid this, but Dr Andrea seemed excited that she was able to have any sort of interpersonal relationship at all – this was behaviour that was bordering on normalcy – so she kept it to herself.

Hannah did however find that having left her old haunts behind, her fever had become less frequent, and she felt lighter somehow. She still struggled to sleep through the night, but this, too, was improving, as she was able to fall back asleep after waking up at exactly 3:24 every night. When Hannah told her psychologist about this, they said it was likely to do with the fact that something was weighing on her, so Hannah stopped worrying so much about it – she had a lot to process at the moment after all, so it seemed logical that this would be a normal reaction.

After a few weeks at her new place, Hannah had managed to push herself to go running and was slowly but steadily getting back into it. She even sent Irish a few screenshots of her tracked runs, which in turn prompted him to get some exercise in as well. This made her feel like they had something in common, which was nice. She didn't hear a word from Kim, who she had very little in common with, which was even nicer.

As time went on, Hannah started falling into a routine in her new life. She'd been constantly working since she was about 14, so she wasn't used to not having to be somewhere, yet she was slowly starting to embrace it. She was able to get her workouts done in the middle of the day, thus avoiding other, more harmonious, people, and although she'd enjoyed working out during the day back when she'd worked shifts as well, she was now able to go harder and longer, as she didn't have anyone to be accountable to afterwards. This also kept her from gaining too much weight from the excess drinking – although she kept it to the days she was messaging Irish, which wasn't very many days a week.

But she *was* starting to feel like the relationship wasn't real and that she would have to make an effort if she wanted it to continue, so after an afternoon of day drinking on a Thursday in the last full week of October, she'd gotten up the courage to invite herself to go see him over in Ireland. She put on her sexiest underwear (i.e. the only set that was matching and had no obvious wear and tear), sucked in her gut and bent herself into a position that made it look like she had a little bit of cleavage and took a selfie and sent it to him, with the tagline:

'So, when are you making room in your bed for this little number? Xxx'

Despite her tipsiness, she fully expected it to take a while for him to reply – it was normally the case that he would be the one initiating any dialogue between the two. Hannah figured it would be easier for her not to drive him off if everything remained on his terms. Yet, this time it only took a second or two before her phone started buzzing next to her:

'WOWZA'

That was the only thing the first message said, then came a photo of his crotch, exposing a visible bulge, and a long string of messages:

'Look what you've done. Total pb'

'pant bulge'

'lol'

Right, calm yourself, lad, Hannah thought, the many separate messages sent in too quick succession, when he could've just sent one text instead of three, threatening to turn her off forever. She took a big gulp of her wine, trying to recreate her sultriness from before:

'I've been looking at buses. Looks like I can get to yours next weekend. Does Friday to Monday work for you? Wouldn't want that bulge of yours going to waste, would we?'

Hannah almost couldn't believe she was being so forward, but she soon discovered her strategy had worked, when he only minutes later sent her a screenshot of suitable departure times that corresponded with his local bus service, followed by a:

'Maybe I'll come get you at the station so you've got something to hold on to for the last leg of the trip'

Hannah figured he was talking about his penis and not his hand – which would have been slightly more romantic – but didn't take offense. They'd been intimate on enough occasions now for this to be more than appropriate texting behaviour, even though she couldn't remember much from what they'd been up to. All she knew was that she'd woken up with no clothes on, next to a man who seemed to have relieved himself of a few swimmers. Either way, it was enough for her to go ahead and book the coach. It was settled now; she was going on a mini break to see her boyfriend. No, that word didn't sit too well with her. He was nearly 50 fucking years old, for goodness' sake. *Manfriend.* She was going to see her manfriend and it was going to be romantic.

When Hannah told her psychologist she was going to see Irish, she squealed with joy:

'Oh my God, Hannah, I'm so happy for you!'

Having Andrea to talk to made Hannah feel almost like she had a friend she could trust, especially on the few occasions when she reacted like this, and it made her feel more like she should ignore the nagging gut feeling that she was acting a little rash, and that she'd made the right decision to invite herself to go see him. Not to mention the fact that if Dr Andrea had known the whole story, her reaction would probably have been quite different. But Hannah wanted to feel like she was more than just a mental patient, so she spun this yarn of herself being in a plot similar to the many, many budget romcoms she'd watched over the years, pretending that that was what she wanted. At least for now.

Chapter 12: November – The familiar call of the abyss

By the time the week of her big weekend away was well underway, Hannah still hadn't heard anything from the trauma unit regarding a second interview, so she mentioned it again to Andrea during their appointment, to see if she'd heard anything. They finally called her, likely upon Andrea's request, when she was getting ready to catch the coach on the Friday morning, to tell her there wouldn't be any second interview, as they thought she'd be better off getting treatment for her OCD whilst her psychologist continued to diagnose her properly. Even though this was the response she'd been hoping for, reluctant as she was to see these two so-called specialists again, she was a little perturbed by the fact that they hadn't shown her – or indeed Dr Andrea – the compassion or respect to let her know sooner. They had known all along how anxious she was, and that her anxiety only exacerbated her OCD symptoms – hell, they'd suggested themselves that her anxiety symptoms should be treated first – so Hannah felt like this further emphasised their incompetency as mental health professionals. Whether they liked her or not really shouldn't impact their decision or their behaviour towards her. It made her feel, again, like a non-desirable candidate, not worthy of their empathy. But she didn't have time to think about this now. She was leaving her reality behind for a few days, in favour of a much-needed sex holiday.

Having dubbed herself a sex tourist in conversations with MJ, Hannah had decided she was adopting a carefree mindset for the next few days. Although, it was quite difficult to reinvent yourself in a matter of hours, so she had a bottle of prosecco as a mid-morning snack before boarding the coach – timing it so it wouldn't kick in until she was safely in her seat – and stuffing her face with mints so she would be allowed to board without the driver noticing the alcohol on her breath.

Hannah had always turned to this trick if she knew she was going to drink and wouldn't be able to eat much, fearing she would look or feel fat. She had found that if she had a beer (or similar) super quickly and then waited at least six hours until she had her next drink, she wouldn't get blackout drunk. Another falsifiable theory, which had proven correct on all previous occasions. Although, you could argue that nothing outside of Hannah's comfort zone, such as sex or other types of real intimacy, had been required of her on those other occasions and that it was in fact Hannah's subconscious that had made her black out when she'd found herself in situations she wasn't equipped to handle and not necessarily the alcohol consumed that was the reason for the blackouts. Either way, today was not a day for introspection. So, as Hannah poured herself into her seat – music blaring through her headphones – she fought her brain down to her last second of awareness before she drifted off to sleep.

Hannah woke up in complete darkness, not really knowing where or who she was, when the coach was still on the ferry between Holyhead and Dublin. She was desperate for a pee, realising she wouldn't be able to hold it for much longer. She knew she would have to find another excuse to use the facilities between the ferry terminal and the bus terminus if she did use the toilet now – never forgetting about the rule of two – but this had to happen before her bladder burst.

To her dismay, Hannah also found that her bottle of prosecco had worn off completely during her little nap, and she was now starting to regret her decision to take this trip in the first place. Maybe she'd have time to grab a pint near the coach station before Irish got there?

Hannah found her sudden nervousness quite helpful in terms of scheduling in another trip to the loo, but rather a bit too helpful now, as she was afraid she would need another one before they docked at the station. She'd never taken this journey before, so she didn't know it well enough to account for time or distance. She decided she'd be better off remaining in her seat, but as they pulled into the terminus and she saw Irish standing at the bay, waiting, she wished she'd gone after all – or better yet, stayed at home. But she got her rucksack out of the overhead compartment and slowly walked down the stairs and out onto the platform, where Irish very publicly embraced her, for far too long for what she felt was appropriate, and planted a sloppy, wet and messy kiss on her, making her feel as if he was trying to devour her. She had no idea if either of them would survive the next leg of the journey should this behaviour continue, so she pulled away apologetically, saying they'd better hurry if they wanted to make their connection in time.

It seemed Irish had forgotten to tell Hannah that they had to change buses again at the city centre, but the silver lining, as Hannah was soon to discover, was that they missed it by two minutes and had to wait for the next one, which wasn't due until an hour later, so they had time to grab a drink or two in a pub around the corner while they waited.

This was exactly what Hannah needed to keep her wits about her, so she happily followed Irish to the warm, cosy pub nearby. He told her he'd never been there before, which at first gave her the impression that he maybe didn't want to be seen with her, but he added that he'd come across it when he had been looking for nice places to show her when she was there. Right now, she couldn't care less about his lack of intentions – all she wanted was something to take the edge off this awkward reunion, and fast.

Hannah was delighted to see that they had a very strong pumpkin flavoured IPA on tap, of which she ordered two while Irish looked for a place for them to sit. Or was he using it as an excuse for her to pay? Hannah didn't really care and decided to ignore the yellow flags that have started popping up in the back of her mind, like weeds in an already overgrown garden.

Irish came up emptyhanded in his search for a table, so they found seats at the bar. Hannah had already taken a pretty big swig of her drink and was finally starting to feel calm enough to start taking in her surroundings. It soon became clear that this was no ordinary station *Spoons*. It was lovely and warm, with a large fireplace at the heart of the room, surrounded by groups of chairs and red Chesterfield sofas around chunky wooden tables, the seats filled with smiling people that were chatting, laughing and relaxing with a drink or two after a long work week. The warm ambiance stood in stark contrast to the grey cold of the late autumn evening outside and had the pub's large bay windows that looked onto a busy street fog up with condensation, making the outside world seem very far away.

Seeing as they had both downed their drinks pretty quickly and were already sat almost on top of the till, Hannah ordered them another round of ale for the road, now almost numb enough for her to not mind the fact that Irish's hand was resting a little too high up on her left thigh.

The little pub was almost like a time capsule in that it was difficult to tell what time it was with the windows all fogged up, so when Irish checked his phone, he discovered that their bus was due in ten minutes. They necked the rest of their drinks and ran for the door. Hannah looked back at the lovely venue one last time just before the heavy wooden door slammed shut behind them and noticed a sign in the hallway pointing to conference rooms and a reception desk – it was a hotel bar… that's why he'd taken her there. No locals would ever go to a hotel bar, at least not where she was from.

Hannah knew she was being silly and that it was the four years of dating a married man, during which they'd constantly had to hide their misplaced affections, that was haunting her. At least this time, she knew they were both single and that he had probably chosen this pub because of its proximity to the station, and likely also due to his perverse obsession with history, as she could also remember there being a plaque of some kind on the bar, celebrating the pub's history as a meeting place for Irish members of the British army during the first world war. Or something like that. Hannah didn't

care much for history and even less for war. She
certainly didn't see it as any cause for celebration.
Regardless, she had to knock this ridiculous suspicion
before it took her over. Why had she spent all that
money on the return trip if she wasn't going to use it as
a nice break from her current everyday life of constantly
analysing her own self?

Their second leg of the journey was decidedly
longer than the first, albeit much easier to endure than
the first now that Hannah had had some miracle juice
shot into her. It didn't even bother her that Irish kept
insisting on holding her hand for the duration of the 40-
minute journey. It was dark out, no lights on in the bus,
so no one could really see, and no one there had the
faintest clue who she was. She could have gone without
him pulling her only free hand towards his little "pb"
every five minutes, but hey. Clearly the alcohol had
done something to loosen him up as well. Not that he
needed any loosening, but hey.

It had started to snow outside, so Hannah was
glad that they only had a short walk left when they got
off the bus, or so Irish had told her. Despite the fact that
it was very dark outside, and they were out in the
boonies with not a streetlamp in sight, he insisted they
take the scenic route. 25 freezing minutes later, he
announced that they were approaching his street –
proudly proclaiming it the last street before the paved
road ended and the forest road started – and Hannah
had lost the feeling in her extremities and some of her
newfound will to live.

As Irish opened the door to his upstairs half of a
semi, Hannah tried to make out her surroundings, but it
was too dark for her to really see anything. While

Hannah started untying the laces of her boots, Irish went through to the living room and started lighting candles all around the room, giving it a welcoming glow. It was still pretty cold inside as well, though, so Hannah didn't really feel like removing any clothing, but thought it might be considered rude if she didn't, so she bit the bullet and took her woolly hat and coat off, casually laying them on top of her rucksack. Her phone desperately needed a charge, but as the signal was pretty bad, she decided to switch it off instead and put it away before she joined Irish in the living room, where he was already pouring red wine into the two glasses that were set out on the coffee table:

'Wine?' he asked, holding a large glass out to her.

'Don't mind if I do', she replied as she took the glass and had a big, long swig of the wine, feeling the warmth of the alcohol hitting her empty stomach and slowly starting to spread through her body, making her limbs come alive again.

Irish excused himself to go get dinner started, so Hannah got a chance to have a look around the flat. It was like a teenage hair metal fan's bedroom – every inch of the walls was covered in band posters and there were dirty socks on the floor. The large U-shaped sofa had clearly just been hoovered – a gesture Hannah appreciated – but it didn't keep her from noticing that the floor underneath it hadn't gotten the same treatment. Hannah stopped her little tour and sat down on the semi-clean sofa, desperately sipping her wine as if it would make the dirt go away. Luckily, Irish poked his head through the door just then and found Hannah's glass almost empty and topped her up before she had a

chance to stop him. Not that that would have happened
in this scenario anyway, but let's just appreciate the
chivalry for now.

Hannah got two more top-ups before dinner was
served, and her mood had lifted considerably. She was
no longer hung up on the cleanliness of this mancave-
cum-80s lounge but was rather surprised to see that
Irish had a lot of plants around the house. If it hadn't
been so filthy and poster infested, she would have
almost thought that a female was living there as well,
based on the number of ornate candle sticks and
greenery alone.

After what had felt like an eternity, Irish finally
called on her to join him in the kitchen, where the
dining table was set for them with an abundance of lit
candles and a box of wine at the ready. The food
smelled like, well, food. The four large glasses of wine
had all but melted Hannah's inhibitions (or finesse)
away, and she thought that dinner was absolutely
delicious – whatever it was. Dead animal of some kind?
Sauce? She had no clue. It looked like food, and she was
ravenous. She didn't even miss her mouth once *and* she
managed to get through another two glasses of wine
with dinner, which she agreed with herself when she
went to the toilet after had been a great success.

They then retreated to the living room, where
they went through his record collection, spinning some
choice 80s bangers whilst downing some more of that
fermented unicorn piss that seemed to make her forget
all about the shittiness of life. And that's about all that
she could remember from the night when she woke up
in Irish's bed the next morning, throat dry and Donald
Ducking it in all of her glory, lying on top of the duvet,

Irish's nose pressed, too close, into her neck. It was impossible to tell what time it was, as the light coming in through the window was a hazy grey.

Hannah winced involuntarily, which stirred Irish awake. Without a word, he began touching her and breathing heavily into her neck, his fingers making their way downwards from her waist until they found a more permanent home a little south from there. He then pulled the duvet loose from under her to cover them both, his head escaping under it to relieve his hand of the work it had started.

Fuck this, Hannah thought and pretended to be asleep, trying to casually roll away from his burrowing head. She absolutely detested it when people insisted on going down on her, and when it became clear that he didn't think she was sleeping and showed no intention of stopping, she tried pushing his head away, saying she didn't think it was going to work, as she had never got off that way. She thought this would be the most polite way of saying 'no' without actually uttering the words, but apparently this "challenge" she'd now presented him with made him even more set on succeeding at what no man had done before him – which, for the record, was completely untrue, but no one believed her when she said she didn't *like* it – and stopped what he was doing for long enough to exclaim:

'I'm really good at this so you've probably never had a proper seeing to. I'll show you how it's done!'

Hannah struggled to stop herself from squirming. His intentions were obviously good, but she really didn't want this, and the sounds coming from down there made her picture images of a pig hunting for truffles. She could feel the bile rising in her throat, but he made no sign of stopping, so she tried to conjure up some fantasies to make this go by quickly so she wouldn't have to suffer through it for much longer. God, how she hated this – it made her feel absolutely disgusting, and as if he'd read her mind, he decided he was going to put his hands to work as well, spitting on her vulva and his fingers to help with the dryness caused by the act she hated. *Nothing better or sexier than being spat on, I guess?!* Hannah thought to herself. She supposed she had the porn industry to thank for that, as it wasn't the first time someone had dubbed it appropriate to put their saliva coated fingers inside of her.

'69! Let's 69!' Irish groaned from between her legs.

What the actual fuck. What's even more disgusting than cunnilingus? Receiving it whilst having your nose penetrating someone's sphincter and at the same time you're struggling to breathe because your mouth is full of hairy onions. Just no.

But then a thought hit her – she could try something to make sure they wouldn't find themselves in that situation again.

'OK. Let's', Hannah said dryly. And after positioning herself just right she took a deep breath and plunged two fingers deep into Irish's arsehole.

'Hnnnnghhhh! Wow! God, yes, fuck me in the ass like you did that first time!' Irish moaned into her fanny.

Pardon??

Clearly, this hadn't been the way to go after all. She'd done it before as well? She had no recollection of that. Crikey... she was running out of ways to stop this and saw no other way out than faking an orgasm. But not until she'd jammed another finger up there to inflict just a little bit of pain to deter him from asking her to 69 ever again. Unfortunately, this just caused him to relieve himself of a bit of methane, so now Hannah was stuck in what could only be described as a makeshift gas chamber.

Struck instantly by the guilt of ridiculing the struggles survived by her great grandparents, Hannah felt even more disgusted, but now also by her own dark, twisted sense of humour.

She wasn't too keen on looking Irish in the eye after this, but her faux moaning and trembling had finally stopped the activity in her downstairs region and she could hear by the sound of Irish's heavy breathing that he was eager to finish himself off, so Hannah expertly plopped herself onto her stomach for him to have easy access from behind.

Good God, make it stop!

And with a loud groan, it did. Disgusted and exhausted – desperate to wash her hands with acid – Hannah rolled back onto her backside as Irish fell onto his beside her. Both finding themselves at a loss for words, although probably for very different reasons, they fell back asleep.

The next time Hannah woke up, it was already getting dark outside, which meant it must be near 4pm. Irish was still fast asleep and snoring beside her, so Hannah grabbed her underwear from the floor and headed for the bathroom to cleanse herself of the sins committed hours before.

Safely behind the locked door of the bathroom, she stared at her haggard reflection in the mirror, grateful for Irish's inability to turn on any electric lights in the house. If only he could have turned the heating on, though, she thought, as she washed her face with the icy cold water that flowed out of the tap, despite the fact that she had twisted the red knob and not the blue. But times were hard, so she didn't blame him for wanting to save money on electricity. And she was a guest in his home – there was no way she was about to start making any unsolicited demands.

When she got back to the bedroom, now fully clothed, Irish had finally woken up as well. Seemingly content with his own existence, he got up to put the kettle on and make them some eggs for "breakfast".

Hannah sat awkwardly at the table, magic flushed from her system with the last of the alcohol, picking at her food whilst Irish was chatting happily next to her, all the while stuffing his face with new mouthfuls without stopping his chatter. Hannah really didn't want to take any dislike to him because of such pettiness as not standing that he was talking with his mouth full, so she was quietly praying he'd crack open a bottle of booze before the urge to run away got the best of her. Seeing as her plate was still half-full when he'd finished his meal, he excused himself to go grab a shower. Hannah, who was starving, jumped at the chance to finish her food in peace and without gagging from the wet noise of Irish's loud smacking.

He emerged from the bathroom topless and in a good mood:

'All of our fucking certainly made me hungry!' he belted. 'But now I could really go for some of that wine. It's the weekend after all', he added.

Hannah couldn't believe her prayer had worked.

Another evening of drinking ensued much like the previous night, but this time, Hannah was able to remember when she'd gone to bed when she woke up around 9am the next day. She went to the bathroom to put some fresh makeup on before Irish woke up and went back to bed, where she laid awake for hours contemplating her own existence before he made any indication of being alive other than the occasional fart and snore. She felt like it would be rude to get up and wander around his flat when he was unconscious in the next room, but as the time went on, she began feeling ridiculous, so she got up to find her phone and charger. She'd need her phone for the trip tomorrow.

Irish came stumbling out of the bedroom at around 2pm, seeming not too pleased to find Hannah sitting on the edge of the sofa instead of lying next to him and his morning wood. Or maybe "afternoon" wood would be a more appropriate term in his case.

Despite his initial annoyance, he went about business much like the day before, but after breakfast he took her on a little tour of the now snow-covered neighbourhood. It really was quite picturesque. There was a little church perched on top of the only hill in the area, with small wooden houses scattered around it, with a little shopping centre and a petrol station at the very edge of the little village. Following another path than they had when she arrived on Friday, they had made it to the bus stop in less than fifteen minutes, which was a relief. They went into a shop in the town centre to pick up some bits and bobs they needed for dinner and then walked back to his the long way around, although this time Hannah didn't mind.

Covered in a layer of clean white snow, the landscape seemed much less harsh and intimidating, and it was nice to get a few steps in. Before long, they were soon sat on the sofa with a beer each, trying to figure out the best way of getting Hannah safely to the coach station the next day.

They'd had a bit of wine with dinner, but certainly not a box between them, which made Hannah think that they didn't really need alcohol to enjoy each other's company. It was rather lovely sitting in his kitchen, eating by candlelight. After dinner, they watched a movie and had a few more glasses of wine before they went to bed.

When Hannah awoke bright and early the next morning, she was almost sad to be leaving and rushed to the bathroom to put her face on before Irish woke up. Back in the warmth of the bed a few hours later, Irish and his little friend both woke up and paid a visit to Hannah's nether regions – without spitting on her too much this time. Which was more than what she could have asked for, really.

When the time came for her to leave, Irish took the bus into the city with her and even kissed her goodbye before she got on her coach, in public in bright daylight, making her think that maybe this was a sort of relationship she could keep alive for a while. With a bit of a geographical distance between them, there would always be the element of going away on holiday, which was a sort of magic Hannah couldn't quite get enough of, so when Irish texted her an hour or so later if she wanted to come back in two weeks' time, she didn't hesitate to say yes.

Back home less than six hours later, Hannah decided to get on better terms with her own body. She was sick of alcohol and made a promise to herself not to indulge until the next time she saw Irish. Hell, maybe they could go a weekend without booze? She called MJ to tell her about her weekend away, not mentioning the bit about the not so accidental rectal fingering of course, and they agreed it was probably good for her to go away for a few days instead of barricading herself in her new flat, however lovely it was.

The first week without alcohol went by in a flash, and by Sunday, Hannah could already notice a positive difference in her appearance; she looked far less haggard, and her waist was coming back now she wasn't so bloated all the time. She took a photo and sent it to Irish, who replied with a thumbs up and an aubergine emoji, at which Hannah just laughed. She felt like she was finally back to the old workout and nutrition regimen she'd followed when she'd gotten herself into shape during the pandemic, and she was ready to prove to herself that she was mistress of her own physique.

Hannah did find herself messaging Irish less and less for each day she went without alcohol, though, and she soon realised she could do without the outside validation. Her own opinion and acknowledgement was what truly mattered to her.

During the pandemic, Hannah had become rather active as a somewhat successful fitness inspirator on social media, but part of what had made her stop posting her wins and highs was when many of her followers had started relying on her to push them. If she didn't post about her Sunday half, people would message her saying they needed her to motivate them. What had once been something fun for her became a task. She hadn't thought anyone would follow her, and she had certainly not started posting content to become an influencer, but she had been happy to know that she had inspired a few folks to get up off their couch and start exercising, but she wasn't in any way licensed to give advice, nor did she have the mental capacity to look after others and help them pick themselves up every time they relapsed in their sobriety or failed to run a sub 60 10k. The unwanted attention had sucked all the joy of accomplishing something out of it.

In hindsight she probably would have been better off putting her accomplishments in a scrapbook instead of resorting to such narcissistic behaviour in the first place, but it was a bit too late for that now.

Either way, she was getting excited about showing off her "new" self to Irish, knowing what another week of clean living could do for her self-confidence. Even her therapist noticed she was looking healthier and for once Hannah took the compliment. Who knew, maybe Irish and her would have a teetotal weekend? He'd mentioned he wanted to show her his gym during her next visit, so she could keep up with her routine while she was there, adding that he knew how important it was to her. So, it was a very hopeful Hannah that boarded the coach less than 14 days after her first trip across the Irish Sea. As she knew which buses to get this time, they'd agreed for them to meet at the village bus station this time. There was only one thing that worried her; surely, he wouldn't want her to 69 again? There was no way she would be able to do that sober.

As her buses were on time this time, she was able to get the express connection from the terminal, shaving a whole 30 minutes off her journey, and as the bus pulled into the village, she could see Irish waiting for her already. It had been raining heavily for the past couple of days, though, so the landscape looked a little worse for wear than what it had done when covered in an insulating blanket of white. But Hannah told herself it didn't matter. The sun had already set for the day anyway. If it stopped raining tomorrow, maybe they could venture outside for a jog.

Irish chatted away all the way through the walk up to his, excited about some breakthrough in his best mate's hospital treatment. Hannah was of course happy for them both, but as she couldn't get a word in edgewise, she had yet to solve the mystery of who this "best mate" was. But they had apparently been one of the reasons why Irish had moved back here, so they must be important to him.

In the same breath as he was first talking about his mate, he now changed the topic to that of his parents, who apparently lived in the next village over.

Did he want her to meet them since he was bringing up the fact that they were at home this weekend? She'd thought about it, of course, but she'd discarded it as being far too soon in their now non-platonic relationship to even contemplate.

As they walked through the door of his flat, the familiar yet nondescript smell of his cooking hit her nostrils. Having fasted all day, though, she didn't mind the aftertaste the smell left in the back of her throat. Not that a smell should have a taste at all, but it was pungent enough. They sat down to eat almost immediately, and when Irish offered her a glass of wine, she decided that just the one wouldn't hurt. Of course, he kept topping her up like he'd done before, seemingly forgetting all about her much talked about sobriety and the positive effect it had had on her, but she didn't stop him. So, by the time they'd finished their meal, she was a little tipsy. Enough so that she was able to ignore the smells she hadn't noticed last time, and the dust and messiness that she had.

They moved into the living room, where Hannah started feeling the weight of the journey and the effects of the alcohol – it was almost strange how much her tolerance had dropped in just two weeks. Before long, she was fast asleep on the sofa, where she woke up alone in the middle of the night. She moved into the bedroom to join Irish, but not without noticing that he'd continued the "party" without her.

Her presence in the bed woke Irish up enough for him to draw her into a seemingly endless penetrative session, of which she wished she had remembered very little – although she had more than tolerated it in her half-drunken state the previous night. It must have been going on for hours, because she felt herself falling in and out of sleep a handful of times during the whole session. There was also the fact that he proudly brought up at their 1pm "breakfast", that they had been at it for *four* hours.

Hannah felt a little grossed out, but she put it down to resentment towards herself for falling so easily back into the drinking again, yet there was something else that just didn't feel *right*. She just couldn't put her finger on it. Or she didn't want to.

They'd decided to take advantage of a let-up in the rain after breakfast – in fact, it was a rather splendid looking afternoon, sunny enough for them to take the bikes out – but not until Hannah had visited the little girls' room, a room she had not till now seen in daylight.

As soon as she'd sat down on the cold plastic seat, she wished she hadn't, because this was when she noticed the flies. The many, many flies on the many brown and decomposing potted plants that were strewn across every shelf in there. It appeared she'd found Irish's greenhouse. She noticed some of them had tags on them: ghost pepper chilli, tomato, courgette, all of which she knew he'd used in his cooking.

She'd been eating toilet *vegetables this whole time?*

Hannah felt a little sick but did her business and got up to wash her hands, only she made the mistake of looking into the bowl before putting the lid down – it was stained with dried pieces of faeces. She felt herself gagging. She needed air. Hell, she needed to clean, but there was no toilet brush next to this particular porcelain throne that should not be.

She tried to tell herself she was overreacting. He had probably had an accident and not had the time to hide the evidence. Right? She slapped on a smile and walked out of there, glad to see he was already waiting for her by the door before she had the chance to start asking herself why he had two bikes as well.

With the midday sun beaming down on them, it became unseasonably warm and a lot easier to focus on the open road ahead and not the dirty flat that made the Fritzl household cellar look like a 4-star hotel. As Irish took on the role as area specialist and tour guide, pointing out his childhood haunts and historical landmarks as they went, Hannah was quite enjoying the ride. They even stopped next to a beautiful old cemetery, where they sat down and shared one of the beers Hannah had brought over from last time, that Irish had put in his little rucksack for their cycling tour. Hannah got the distinct feeling, once again, that they were in their own little bubble. It was nice.

As they got up to leave, though, Irish got a phone call. It soon became clear that his mother was on the other end, and as he walked out of earshot of Hannah to continue his conversation, the last thing she heard before he was too far away was that she 'shouldn't come over this weekend', as he wasn't going to be there. Needless to say, Hannah didn't like this one bit, as she now got the distinct feeling she was being kept a secret again. She didn't give two shits about meeting the parents – it was far too soon anyway – it was the lying that bothered her. She was being kept secret, hidden, *again*. When he'd finished chatting to his mum, they got back on their bikes and cycled back in silence.

On their way back, they stopped at a supermarket to pick up some stuff Irish needed for dinner, including some more wine, but when it came time for them to pay, he just walked past Hannah to start putting everything in bags, leaving her to sort the payment. It was only dumb luck that she'd brought her debit card at all, but she simply swiped it without saying anything.

It was starting to get dark again now, and as they cycled up past the church and down the last hill, Irish's phone rang again. He didn't pick it up that time, but waited instead until they got back and he'd sat Hannah down with a whisky to warm her up. Not looking down at the no doubt filthy glass, she downed her drink in two long gulps whilst listening in on his conversation. It appeared to be a child he was speaking to this time, and Hannah didn't know what to make of that. She knew that his sister didn't have kids, nor did he, so who could this have been? She got another uneasy feeling but decided not to investigate any further. If he wanted to tell her, fine. If not, she'd be out of there soon enough and no one could make her go back.

When Irish returned from his conversation, he handed Hannah another of her beers and explained that it had been his best mate on the phone and that this "best mate" was a thirteen-year-old boy with severe learning difficulties, that he took care of when his mum was too overwhelmed with work during the week. Hannah thought it was a bit odd that he hadn't mentioned this before, but thought that him being a carer sort of made sense in the way he'd treated her when she'd had her anxiety attack just over a month ago. She still thought it was weird that a 47-year-old man was best friends with a teenager, but maybe he didn't put as much emphasis on the term best mate as she did. Regardless, it was none of her business and the whiskey and beer was beginning to kick in.

They had beer with dinner as well, which didn't have the same effect on Hannah that wine did, so instead of getting tired and/or mega horny, she found herself becoming more inquisitive and even argumentative with each sip. She did manage to keep a lid on her innermost thoughts for the most part, though, so they made it through the meal without any casualties. Although, after dinner, Irish asked her to do the washing up, which by the look of things was the washing up for the entire week, and Hannah could feel her inner slugger squirming to get out. But she did the housework, in part so she would have an actual clean glass to drink out of by the end of it.

It became clear that Irish had another night of debauchery in mind, as he'd set up the living room with an array of wine, beer and spirits, snacks and a selection of albums for them to listen to, but Hannah had almost had her fill of alcohol and didn't really feel like another party. Why waste so many calories on something she was bound to forget if she kept drinking?

Yet, they listened to a few albums before Irish started sensing her disinterest and suggested they watch a movie instead, so they put on an old action movie and Hannah fell asleep within the first 20 minutes. But when she woke up to him watching some fascist supporting conspiracy theory bullshit a few hours later, she completely lost her ability to hold her tongue:

'What the *fuck* are you watching? You don't condone this propaganda, do you?' Hannah hissed, with venom in her voice.

'You've gotta admit this is pretty funny', Irish laughed. 'And you have to wonder where it all comes from. They've good a good point'.

Hannah didn't know what to think. She'd let this person, this filthy, disgusting, best friends with a child, manchild *inside* of her. She felt sick and suddenly feverish.

'I need to go to bed. I don't feel well', she muttered and got up on unsteady legs and went to lie down in the bedroom, where she fell asleep pretty quickly. She woke a few hours later with him panting next to her, but this time she pushed him away.

'What's wrong? Did I do something? I can feel like something's changed'.

To be fair, Irish was giving her a pretty easy out here, but she couldn't handle it right now. She wanted to take the out, but it was impossible for her. There was no bus out of there until Monday morning, so she'd have nowhere to go for the next 24 hours. She *had* to pretend everything was fine. But she did feel like she was getting a fever, so she played the illness card.

'I'm really sorry', she whispered, 'I feel like I might be coming down with something and I don't feel very well'.

And then she fell back asleep. When she woke
up again it was dark, and she had no idea how long
she'd slept. Irish was no longer in the bed next to her, so
she got up to use the bathroom and she heard him
stirring as she passed the kitchen on the way there. She
noticed they were almost out of toilet paper, so she used
as little as possible. What grown man has a woman over
and doesn't get extra bog roll? Either way, she quickly
washed her hands and face – neglecting to top up her
now ruined makeup – and let herself out of the
bathroom and into the kitchen.

'So, I think I'm gonna take the 9am bus
tomorrow morning', she started.
'Yeah, I think that should probably work best for
me as well. I've got work to do', he replied.

*What work? She hadn't seen a computer or
tablet in his house since she'd been there and there
were no offices in the village, outside of maybe the
library next to the bus station. She didn't care. All she
wanted to do now was to go home to her lovely,* clean
flat.

They had some leftovers for dinner, and Irish had
a few of the beers that Hannah had brought. She didn't
touch a drop, saying she wasn't feeling great. She
offered to sleep on the sofa that night, but he wanted to
watch a movie if she was 'just going to sleep anyway'.
Hannah began to think that maybe he did have a lot in
common with a teenager after all. She held her tongue,
though, and went to bed, but she couldn't sleep.

After having forced constipation on herself in fear of Irish not liking her if he discovered she had actual bowel movements, she had thought she'd remain in this state until she'd at least crossed the border, but she could feel a turtle head starting to poke out. *Shit.* She opened the bedroom door slightly to see Irish fast asleep on the sofa, and with the coast clear, she tip-toed towards the bathroom not making a sound and let herself in to lower her overfilled behind onto the cold, cold toilet seat. The birth was well underway when she noticed: there was no more toilet paper. FUCK.

By some miracle, the drop had consisted of a very long, hard and solid piece of stool that had snaked its way out of her – more or less devoid of sound – and into the toilet, so there was no mess to clean off or wash away, and a clean break at that, but she felt dirty as she bid it farewell with a double flush. The alcohol must have been what had kept it in there for so long, she reasoned.

Regardless, she took her filthy self back to the bed after washing her hands and fell back asleep for another few hours. She awoke again to see Irish having turned in as well, so she got up and moved herself to the sofa, where she spent the few remaining hours of her stay in a staring contest with a spider that had taken residence on a spot on the ceiling directly over her head. She got up and began to get her stuff ready for the trek to the station at about 7.30, careful not to wake Irish before she absolutely had to. About ten minutes before she had to be out the door, she woke him up to tell him she was leaving.

He opened his left eye to look at her and said that he could feel that she was being weird. Again, she blamed it on feeling a bit fluey. Despite the fact that she wasn't feeling well, though, he was clearly done with being a gentleman and didn't offer to walk her to the bus. Which was of course fine, they'd never make it there in time if he had, so Hannah simply let herself out with an:

'Oh, by the way, you're out of toilet paper'.

As she turned the corner, she knew in her heart that she would never return here again.

Finally on the bus, leaving the village in a cloud of dust behind her, snowflakes starting to fall gently from the sky and Hannah left to her own devices, she started to reflect on her love life. Or rather her understanding of the concept of love. Of the emotions she felt but had no words for or any way of recognising by something other than patterns of her past, but also on her unflinching ability to cut ties by the drop of a hat once she'd had her fill. She knew from experience – but mainly observing others – that falling in love and making a relationship work could be hard, but for her maybe even more so, as she didn't know what it would feel like to be loved in return. And, when someone falls in love with you and you're incapable of recognising the signs, you might just find yourself trapped in a situation it can be very difficult to get yourself out of.

Hannah begun to think that maybe this "love" business just wasn't for her. Not that she was confusing her most recent experience with love. That's definitely not what this had been. But still.

Sure, she could see how love might work for other people, but she had never once had anyone tell her they loved her when she'd needed it as a child, so she had always sort of looked at other people's love for one another as something utopian – the fact that she hadn't become a serial killer (or worse) should come as a rather lovely and surprising bonus. Also, if she had to get drunk to convince herself that she was capable of such emotions, it was pretty clear to her that she had gotten the wrong end of the stick somehow.

This time, she'd gone into it knowing that she wasn't in love with the person, but it was far too easy to let yourself get lost in something when you already harbour feelings of love for someone, platonic as they may have been. But this kind of "love" very quickly turned to hate or resentment in Hannah's case, once she realised that she had played a dirty trick on herself, meaning she couldn't trust herself not to go behind her own back and fuck things up, and to protect herself from her own wrath, she'd let her self get caught up in trivialities and minor details to make her despise someone and get out of a potentially bad situation before the other person had the chance to suggest they call it quits first. It was as if – like with so many other situations in her life – every relationship she embarked on was a race. But every race has a finish line, and you can't start a relationship with good intentions if you think it's going to end before it's even begun. She *knew* this.

So, why had she denied herself of love on the one occasion in her life she had been presented with the prospect? She'd rather not think about that, and she'd been able to avoid thinking about it for almost ten years now. But if she was going to get past this, she had to confront her own fear. She was afraid she wouldn't be enough and that she'd be the one that would be left behind by her true love. She knew he was out there, because she'd already met him. She just didn't have the guts to believe that he would be able to handle her when things got tough. Because of her issues, her evasiveness, her constant need to please and not let people see her human side. She'd become this way because she had been treated like shit for so long that she'd started craving it, and to some extent sought it out. Well, not 'to some extent', more like in any way possible. But it wasn't fair of her to hold on to that mindset anymore, when she had the choice to leave her past behind. Learn from it, yes, but also forgive the people who hurt her, forgive herself for wallowing and prolonging the hurt and to get the fuck on.

What was it that she was constantly telling herself and others? At the end of the day, the only person that *has* to live with you is *you*. The one person you can rely on. So, you'd better start treating that someone with compassion and respect if you want to feel like you're worthy of positive changes in your life. Words to live by, right? Too bad it's so fucking hard to do so. But, as Hannah was starting to realise, life wasn't a race. Like relationships, it was a journey, with all of the dead ends and knockbacks and hills of doom that were so often part of it. But, without the bumps in the road, all the shit days and the sorrow, the impact of the truly joyous occasions, the wins and the laughs wouldn't matter.

She was slowly coming to terms with the fact that she really was mistress of her own reality. And, with that, her phone rang. It was her mum, of all people. They'd had a deal for some time now, that she wouldn't ring her unless it was important. Hannah hated talking on the phone, and her mother had the unique ability to rub her the wrongest way possible by saying something to hurt Hannah, whereupon Hannah would say something she'd regret, too, making her mum upset and then in turn leaving Hannah with so much guilt she would have to find oftentimes unhealthy outlets to deal with the aftermath – so their agreement was that she was *always* to text first, to see whether it would be a good time for a call or not. It was only okay for her to make a call like this if someone had died – or worse – so Hannah picked up, fearing the absolute worst:

'Hello? Is everything alright?'
'Oh, hi! I just wanted to hear my daughter's voice, that's all!'

Hannah had to sit on her hands so she wouldn't throw her phone out the window.

'Mum, we've talked about this… you really gave me a start. Is everything alright with Nan? I haven't heard from her in a while'.

Feeling vulnerable all of a sudden, Hannah had already started making excuses for snapping at her mother.

'Oh, you know. She's getting on. Can't remember her name most days due to the Alzheimer's, but that's how it goes, you know'.

Yeah, she did know. She'd suggested to the family that they have her see a doctor about her early onset dementia years ago, but they had told her to butt out as that 'clearly wasn't the case'.

She'd always been a bit loopy, that much was true, but there were days she'd be on the road and forget how to drive and she'd just got out, left the car in the street and walked home. But when Hannah had brought up that she might be suffering from something other than your bog-standard whimsy, they'd told her:

'You're no medical professional like your uncle here, so mind your own business'.

So, she did. But it was so advanced now that Hannah was afraid she'd hurt herself – or, God forbid, her great grandchildren. So, every time the phone rang more often than the usual once every six months check-in chat, Hannah's heart understandably leapt into her throat. Either way, back to the call.

'So, how are you? I understand you've moved *again*? When are you going to settle down like a normal person?'

Fuck off.

'Maybe when I win the lottery. They don't give away houses anymore like they did in the seventies, you know.'

'Well, maybe if you would have stood up for yourself once in a while, maybe you'd be able to hold on to a relationship and have the money for a house before the market blew up. All three of Alfie's kids have their own houses, you know, and two of them are on benefits.'

What?

"Alfie", her mother's partner, who she had fuck all to do with, who incidentally had been the person to decide that her mother shouldn't act as a guarantor for Hannah the one time she'd asked for some financial support was the last person she wanted to be reminded of right now. Hannah may have been pissed off before, but her blood was boiling now.

'How lovely for them. I need to find out where I want to live before I can start thinking about that stuff anyway, and seeing as I don't even have a job, I'm not eligible for a loan anyway.'

'Right. Well, you're going to sort that out, aren't you. How's the treatment going? I've still not heard from your psychologist. When can I expect to hear anything?'

Ah, so that's why she called. To nag her about something she had no way of controlling.

'It's all a bit up in the air now, with evaluations still ongoing, so I don't know. I'm not in charge of my psychologist. She'll call when she has the time, I suppose. My evaluation with the trauma team didn't go very well and I suspect they didn't like me much because they suggested I seek out other treatment first.'

'Oh, it's always someone else's fault with you, isn't it?'

'Pardon?'

'You've always attributed qualities to other people they don't really have so you can feel sorry for yourself'.

First of all, *always*? Hannah hadn't told her a single thing between the ages of 11 up until the one time before today at 27, when she'd told her about one of her suicide attempts just to make her shut the fuck up, so how did her mother think she even knew her, never mind knowing about things she "*always*" did? No, the only thing that had been a case of the *always* with their relationship, was her mother gaslighting her. And Hannah had finally had her fill. Time to cut the cord. And for the first time since she was about five, Hannah stood up for herself and said calmly, but firmly, her throat swollen, but not caring if the person on the other end heard that she was on the verge of tears:

'Right. This is the kind of behaviour that has made me believe that it's okay for people to treat me as if I have no value. I don't need this right now. Or ever, as a matter of fact. You can't say that experiences I've had throughout my life never happened, because *you* weren't there. I am 41 years old. I can tell when someone dislikes me, when their pupils are constricted to the size of sewing needles. And I especially don't need you to tell me that my reactions or feelings are *wrong*. If I am having a feeling, something has caused that to happen, and my perspective on reality or subjective experiences will sometimes differ from yours, but that doesn't mean that I am *wrong* to feel something or that what I am feeling or experiencing is indeed wrong. My feelings are my own and you cannot tell me that they are without merit or value. Goodbye, mother. I do hope that you have a lovely rest of your day and that you won't let our conversation ruin anything for you. But I need to go now. Bye.'

And with that, Hannah shed 240 lbs of crippling deadweight.

Epilogue

So, my dear reader, the story doesn't really end here. It's actually only the beginning.

We can both probably gather that the old Hannah would never be truly happy. She had spent most of her adult years desperate to hold on to her grief in order to protect herself from opening up to the world that she simply wouldn't let herself be capable of happiness. Or love. She saw it as a concept, for goodness' sake!

Naturally, the only way forward for her was to take a step back and evaluate her own approach and to realise she had to forgive and let go. She had to kill the part of her that held onto the bad like a sort of protective shield. It's euthanasia, really. The old Hannah had to die for the real Hannah to stand a chance. So here we are, at the end. Which, for Hannah 2.0, is only the beginning.

And finally, a word from Hannah herself:

'I don't think I would consider myself suicidal back then. Maybe I wanted to kill the person I'd let myself become – not end my life, but rather begin living my life on my own terms. For this to happen, simply shedding my skin wasn't enough. Like one does when cauterising a wound, some pieces had to be cut away for me to fully heal and find my way back to the self that had been screaming from the inside to come out for almost 40 years. The child that never got the chance to live. Today, I'm more "me" that ever, but me, myself and I are still getting to know each other. I may have a big scar and a body that is finding new and inventive ways to trip me up, but I'm getting to terms with the fact that there are aspects of it that can be considered beautiful as well. So, I am working my way up to a level of self-compassion that's more than tolerable. I am starting to think that I can be worthy of good things. And my nephews deserve to have an aunt that's confident enough in herself that they'll trust me enough to be themselves around me. We all deserve to feel like we're in harmony with the universe – that way we won't be so busy thinking about doling out revenge or spreading hate. Happy people tend to treat others with the respect they deserve, so that's the way I've chosen. I'm not saying I'll always choose the high road – sometimes it's not even the better choice. But I will definitely make sure that I take care of myself in a way that will allow me to become – and remain – a better version of me. Despite my past, but not *in spite* of it.

And I'll be damned if I let another human being spit on me again – whatever the context.'

– Thank you for coming on the journey with us, we're not done yet–

Special thanks

Without the help, feedback and constant encouragement from two very special people – namely Kris and my very own MJ – this book would never have seen the light of day. With you two in it, life takes on an undecipherable, magical hue, without which I would have been completely wayward, adrift and very alone.

I'd also like to give thanks to all of the musical artists featured in the book. Each and every one has lent endless inspiration and helped me set the stage when there was no light. Without music, my existence lacks dimension, colour and shelter.

To the town of Edinburgh, for always being home – even when I had none.

To Bri, for making me laugh when I really, *really* shouldn't – or have no reason to.

For Chris, for being a real-life unicorn.

For C.S. Lewis, for giving me a portal to another dimension when I needed an escape.

Last, but not least, thanks to my Opa, the OG ORB, simply for coexisting with me – if only for the briefest moment in time.

X